THERE OUGHTA BE A LAW

By Lois Fowler Barrett

Author of When The Earthquakes Spoke

Preacher's Son & Henry Brown

Published by
Brick Hill Publishing
1413 S. Webster St.
Harrisburg, IL 62946

Online Address
www.brickhillpublishing.com

Cover Design
By Velma Crow

Cover Background
Front cover: Sheriff portrayed by Lewis Kessler
Back Cover: DeWitt County Texas Courthouse photo by Lois Barrett

Library of Congress Control Number

International Standard Book Number (ISBN)
paperback 978-0-9762356-2-0

Printed in the United States of America
1st Printing

Background set in Cuero, Texas but any similarity to fictional characters living or dead is pure coincidence.

ACKNOWLEDGMENT

This book is dedicated first and foremost to God and His mercy without whom this endeavor could not have been completed.

Second, it is necessary to acknowledge the following for assistance in creating this novel, I most ardently thank the officers of the law in the State of Texas: most specifically Defense Attorney Elliot Costas, Victoria; Cuero Chief of Police Glen Mutchler; DeWitt County Sheriff Jode Zavesky; the DeWitt County District Attorney's office; the Texas Rangers; Justice of the Peace Peggy Mayer; Cuero City Library personnel; and tour guide Sterling Billings. A special thanks to Illinois' Saline County law enforcement and judges who were helpful in preliminary findings for a law and order role in justice.

Third, many thanks for the editorial assistance from Author and Minister Velma Crow and Kathy Branecky, Texans.

"Do not repay anyone evil for evil. Be careful to do what is right in the eyes of everybody. If it is possible, as far as it depends on you, live at peace with everyone. Do not take revenge, my friends, but leave room for God's wrath, for it is written: It is Mine to avenge: I will repay," says the Lord.
Romans 19: 17-19 NIV

"— It is not good to show partiality in judgement.
Proverbs 24:23

Chapters

Chapter 1

Missing

Raleigh King jerked awake. He leaped up in answer to loud knocking on his door. He was scared and rammed his fists into his sleep-filled eyes rubbing them awake. He attempted to clear his nose and throat of the grey cotton fibers that always caused asthmatic lungs to go into fits of coughing. His house on West Lacy Street was always full of the fibers. Every weekend he could sweep up a bag full of the stuff and show to his Ma. She said there was nothing could be done, but when his computer quit working, she took it to a shop and the man there showed them it was full of the fibers. Ma said if they reported it, and the factory was shut down by the monster EPA, all the people who worked there would be mad. Besides, the cotton mill people were the only ones who would hire him with his problem.

Raleigh grabbed for his inhaler from a table beside the door. He should have kept it in his pocket like Ma said. He took two good puffs, put it down and frowned. A hard week at the cotton mill left him in no mood for a visitor. It had to be his mother—no one else ever came. Hitching up unbelted jeans, he dragged his aching, slender body to the peephole in an always-locked door. Outside stood a very young girl, or at least he thought it to be a girl. The face was distorted from the magnifier in the peep hole.

"She's not supposed to be here. I'll get into trouble," Raleigh whispered. His mother had made it plain, reminding him that he was labeled " mentally challenged" and had to think before acting. He didn't mind—Ma loved him anyway. She made sure he was taken care of and put through school like all other boys. Cautiously, he inched the door open enough to peep out and say:

"Go away! I'll get arrested and sent to prison for you being here." He knew that much about why he couldn't be around young girls.

The teenager forced a hand through the opening and begged

"Let me in, Mr. King. I need a place to stay. I'm in trouble at home and if they find me, I'll get a beating! You know me, my grandmother lives on Esplanade. Karly Young." The teenager's nature left her friendless and no place where she could hide. This was her last hope.

Compassion for anybody who could suffer a beating overrode head knowledge: Lord knows he had suffered enough himself. Raleigh slowly opened the door, looked up and down the street, carefully studied the grass-lined blacktop, then pulled the teenager inside. His sense of rescue overcame his intelligence. He was a registered sex offender. It was 2004 and he had been registering for years. This girl looked almost like the one who got him into trouble when he was a teenager. *Oh, boy, what would Momma say?*

* * *

On Monday, hot as Texas can get in the Summer, Art Simonds was leaning back taking a well-earned break from his duties as sheriff when the door flew open. A red faced woman burst in slamming the door behind her.

"Have you found my Karly yet?" Leona Broughton yelled as she crowded into the male-smelling undersized room.

Dang! Art asked himself, didn't I lock that door? Where's all the security we had installed? Security better than this had better be in the new building the county is planning for the near future. Maybe I've been too easy on her and the staff thinks it's okay to let her in. It was the third day of her thirteen year old granddaughter's disappearance and she was Jalapeno pepper hot.

"You call yourself Sheriff, Art Simonds," she yelled, "and nothing done about Karly's disappearance?"

Snuggled down, hat over his face, feet propped on the desk, snores ripping the silence, Art had relaxed in his homey office deep in a heretofore quiet little town. He slipped off his boots to ease the pain associated with an old injury when he dropped a fence post on his left foot and didn't seek medical treatment or surgery. He reached down and pulled on the boots, careful to hide a toe sticking through the sock end. Embarrassed, he picked at his jeans until they were straight on his boot tops. He glanced over the desk to see if Leona had adapted to western boots yet. She hadn't. Northern boots were her style, with the zippers up the side to ease pulling them on.

Discomfort wasn't the word to describe how he felt with blue ice staring holes through him. Half-awake, he waited for her to tell him again how anybody who touched her kids or grand-kids would never live to go to trial. Art swallowed. His office was not large enough for noise and it was hot. The AC wasn't putting out like it should, but maybe he could do something about cooling it off in here. He reached around and placed a heavy hand on the back of his chair to lift his past middle-age body and turn on the overhead fan.

Dang! The back of the chair broke off! Art landed flat on his back, papers flying everywhere as he grabbed for the desk—feet kicking in black leather boots like a turtle on it's back. *Heck, a man's got no dignity when he's old.* Leona burst out laughing: the tension was gone.

When he managed to roll over in spite of too-tight jeans from his latest weight gain, he grimaced from the pain of kneeling on bony knees. Elbows stiffened like a recruit doing push-ups he rose off the floor peeping over the desk top, his grey eyes red-rimmed from the nap. Art pulled himself to a standing position, put the chair back together, picked up papers and tried to rearrange his desk. Cold eyes were on him the entire time in spite of his drop-in visitor's amusement at the accident. He jammed his hat down where she couldn't see so much of his eyes, but his beak of a nose stuck out from under the brim. He was conscious of sweat stains under his arm pits. To clear Leona's mind of the embarrassing situation, he answered the question she probably forgot asking.

"No Ma'am, we ain't located Karly, but we're close," he said. "We put out an Amber Alert, and as you know, that's a disappearance vehicle. If she's in town we'd hear. Apparently nobody's seen her. Besides, we don't have any description of a perpetrator or a pedofile or a vehicle." Art changed the subject. "Take a load off– have a cup. " She waved the offer aside, loose skin sweeping the air in a sleeveless tank top.

She shouldn't wear that thing, he thought. He smoothed his

untrimmed mustache, reached up to push back the sweaty hat and ran the same hand over a handful of thinning hair; automatically ran fingertips slowly across and down scalp-line scars. Faint now, they resulted from from a head-on collision when he was chasing a perp into the blinding sun years ago. He had amnesia for several weeks after leaving the hospital. Sometimes thoughts just disappeared.

He was glad he had enough hair left and a lean enough body to keep him from looking like the retired Texas ranger on television serving up chili in a bar and grill. Nervous, Art let the same hand drop on a little pot belly that came with age and sitting behind a desk too much. He admitted to love handles, but said often enough "I ain't fat." This statement had always made his wife flinch when she saw him jerking his favorite big buckle up over the pot. He missed her criticisms—wished he had another chance. Glancing down at his littered desk, Art searched out a stained mug, his favorite with the western scene baked on the ceramic sides. He reached to the left, found coffee and addressed his visitor.

"Leonnie, ma'am, I know how you like jelly beans. Take some of 'em." he said, pushing the jar closer. "I know you're partial to black. Me, I favor lemon or orange. Lime's okay, cherry's okay, but they don't leave a sour enough taste so you don't notice the sugar as much. We don't have to have coffee."

"Art Simonds! Are you listening to yourself? I'm talking about my granddaughter's kidnaping and you're in another world about candy. Stuff your jelly beans where the sun don't shine!"

"My, ain't we in a mood?"

"Are you trying to buy my silence with jelly beans?"

"No, ma'am , just thought I'd rent it for a few minutes," he tried his charm.

They laughed. Her face grew serious again and Art knew he better have an answer.

"Back to Karley's disappearance, didn't you say she's hard to handle and always threatening to run off?"

"That has nothing to do with the lack of response on finding her and you know it."

Art popped a lemon jelly bean in his mouth and rolled it around on his tongue. Dang. He hated his new teeth even though a friend had taught him how to roll candy and gum around to keep it from sticking. "You just have to keep it moving," he had said, but Art knew that didn't work with jelly beans. They had a tendency to glue teeth together.Still he couldn't leave them alone for some unexplained reason. Didn't everybody in Texas have jelly beans handy?

Leona was tired of the fun-loving good ole boys of Cuero. She was no longer amused by the chair incident or renting her silence with her favorite liquorice jelly beans. She wanted to reach out and knock some sense into his head.

Realizing Leona no longer was amused by the turtle on the floor incident, he leaned forward and lied: "We have a pred-o-file in mind, and we're closin' in on his where about's. What've you heard when you're out and about? Ole northern reporter like you, I know you been lookin'."

He could hear her breathing hard on the other side of his desk as she eased herself farther down into the chair. He hoped it wouldn't fall apart too.

"I'm too old to chase around anymore," she said, looking down on age-spotted hands, "and where did you come up with that word Pred-o-file? It's a new one on me and I'm a journalist."

"Wasn't hard, Ma'am, I just wrapped predator and pedofile together. It fits the bill, don't it?"

"Art, back to your statement that you know I've been looking. It's your job to catch these monsters, but I know from experience some dedicated defense lawyer will just get whoever it is off on a technicality. Art, this time you'll dot all the i's and cross all the t's, won't you?" Even with her red nose and swollen eyes, age creeping in, she wasn't bad looking.

Dropping his gaze, he hoped she wouldn't cry here and wipe out whatever reserve he had left. He reached for a handy fly swatter in case he needed a distraction.

"Don't let the judge turn your so-called pred-o-file loose on a technicality," Leona continued. "We're talking about my granddaughter here."

"Wait a minute, Leonnie," he said and indicated the extra cup he had on the desk. She waved away the office coffee again; said she had tasted it before; refused again the jelly beans he slid toward her. Art didn't mind when she said:

"You know reporters don't accept coffee, just go for the jugular vein." She smiled, mouth all twisted to one side and he knew she was spoofing. They often had coffee together. Their friendship began when she arrived in Texas in the early Nineties and stirred up a mess about some dude following her; harassing her on the highway coming from Victoria.

Leona pushed her weight out of the chair where ample hips hung on the arms, rose slowly—an eternity—and stood staring down at Art until he swatted an imaginary fly.

"You ain't a bad lookin' woman for your age," he offered, hoping to change the subject. "How come y'awl never married again?" He always drawled when talking to a Yankee. It made them fidget. This Yankee kept herself up with makeup and dyed hair.

Leona resented his hem-hawing around. He didn't have a clue about her granddaughter. She could see Art wasn't in a hurry to move his tired body right this minute to find one. Although his mind was always on the job, she knew he mostly left everything up to the deputies in these last days as Sheriff this year. And where did he come up with such a word as pred-o-file? She thought about it for a moment, then decided she actually liked the new word. It was a perfect description for the sex offenders on the loose. Leona could live with the knowledge of him relegating jobs to the deputies if he kept her updated.

Watching his older friend's face, Art flinched internally when she said "To use your down south vernacular, Art, it ain't your kin disappeared."

He knew Leona being a northern lady would never use the word ain't in a sentence, although Art delighted in tormenting her with a slangy contraction each chance he had. She never failed to frown when he did so.

"Ma'am, if you leave me alone, I'll do this like in the old days. Bull-doggin' me on what I'm doin' ain't gonna win you any prizes." She didn't answer, just stared. Her reputation for digging around followed her down here and the good sheriff wasn't above checking on her when she showed up in town some years ago nosing around. He thought she should've been a cop or a private detective, maybe even worked for one of the rag newspapers, or even locally.

What was the difference what he thought when Leona's granddaughter became a no-show? Well, she was like the rest of the people—she had a PC and there wasn't much anybody could hide from her. She could click on the internet for a list of sex offenders' names in her own close-knit neighborhood, just down the street from the church she attended. Maybe a pedofile took Karly. He hoped not. Karly was young to be a runaway, but old enough to get caught up in a chat room.

"Ma'am," he questioned, "didn't you tell me this girl had a disagreement with her parents Friday when she didn't come home?"

"Yes, but what does that have to do with her being gone three days?"she shot back. Leona was becoming more than perturbed with Simond's cavalier attitude toward her Karly's disappearance. She held her tongue. It wouldn't do any good to make an enemy.

"Well, maybe somebody hid her, or she found a place to stay," Art said. "I know of a case where a girl disappeared and turned out some church people were hiding her because she lied about her parents. Have you called her friends? Have you looked among the less fortunate people in your surroundin' neighborhood?"

"You know we have, Art. Knocked on every door. Why are you wasting time asking inane questions and sitting around this hot office? Are you too lazy since your time is almost up as sheriff?"

"It ain't only that, Leonnie," Art evaded, "you have to consider that livin' inside the city limits, our Karly Young's disappearance would first and foremost be the city's case. Even if it is, I can influence, but I cain't take over. Give me some slack here. I'm still workin' on the death of the man who bought your big van last year. You remember, the stranger we found shot in the face and mutilated in the back of the rig?" He stared into her face, but no reaction–nothing registered.

"Well," he ventured, "whoever tried to burn it didn't get the job done, but then forensics couldn't fingerprint him what with his hands chopped off. His dental work was a mess with a hole in his mouth. He wasn't in the system. We picked up an I.D. from the title of the van, but it was fake. He dropped in here from another planet I reckon. It's one cold case I ain't gonna see an end to. Forensics had no idea of where to look for matching DNA."

Leona stared at Art, said nothing and turned her head. She realized this law man apparently couldn't concentrate on what she wanted; might as well leave.

Art couldn't read anything in the move of her head. He wanted to say more, but nothing came out, opening the way to stand and let her know time was up. She frowned, opened her mouth, once again said nothing. Art watched that crafty old broad with her snow-white hair waddle out the door. She shouldn't have worn jeans with that hump, he thought. A loose cotton shirt didn't hide much. He knew her, she'd find that perp and call. She could never leave anything alone. He wouldn't even have to move from his chair. Besides, he had this deputy who was ready to be sheriff; election was coming up soon for 2005. Art gave his deputy that chance. This sheriff was too close to retirement to get hung out to dry on a kidnap case, but .... well... maybe for a last roundup, if it would keep this nag off his back.

Besides this, Karly Young was not yet fourteen. There ought to be a rule that says the law could hunt the first hour, not wait. The Amber alert was always used, and darn successfully, but didn't help in this small town if the law couldn't locate a witness who saw what, when, where, why and who. It worked for some – not always for others. It wasn't hard for teens to get caught up in a pornography site nowadays. His opinion was that Kids had access to the net and chatted with some of the perverted characters Art knew about.

The sheriff's thoughts were interrupted by parting Leona who turned and minced out: "But here you sit with my granddaughter maybe going through hell!"

Art stifled his thoughts and yelled at the chief deputy when he thought she actually left.

"Tom, get in here!" He knew Bridges was always outside the door listening.

Tom strolled in with "I ain't been listening, boss" on his face, ignorant of everything Art and Leona said, but he was grinning and trying out the sheriff's new word: Pred-o-file. Art laughed to himself at the way Bridges always tried to look innocent, but gave himself away in little ways like trying out the new word.

Bridges had a sideways smile on his dark face; strong white teeth and a dimple on the right side. He was smiling for more reasons than one: at last he was being relieved—taken off the stolen bull case. Yesterday Art had busted out laughing when Tom came sloshing in, boots full, clothes stinking, hat gone, sludge dripping down his face.

All because of a stolen Brahma bull Bridges was ordered to chase down and hunted for three days. His suspicions led him to climb a fence just south of Cuero where trucks rolled in and out unloading full tanks of fresh oil. He didn't dignify Simonds' laughter by telling him what happened. Let him guess.

He had just headed across field, careful to avoid fire ant mounds, rattlers, and fresh cow dung, but almost stepped square into one of the biggest chips he ever laid eyes on. What could have made a pile as big around as a ten-gallon hat? He made his way to an oil tank and climbed up on the fire wall to get a better look-see when the sound of thunder jerked him to the right.

Out of swirling dust came a whale of a bull, snorting and galloping straight at the deputy. Bridges scrambled, slipped and fell head first down the bank of the ditch. Head under thick, slimy water, fancy booted feet kicking, he thrashed about trying to regain his senses enough to roll over and get his head above water. He'd swallowed enough to make him sick, and what little he spit out, sputtering and coughing, scared him. He thought he might die from the stagnant mess. He would have to change his pants for more reasons than one.

Finally, by twisting and thrashing around until his knees supported his body, he was able to lift his head out of the water long enough to get a decent breath; raise up on his feet and climb the slippery wall. He could've drowned, with nobody but him out here and his body not found for days. The bull snorted, turned and galloped back the way he came. Lucky for Tom Bridges Leona Broughton picked today to yell about her granddaughter and he could leave the stolen bull case to a deputy raised on a ranch.

"We've got us a case I want you to loop onto and leave everything else alone," Art said, pulling the deputy's thoughts back to the matter at hand. "Tom, you know Miss Leonnie's granddaughter's been missin' for three days now, and her grandma is worried. Leonnie's who and what she is. You know what I mean. Drop that stolen bull case and concentrate on Karly Young. She's immature enough to be a runaway. Find her, however, whatever, has to be done."

"Yes Sir!" Bridges agreed so brightly, the sheriff paused to look Tom's way, started to say something, then waved the deputy out the door.

Art watched Bridges hesitate like he had something to say, but left with the sheriff's mind busy replaying thoughts on the Karly Young case. Art had planned on doing all he could for Leona, but his hands were somewhat tied if the action took place in the city limits. He always waited for an invite. It was the same as when the department never solved the case of the murdered van owner in 2003. It was Leona who sold the victim a van with a queen-size bed in it, a TV, a video player, mood lights: an all out love machine. She said she didn't know the buyer and was furious when she found out he was a sex offender.

Art never considered her for a second to be the killer. She was too sane for that. The only thing that stuck in his craw was how she knew the man was a sex offender. He hesitated to ask. If and when a jury found sex offenders not guilty or the judge threw out a case, there was nothing anyone could do. Maybe the city could charge whoever might've taken Karly with harboring a runaway if that's what this case was about. If the kid was found inside the city limits, and with a known sex offender, it would still fall mainly on the local boys. The perps were all required to register at his office, still —

He asked himself why ain't she over there at City Hall bothering them? He could keep Leona posted from a distance he reckoned. From past visits he remembered her talking about how hard it was to keep track of that maverick child who wandered all over the neighborhood curious as a cat, but with no show of interest in boys. Art wondered.

"Tom!" he yelled at his deputy as Bridges finally started out the door. Bridges stopped but didn't turn. "Start with Leonnie's neighborhood, and keep me apprised of your findin's. It ain't like we don't have enough problem patrollin' 900 square miles in this county, and watchin' after more than twenty thousand citizens and over seven thousand households— now we got to be babysitters for the parents. Dang! It would make our job a lot easier if Texas passed a law requirin' sex offenders to have a special color license plate so kids would know not to accept a ride with one of 'em." There's some states considering just that, Art thought. He remembered one was green. He reached for the jelly beans—green was one of his favorite colors.

Tom grinned and scraped across the floor in fancy snake boots. That had been the worst part about yesterday—muddied-up expensive boots. Took two hours to clean them up like he wanted. He was growing a lip cover like Art's, but he wasn't pot-bellied yet. In fact, some might think him handsome with his thick head of curly black hair and light brown skin. He would be the first black sheriff of DeWitt County.

Tom Bridges was aiming for a higher profile than Art ever had as soon as he became sheriff in January. He was confident he had the election sewed up. Democrats held this county in their palms and he was smart enough to seek a blessing from the party. Art was an all right sheriff, never making waves, fair at solving cases, but nobody outside this county even knew who or what he was. Tom knew he could solve any case without the help of the Rangers when it came down to it and he would show this county. His name would be known. Word on the street was Simonds had grown soft and wasn't strong on arresting friends. Well, that would end with Bridges' regime. He promised the Party.

He grinned under a short upper lip which shouldn't wear a moustache, thinking how Art was so tied up in a retirement plan he failed to notice his chief deputy taking over one case at a time. If this Karly Young case was handled right, it could propel a good sheriff into state wide fame and acclaim. While ole Art was relaxing on that scraggly piece of property he called a ranch, Tom would take over the department and run it like it should be; leave cattle rustling to somebody else, maybe like the newest deputy. He almost giggled, thinking about the word pred-o-file Art invented, but grown men don't giggle, they snicker.

* * *

Oblivious to the deputy's and Leona's thoughts, Art reached for the phone to call Chief Richard Brown. Surely he had some news, but Brown was rumored to being on the downhill side of investigation since last year when he had to shoot and wound a close friend's son. Maybe the two of us should pack it in, Art thought. This ain't like a law and order show on TV with cops arresting and the courts taking over. Although —

Chapter 2

Meltdown

Outside, Leona Broughton cared less about sheriff elections just now. Easing into a ten-year-old red sedan, she looked back and scowled at the steps she had descended, then slammed the car door. It wasn't the stiffness in both legs, or resentment for the lack of ground-floor entrances; it just seemed somebody, someday, would offer a place to call on law officers which wasn't a chore for older people to climb into. The city hall also was off the ground and the building just as stark as the county sheriff's structure. They were in such contrast to the beautiful old courthouse with their square looks. At least the other offices of the county across the street were housed in outstanding design of an another century building.

A lover of age-old landmarks, in any other situation, any other time, Leona rarely missed an opportunity to stand and admire the cream and red sandstone design of the courthouse topped by pyramided roofs. Normally, every time she drove down the hill on Broadway from Wal Mart, the six-story high clock tower protruding from majestic tree tops greeted her eyes, especially when the sun was right. This sight kept her from resenting the drastic slow-down in traffic at the high school just before dropping down a steep hill where the tower was hidden from view.

The lovely building would be renovated starting next year. Just last month when she was required to visit the courthouse on business, she had asked another admirer: " Would A. O. Watson, the architect who built the structure—with such a labor of love that he went bankrupt as a result— be happy or saddened by still more work on his beloved building?"

"I don't know," came the reply. "I never wondered about how the courthouse got here, just appreciated the beauty."

Leona's question came on the heels of a pleasant afternoon spent at the library reading history of the courthouses in Texas. She wondered at the time if Watson turned over in his grave when the courthouse was refurbished in 1956 by a San Antonio construction company modernizing the interior. The intrusive new central air conditioning and space-using elevators would never have been in the mind of an 1896 architect. She thought he late architect might be proud, however, that his accomplishment withstood the added weight.

Today, the intense agony of Karly's disappearance blinded Leona to things of history. Her anger over perceived lack of concern on the part of officials drowned her in self pity. She looked down at the ignition, started the car and frowned.

Art's suggestion of questioning the Cuero police aggravated her. She had already—before talking to Art—visited Chief Brown. He told her the same things the sheriff did, but she had to make a point: nobody was concerned enough to please her in the disappearance of her thirteen-year-old granddaughter.

Of course she knew Karly lived in the city limits, but she also knew county and city worked together on such cases. Nowadays looking for lost children wasn't taken as lightly as a few years before. Almost sixty years ago her life was ruined by a man nobody prosecuted to the extent of the present laws. She wouldn't forget.

Unexpected emotion tore at her as tears gushed. Squeezing her eyes, she sat with hands shaking on the steering wheel. *Not now! God don't let this feeling come back now! I don't want to hurt this way — I don't want to remember.* The feelings came anyway. Sobbing uncontrollably Leona couldn't move from the spot. Pain gripped her throat and she knew she was either choking to death or having a heart attack. Fifty years became yesterday. Abject fear gripped her mind and she knew it was going to come flooding back— the hands on her eleven year old body, the whispers in the night, the filth in her mind—none of it leaving her as her head banged on the steering wheel.

God, help me! I cannot go there again! Not now!

Leona came to herself long enough to throw the car into reverse, screech out of the parking space onto Live Oak as heads turned to see who the fool driver was. She didn't care and couldn't see. Saliva dripped from her mouth, tears ran down and mixed with the dripping of her nose. She gasped, sucked in air and flailed at the wheel.

At the corner, Leona turned left on Clinton and then right, ignoring the stop sign on Broadway. The wheel almost got away from her but determined fingers gripped and the car righted. As she entered traffic headed up the hill toward Wal Mart, a driver screeched to a halt, sliding into the other lane, and bore down on his horn as though the sound would stop the crazy old woman at the wheel.

Who did that old lady think she was, anyway? He chased her up the street but she saw nothing and raced on. He dropped the pursuit. He was at K&N where he had headed to begin with. Thoughts of a shrimp basket and a frosted mug root beer drove away anger. He would report her on his cell phone and let the cops take care of her.

Leona sped toward Victoria at full throttle, never fearing or caring if she died. Mind blank, unstoppable tears, choking, numb from the brain down, screaming over and over at God, Leona was bent on outracing the terror inside. Dread of the memories of the awful treatment she received when eleven years old. *God, don't let Karly go through what I did – please!*

* * *

In Port Lavaca a policeman tapped on the window of an old sedan sitting in the sand, tires spinning, going nowhere. A wild-looking face turned toward him and he swung his club to smash the window in back of the driver. The crashing noise jerked Leona back to reality. The officer climbed in the back, reached over the seat to turn off the ignition and grabbed her hands.

"Lady! What the heck are you trying to do? How did you get between the posts and out on this beach?"

Leona was unaware of her location. She didn't realize the roaring sound in her head was the ocean pounding wave after wave on shore. *What am I doing here? How did I get here? Lord, help me!*

Another vehicle, a county squad, slid up to the edge of the parking lot. The driver jumped out as his siren stopped.

"What we got goin' on here, Officer?"

"Heck if I know," the first law on the scene answered. "I observed this vehicle race onto the beach. I followed, observed the woman driver inside revving the motor and spinnin' the wheels like a crazy fool. The doors were locked so I beat in the back window with my stick and entered. She wouldn't or couldn't respond to me tapping on the window."

"Search her purse and get some I.D. Maybe we can notify her kin or the law wherever she hails from. Anybody you know?"

"No. I don't recognize the vehicle, the driver or the tags. I'll get on it and let you know who she is," the first responder offered. He moved to his car and radioed in the license. The answer came back for a Leona Broughton of Cuero. Sheriff Art Simonds answered the call.

"Wow, she come a long way for her age and the shape she's in," the caller told the Calhoun County deputy. "The DeWitt sheriff's on his way over here. We better stick with her until he gets here. He said he'd bring her son if he could find him. Okay?"

"Yep. I got coffee in a thermos over there in my squad. I'll get it, we can sit here on the beach until somebody comes. It's an hour and a half trip, ain't it? Want somethin' to eat?"

Chapter 3

Girl Found

"Broughton here," a crabby Leona answered her phone at 7:30 a.m. on the fourth day.

It was Sheriff Simonds. She didn't want to talk to the man who came for her yesterday evening in Port Lavaca where she stupidly mired down on the beach. It was just a temporary meltdown. Too much, too much. Good Lord, a woman's only got to take so much before she cracks. Don't any of them ever get that way?

"Ma'am! Leonnie! Your granddaughter came home!" Art shouted into the phone like Leona was deaf. "She's out here at the hospital! Get over here! She's contrary and dirty-mouthed. Nurse said she won't talk to any of 'em. Her parents are here, and they won't let me talk to her. The city's already been here and told me little. Had to get all the news from Bridges."

The sheriff hung up, leaving Leona —in a state of agitation —hanging onto her phone.

It wasn't the right time for Art to mention a strange tip his office received at four a.m. today. He wanted to talk to Karly without her parents in the room, and racked his brain for a way to get them out. He was sure by now since she came home on her own she was led away through the internet. He wished parents wouldn't let kids on the thing until they're older, but it seemed responsibility meant using computers for baby-sitting.

* * *

Art was leaning against the nurses' desk, both elbows planted firmly to keep from sliding down the slick top. He was talking to the city boys who took over the case when raw-boned, hippy Leona came busting through the door, hair uncombed, baggy clothes making her look twice her size. These were the same clothes she had on yesterday when they talked in Art's office: the same clothes she had on at the beach in Port Lavaca. Wow! She must be in worse shape than he imagined. Maybe his news would bring her around to the coffee buddy he knew.

Leona noticed Art sizing up her five-foot eight-inch frame and down, realized she had put on the first thing to touch her hands when he called, but cared little.

"I only took time to jerk on a pair of jeans and a used shirt dropped onto the side of the bathtub from the day before," she volunteered. " I guess in the excitement I didn't care if they smelled or if I looked bad. They were handy at this time of day."

Heck, Art thought. So what. He took showers himself instead of putting his "old bones" down in a tub. Unused bathtubs seemed like a good place to pile clothes, except for the time he was spider bit. He guessed spiders liked damp, smelly clothes. But, he wasn't volunteering his feelings on the subject. It was no surprise the way she looked today. He and Bridges only got her to bed at three this morning.

"That was some stunt she pulled yesterday after she left my office," he had said to Bridges. "Never would've believed cool-headed Leonnie would have a meltdown like that."

"I'm looking for Karly Young," Leona said to the desk clerk, ignoring Art's presence as if that would change the situation of last night. Then she remembered Tom and Sue, and asked, "Have you notified her parents?"

"Ma'am, the sheriff said he had it covered," the clerk answered, looking to Art. He nodded and she handed Leona a slip of paper with Room 300 penned on it, but then jerked it back, asking: "Ma'am, are you a relative?" By now, everybody in this small town hospital knew Karly belonged to Tim and Sue Young; worse, to Leona Broughton. Only a new nurse wouldn't know Leona from prescribed weekly visits.

"Yes! Give me that number," Leona growled. She reached across the counter, grabbed the paper from the pinched-face clerk in the bright colored tops they all wore now. Gone were the days when white was uniform in hospitals and clerks were nice. She frowned with disapproval, turned and swished down the hall as fast as arthritic legs would carry her. Art followed, with the clerk's whisper in his ears of "the little brat in 300."

"Grandma!" screeched Karly. She glared at her kin when Leona pushed into the room, obvious she was unhappy to see her grandmother. Her voice reeked of resentment as she growled "Grandma don't belong here." Karly's parents, father, Tim, and step-mother Sue, were at her side. Art didn't get to question

Karly like he wanted. Who told them was not important. The two of them were here in the way of his promise to Leona.

Karly had little to endear her to anybody and stringy blonde hair squirreled over the pillow did nothing to boost her looks. Added to that, she was baby-fat pudgy with beady eyes staring out of a blotched face. Standing back where the parents or Karly couldn't see his face, Art frowned.

"What're y'all doin' here?" asked Sue. "We told the deputy not to bother." Karly didn't get her looks from Sue because she wasn't her mother, but body shape to those who didn't know this would have identified Sue with Karly. Art wondered what Karly's mother had looked like. It wasn't his business; he just wondered in passing.

"Too bad," Leona responded to Sue's cross words. Spitting venom, the mother-in-law said "I have friends in high places."

Art was glad she didn't mention him.

Leona said "I'm here and you can't do a thing about it." She turned a smile on Karly who didn't smile back.

If the two had known about last night at the beach—Art was glad now he didn't find Tim Young—they wouldn't be so cavalier about aggravating a woman on the verge of murder. He knew they didn't have a need to know when he saw Karly lying back in her hospital bed with a scowl of annoyance rather than a scowl of violated body. The little ingrate.

What Leona suspected but wasn't told was that Karly's parents knew exactly where their daughter had been; exactly what happened.

Never let your right hand know what your left hand's doing or some other such nonsense, Leona told herself, and that applies to the incident at the beach also.

Art didn't comment on Leona's remark about friends in high places to her family, just wondered: is that girl in bad shape or just plain ornery? Was she hiding something or was he getting suspicious of all young people?

"Y'all don't belong here," Karly grumbled, ugly on her face. "Daddy, make 'em leave. It's none of *her* business," she said, pointing at her grandmother. It was again obvious she either hated her grandmother or dreaded her condemnation. Art couldn't decide.

Karly just wanted the *old witch* out of her sight. Leona Broughton was just too much of a disciplinarian. The old ways didn't fly with this modern teen. This old woman was exactly the reason she hid.

Tim's wife, smothering the fact that she ran everything in the family—like all good Texas women do and think their men are in the dark—ducked her head and let her husband do the talking. He always did what his wife said, or so Art reckoned and believed. No doubt they discussed Leona before she showed to put in her two cents.

"Better let it go, Mom," Young said. He wanted to keep the peace between his wife and mother. Tim had never been a fighter, just meandered along letting life slap him in the face as he struggled to make a living. He could never live up to Sue and her family's expectations no matter what he did. She wore the boots as they say in Texas. He ran a hand through brown, wavy hair and tried to smile away the knife-cutting tension . He failed.

Art wondered if Young was the least bit aware of the talk about his daughter and how his own mother said she was easily lead astray if somebody had a dog. Didn't the city boys say the alleged perp had a cute pup? Anyway, Tim acted nothing like his mother, nor did he resemble her. He was a dark-haired man, so Karly wasn't his look-alike. His tall lean body belied the fact he came from Leona's loins, although the smaller nose he sported resembled his mother's. Her first husband must have been a looker.

Again Art frowned; looked away. He wouldn't betray his disgust at a child. Art wouldn't want his daughter, if he had one, to confess she went there willingly, but by Grib he'd bet his boots Karly did. It remained to be seen what would come out in a trial if there was one. Mind rambling, he was hoping his deputy who was along for the ride didn't walk out and leave the pup alone to starve.

He jerked his thoughts back to the matter at hand in time to see Leona coughing and gagging into a man-sized handkerchief. Ted Broughton's, he supposed. It touched Art to see her carry something of her dead husband's, but he thought she was gonna puke. Could it be the cancer or anger? Boy, how her son had changed since he married Sue Clements. She hates Leona, Art thought, but I know her type, jealous of mother-in-law. Leona will wind up to the good and Sue Young could go —

"Grandma! Get out!" Karly interrupted his thoughts, and nobody corrected her.

"Dang!" he said aloud and could have bitten his tongue. He recalled when a kid talked like that instead of addressing grandparents respectful like, they'd get their jaws smacked. The little brat was ripe with resentment. He was tired of the tension in the room.

"You can all go to hell!" Leona yelled, face red, compassion gone. Her outburst caused Art's thoughts: now that ain't no way for a church-going lady to talk. She was a regular at the big church going north out of town. Never been there himself. He heard there was some mighty unusual things going on out there.

Probably the man who had Karly was surprised when he took in an ugly-mouthed thirteen year old who had been known to accompany her grandmother to church. Going didn't wear off the smart mouth. Her captor probably got tired of fighting her and would've thrown her out by the time she showed up at home.

Anyway, Art decided, Karly's "kidnapper" let her leave or she escaped. It's a good thing Leona loved her family or she'd have them for lunch, especially after she dug around and found that little heifer. He smiled to himself thinking his old friend probably called on the alleged pervert and told him what would happen if he didn't turn Karly loose. In fact, he wouldn't put it past her to walk right up and knock on the door —gun in hand. He reckoned she was sorry she pulled her son down here from the north to marry that bossy Sue. That move put Karly into a bad situation. She lost her mama up north in a car wreck and Sue wasn't going to be another mother.

Sue Clements was on her fourth marriage. She snagged Tim Young when he first arrived, grief-stricken and lonely. She was sweetness personified. According to Leona, he fell for it like a ton of bricks remembering Karly's mother and her hateful ways. Art hated to think of it, but the world was better off when the alcoholic woman hit a car head on and died in the crash. Karly wouldn't remember the bad, just the good and she probably compared Sue to that good. Art met one of Sue's husbands—a man who had nothing good to say about her except her folks had money. Oh, well, the sheriff had other concerns.

* * *

Art's thoughts returned to the situation at hand when Leona tried to slam the door on her way out, but hospital doors were not designed to slam anymore than the windows were made to open. He followed, letting the door do its thing. He wanted to tell her that Raleigh King, the city's suspect, wandered around town at will and would be familiar to kids. If Karly knew him, she wouldn't have been afraid. He grabbed Leona's arm. She swung around, fist in the air.

Throwing up an arm, he said "Ma'am, accordin' to Bridges, there was fast food sacks all over the house and it looked like she ate some of it. My deputy was with the city boys," he explained to the question in her eyes.

Leona didn't answer. She wouldn't admit her granddaughter was a gullible fast food junkie and might walk off with anybody carrying a sack, which explained her weight problem.

Nobody asked Art why he talked to Leona instead of Tim and Sue. That would be obvious to anybody who knew them. They were too "hi-ka-falutin'" to talk with the "un-monied," little people of town of which he was a part. He knew her folks, Fred and Hilda Clements. They didn't impress him, but Fred could become a very formidable opponent if Art again sought office.

Leona never mentioned any quarrels with her son since Tim married into what Art's deputy described as "the pseudo aristocratic Clements family. No good blood ever came out of the bunch. They were just new money, with common written all over 'em," he'd said. Art kept an opinion to himself.

Did it matter when Tim and Sue could afford to let Karly eat where she pleased and go where she pleased? It was easier that way for some parents. Generational ranchers fed their kids decent food. Another difference, old land ranchers were polite and relaxed. But then, most of them hired help to do the cooking and chores. Heck, the help even lived on the big ranches in their own cottages. But no use thinking along that line. Sue didn't look like she would enjoy healthy food herself. Too broad in the backside. Leona's son put on weight, but still had looks.

* * * *

That afternoon Leona called the office.

"Well Ma'am, what did you think of our detective work?" Art asked, smiling because he knew. "Chief Brown invited us along on the search when we notified him of the tip we got. They obtained a warrant, arrested your suspect and charged him with suspicion of rape just like you knew they would."

"What do you mean, just like I knew they would?"

"Yes Ma'am, like you didn't. Bridges recognized your voice on the phone. Your northern twang wouldn't fool Tom or anybody. Out of curiosity, how did you find King? It was three in the morning when we got you back to Cuero. Stay up the rest of the night, did you? Find him on the PC, on the sex offender's list? I know you're aware of Megan's Law and the registration list."

Silence from Leona's end.

"No matter," Art said, "good thing is Karly's back and the man who had her will go to trial." He was proud of the department's part in the arrest, and hoped Leona was satisfied.

"You know from me talkin' about girls wanderin' loose around the neighborhood and you lookin' on your list of offenders and findin' the one you told us about. Lived a few blocks from you, inside the city limits as you know."

Leona asked him a question. He repeated it to give himself time to hunt an answer. "Why didn't he have a sign out in the yard? Well, now ma'am I'm sorry the ordinance the city passed don't effect these known offenders. It don't take effect until December O-Five. Only the ones convicted after that or movin' into town are required to have signs in the yard." He waited for her to say something but she didn't. "We had to join the city boys on this, Leonnie, 'cause it's in the town limits."

She offered nothing.

Art added "Raleigh King must've had her, like you know, but I don't know if or how much damage he did, nor how he got her to his place. Maybe, Karly bein' thirteen, prob'bly wasn't very cooperative and he had to get physical with her. Her doctor's being secretive on that at Tom and Sue's request."

Still no answer. Maybe she hung up. No, Leona sat gripping the phone, thinking you can kiss where I can't.

"Are you still there, Leonnie?" No answer.

"Leonnie? You still there?" She grunted. "Okay," he sighed. "Well, you know your granddaughter, Leonnie. Why would a kidnapper let her go if she could identify him? Maybe he thought good riddance and pushed her out the door. Maybe she was there of her own accord. She's somethin' else, huh? But then, she's a lot like Grandma."

Art laughed at the thought of the dishwater blonde teenager with pasty complexion not yet browned by a good Texas sun.

Leona didn't see the humor. She slammed the phone in his ear and left his head ringing.

* * *

Using Karly Young's deposition—her folks objected to a public appearance—of kidnap and rape, a grand jury indicted young King days later in the teenager's disappearance. The court system had followed procedure to the letter as far as Art knew. It was policy as well as the law: dotting all the "i's" and crossing all the "t's" as Leona had requested of the sheriff.

Judges, attorneys, court clerks, and law enforcement personnel were hurriedly using up what little time they had left before the landmark DeWitt County courthouse was closed off from the public for renovation. They would be using an abandoned car dealership building up the way, rebuilt and structured inside to accommodate courthouse proceedings.

The magnificent sculptured block courthouse, like many others in Texas, was being renovated and structured inside to handle business as usual after the renewal was completed. Art believed it would take more time than anyone imagined, but the landmark was, and would be, the center of attraction in Cuero. For years visitors topping the hill from the southeast on Hwy 87 were met with the awesome red-roofed steeple and clock tower sticking above the tree tops of the town. Art, like Leona Broughton, would never get over the feeling of expectation each time he topped the hill and dropped suddenly to enjoy beautiful old houses on wide streets restructured from bygone days. God, if you're there, he thought, I thank you for this town.

He sucked his wandering mind back to the city's investigation of Karly's alleged kidnaping. City Chief Brown's department checked out the tip Simonds' office received and relayed. Art never revealed who he believed called in the tip about Leona's granddaughter.

King had been promptly brought before the magistrate and arraigned. He was told what his charge was, and indicated he understood. King had no money: everybody in town knew that. Public defender Neal Sturm from Yorktown was the one appointed from a pool—no choice in the matter. King was returned to his jail cell across from the courthouse.

Art's attention was drawn to an insistent Deputy Jose Gomez who had something to tell the sheriff on the lost bull case Bridges was so eager to drop.

"Sheriff," Gomez said, "I solved Bridges' lost bull case for 'im. I discovered Wayman Prescott's Brahma bull on FM 263 going towards Victoria just inside the county line. I was going along counting road kills to pass the time and saw this big tan and grey object the size of a small car sticking half in and half out of the ditch right alongside the highway. I thought I saw four black tires shining in the sunlight and got concerned somebody might be trapped in a car. Dang if it wasn't that big bull Bridges hunted before all this hullabaloo over the Young girl interrupted. That crazy thing had wandered almost to the county line—must've been hit by an eighteen wheeler. It was on its back, four black hooves sticking in the air, bloated up in the heat to the size of a small car."

"And how do you know it belonged to Prescott?"

"Put a bandana over my nose, twisted an ear and found the chip saying who owned it," Gomez proudly proclaimed. "Whatever hit it surely had some damage, but I wasn't goin' to look for a wrecked truck all day. I told Prescott and he said he'd take care of it."

"Good job, Gomez, be sure and tell Bridges," Art said. "He didn't want to be involved after his accident he failed to report."

"What accident?"

"Oh, you know, the day he came in slimed from head to toe and a mess on his fancy snake boots. I figure he fell into one of those salt water traps or something. You know, the day I had a run-in with Leona Broughton about her missing granddaughter."

"Yeah, you're right, Art," Gomez said and laughed. "Sure did smell, didn't he?"

Art had other things on his mind such as the King trial and his defense attorney appointed by the judge. He waved and left.

Chapter 4

Justice Begins

Filled with trepidation, yet ever-seeking justice, Defense Attorney Neal Sturm turned his attention to the charge of attaining freedom for his latest client. At his office in Yorktown he called in an assistant and opened the file picked up from the city. A photo clipped to the jacket revealed a twenty-seven year old alleged sex offender, Raleigh King. The charges were there; an arresting officer's report; the city's finished report alleging a confession; and unnecessary, but helpful, a report from the county sheriff's chief deputy who had been present at the time of arrest.

"King's been charged with aggravated kidnap," Sturm told his assistant, Brad Jones, "and if he committed this conduct with intent to violate or abuse the Young girl, our case won't be easy. We have District Twenty-four Judge Tobias Black to contend with."

The assistant noted that someone had photographed the interior of King's residence, focusing in on a messy bedroom mostly cluttered with remnants of fast-food wrappers, sacks and soft drink cups.

"What did this mean, if anything? If the girl had been in the photos, it would have meant a lot: it would have provided indisputable evidence," he said to Sturm who nodded.

The file contained very little in the way of past arrests, other than the years-old statutory charge which led to King's requirement to register as an offender every year on his birthday. The only other noticeable blotch was driving without a license when he wrecked his mother's vehicle. All this filled a paragraph on the pre-sentencing report. Not much to hang a man with.

He removed his glasses and rubbed his eyes before dragging a hand down bearded cheeks and onto his chin where he allowed the small beard to cover a deep cleft. He'd always liked the cleft since college when he learned girls traced the indentation with soft fingers as thrills of youthful anticipation coursed through his body. They weren't bothered by thick glasses when approached.

Brushing these distracting thoughts aside, he realized if King was guilty—which Sturm doubted from the circumstantial evidence compiled with an un-provable, unsigned verbal confession—he nevertheless sighed over what could evolve into a plea bargaining session. No mileage there.

"The main thing against this new client is the glaring fact of him being a registered sex offender, a title he acquired at age seventeen over a fourteen- year-old's mutual consent for sex, a 'low risk' offense at best," Sturm said to Jones. "The man, mentally a boy, confessed in writing the first time, not knowing his rights and without sufficient financial backing to hire an attorney. There was no trial, just a plea. Each year since, King dutifully registered as the law required. Added to that, he was on medication for obvious mental deficiency."

Sturm pondered whether this would be a case calling for mental incompetency while his assistant waited. That information could make the defense more difficult if it came to trial.

The attorney was fully aware that his job of defending alleged offenders was considered abhorrent by many victim's families who sought justice, but somebody had to do it. It was a mantra many public defenders and defense attorneys wore. Some said it bordered on idealism.

Rationalizing was a plus for Sturm: he came by it naturally. Presently this ability assisted in his quest to keep cops honest—making sure the constitution was obeyed—as these erstwhile law keepers made arrests. Looking at the file, Sturm wondered again if this could be a case for mental incompetency.

He rarely found in this small county of DeWitt instances of malfeasance by authorities but this possibility sometimes loosed a client before the trial became serious. There was always the ninety-nine out of a hundred who were guilty, leaving that one totally innocent soul to rejoice over. This made his job worthwhile, finding that one unjustly accused person innocent, who was merely caught up in a bad situation.

"Everyone deserves justice, no matter their status in life;

their guilt of other crimes; living on the fringe of society, stupidity and ignorance keeping them always in trouble, most unemployed," Sturm told his assistant-in-training. He proceeded to go into detail about the average perpetrator, unlike King, and how the facts didn't alleviate responsibility to convey legal advocacy on the lower class of which King was a definite part.

"Born under illegitimate circumstances, according to his file, King surely had the very essence of goodness, love existing in everyone from their Creator," he said once again to the aggravation of his assistant. Sturm was not overly religious, but he believed all of God's children—poor, middle class or rich—deserved his utmost to exonerate them: at least represent them to the full extent of the law.

"Haven't I heard this before, Neal? Don't you say this to me every time we do an alleged felony case?" Jones was bored with the speech and bored with Neal's story of "why." Jones was fresh out of law school and eager for glory. His dimples and black eyes set in a lean face topped by gel-stiffed black hair would do for the ladies he could lure into his four-wheel drive jeep.

Ignoring the interruption, and because of it, Neal once again reminded himself how and where he acquired his beliefs when cases such as this blew his way. How did he get into this profession? He knew the answer. Sturm's father was unjustly accused of a crime, "railroaded," due to lack of money—at least what Sturm considered railroaded—into prison where he died, breaking Sturm's mother's heart. His devastated father man over and over proclaimed innocence.

It was one year after his father's death, while in law school, Sturm proved his father's innocence. The decision was made. He would tirelessly defend the accused, innocent or not. Justice was served when his mother won a tidy sum to recompense her husband's untimely death.

More than once, after defending a client, Sturm had to face them again with their dog-eyed look, seeking absolution of a new crime, a chore he dreaded but often accomplished. Back when his father went down in disgrace, Sturm developed a self-deprecating belief that he was little better than the accused.

Therefore he would avenge his father's miscarriage of justice through a better system of defense, thus exonerating himself.

The weary defense attorney sighed again as he closed the file for the present. He was tired, having just finished a case concerning vehicular homicide: his client found guilty. Not a good way to end yesterday, and now this. Sturm determined to go home early today to sweet forgetfulness in his new bride's arms. She made life worthwhile, her and the dogs. He had dogs before he had a wife so they almost came first, but not quite.

He left his Yorktown office, drove to Cuero, with little else on his mind, wearily climbed the steps to the jail and entered. Recognized as a frequent visitor, he wasn't challenged.

"Neal! Wait," a voice at his side interrupted. "Are you ready to enter a plea, counselor?"

It was District Attorney Terrence Trent, a natural-born prosecutor running for re-election, a handsome and confident individual.

"See you in court, counselor," Sturm replied.

* * *

Trent followed the shorter defense attorney's departure with a smile as Sturm suddenly turned and purposely strode toward the door leading outside. He noted the cheap suit of King's advocate. Too bad. Maybe someday he'll make it to the top. But this was one case cut and dried, Trent believed. King was reported as having confessed to the city boys and that lessened this prosecutor's job fifty percent no matter what Sturm did. Sweet revenge.

Since this would be the last case in the beautiful, landmark courthouse until renovation was completed, Trent wanted to take advantage of the surroundings if and when the news media came into play. He photographed well enough, but the background would enhance ads for the next political campaign.

Without desiring a replay of yesterday, Trent's mind flashed back to past encounters with Sturm, that self-appointed savior of underdogs. Neal wouldn't win this one either, Trent assured himself. Vehicular manslaughter was one thing, but Sturm lost out to Trent on vehicular murder when the prosecutor proved beyond a shadow of doubt that Sturm's client purposely ran over his wife's lover. Hah! This case wouldn't be any harder to prove unless the city had slipped up. They assured him before he allowed the case to go to the grand jury for indictment that King had confessed, and on tape. He hadn't seen this in person, but rested on their word.

"It's on tape," Chief Richard Brown had insisted.

"I'll want to view that," Trent had answered without immediate follow up. He had heard rumors about Simonds and Brown getting lazy in their jobs, but didn't believe the tales.

"Okay," Brown had said. The two left it at that. Brown failed to mention he had something else needing attention and left a rookie and his partner in charge of the taping.

This replay led Trent to reflect on his own reason for becoming a prosecutor, an elected position. He was fully aware of the political advantage in finding most, if not all, alleged perpetrators guilty as charged. Pleas were good, but winning a hard case better.

Still, confidence was lacking in the King case. Something bothered Trent. The innocent-looking, blue-eyed young man wasn't any trouble to women he worked with at the cotton mill. Of course they weren't teenagers, but why would he select thirteen-year-old Karly Young for a conquest? Her parents were vehemently against her testifying at a trial, but he would just subpoena her. That was no problem.

Well, no matter, she was in King's house, according to Deputy Tom Bridges. This information came down from the girl's own grandmother to the sheriff, Leona Broughton, herself a sex offender's victim in her own right some fifty years ago in another state. Trent would see her avenged over her granddaughter's plight.

Simonds had apprised him of the grandmother's desire to see King punished, and if not, she had threatened to avenge Karly herself. He hoped this wouldn't be the case, and was glad Art filled him in. The threat caused Trent to call for DNA evidence beyond what was ignorantly destroyed by over-zealous parents, and anything else to prove his case. Precinct One Judge Kate Sorensen called in a forensic team from San Antonio, not in town yet, but well on his way.

Unfortunately, several factors were picking at Trent's conscience. Chief Brown had assured him the confession was taped, but—quite by accident—no writing or actual signing was filmed in the confession to convince a jury. Trent had to trust that just the picture of King shown writing and talking would do the trick.

The prosecutor would be more than diligent in choosing jurors who had no axe to grind; who would take the case as just another blight on their close-knit community and find King guilty. The officer in charge assured Trent that King was given his Miranda rights when picked up at his residence. One of them said so, Brown said.

"Will he testify to that, Brown?"

"Oh, yeah, if he wants to stay in my good graces," Trent was assured.

King, a misguided soul, had asked for a bench trial not knowing how the system worked and he had seen it done on television. Trent wondered who put the idea into his dim-witted head, or if maybe the man had watched too much TV. No matter, King would be found guilty and Trent would have a second win against Sturm in a year.

However, Sturm and the judge both encouraged a jury trial: a sex offense being such high profile. No one, including Trent, wanted King to be able to appeal later. It would be a negative in Trent's career and a blight on the very art of prosecuting, but looked forward to judgeship.

For now, it was his duty to right the wrongs of his world here in one Texas county. Let the others take care of their duties and his sense of right and wrong would spread over the miles to inflame other attorneys into action against the common crimes of the day. He would be remembered as "protector of the helpless," his sworn duty as a prosecutor. Idealistically his county would be one of the few where people could live without fear: his goal for life.

Trent turned, swaggered and strolled toward the open door, jauntily descended the steps, crossed the street where he walked to a Lexus passed down by his well-known attorney father, and carefully slid in without wrinkling his finely pressed pants. He glanced in the rear view mirror to assure himself he was the best looking attorney in the county, dark wavy hair, dark blue eyes. At least the beauty he married and had children with believed him good-looking. That was enough.

* * *

Early on, Sturm realized some one appeared to be leading on the alleged sex offender in his decisions concerning a trial. King had indicated he would like to waive appearing before a jury, but Sturm hurriedly brushed this move off after talking to the magistrate. King was apparently incapable of understanding just what this waiver meant, Sturm said, and the magistrate agreed. Prompted by Sturm, King had pleaded not guilty at his arraignment.

An anxious sheriff sat in on all proceedings, watching a blonde-haired, blue-eyed "man-boy" of twenty-seven looking innocent. King's defense had asked for and obtained discovery to scan the information on the client, looking over the case the city boys had, and the alleged perpetrator's rap sheet among other things. Art was glad Sturm was on the case, looking at an angelic face, dimples, an anxious boy ready to please; a boy in a man's body; a boy-man a teenager could fall for, age forgotten.

He thought about King's family. Besides Suzie, the mother, there had been Suzie's step-father—rumored to have molested her but unproven; incest evidenced by the production of many half-wits roaming around a run-down cattle ranch—and a grandmother of questionable parentage. Sure didn't make for a well-adjusted background. Nobody was surprised when Suzie King came up pregnant. Art reminded himself he wasn't here to give history lessons on behavior.

The sheriff heard that Raleigh King gave a confession to the city boys and on tape. It wasn't mandatory to tape an interrogation, but in cases like sex offense, Chief Brown knew it was good policy and the sheriff agreed. King was reported to have said: "I don't bother young girls. She came on her own." So far, so good. How would that statement set with a father of daughters?

* * *

Raleigh King dared to glance around the courtroom. He

admired the smooth wood of the bannisters, the tables, all shined and clean. He had been here years ago— when he was seventeen— he wasn't afraid. Chief Brown said it would be all right and the slow-thinking young man trusted his new friend. Years before there had been a different policeman. Raleigh's gaze traveled to the right where he saw another new friend, Mr. Trent. He smiled, but Mr. Trent looked away.

Behind Trent Sheriff Art sat staring straight at Raleigh. He had been kind when Raleigh wrecked his mother's car on a live oak tree in the middle of Hunt Street when he was confused. The sheriff said he did the same thing once when he was young. Raleigh smiled, but Sheriff Art didn't smile back.

I must be in real trouble if nobody's smiling. I bet he ain't gonna offer me no more jelly beans. He knows I like liquorice. It stains my teeth, but Ma don't care long as I keep 'em brushed. Why ain't nobody smilin'?

He knew he had done no wrong, and when the men came knocking at his door that day, he gladly let them in. They asked if Karly Young had been there and he said "yes, but she's gone. She up and decided to go home." When they asked what he did to her, he told them the truth: "Nothin'," but they jerked his arms behind his back and handcuffed him all the same.

Raleigh went along with them to the police station quietly, just as his mother told him to if he ever got into trouble. So now, why did nobody smile back? He swiped at a tear sliding down his cheek.

Behind the Sheriff Art sat the mean old woman Karly called Grandma. Raleigh believed he did a good thing when he hid the teenager, but look where he was sitting now. Karly lied, but she had to: so the old lady and Karly's Daddy wouldn't beat her for being herself. Raleigh knew what that meant. Only the people at work treated him good for being himself.

Mrs. Broughton had a mean look on her face today. So did the man sitting up behind the big desk, the judge. Everybody looked mean today. Hadn't Raleigh done everything they told him to? His mind was slow, but he knew when people were mean. Where was his mother? She must be ashamed of him being in trouble.

Where was Karly? She could tell them he only let her stay at his house because she was afraid. She promised when she left. She had fun, didn't she, playing with Squeaky, his little puppy? The dog liked Karly and kept going back for more bad treatment when she tossed him away and he rolled and slid across the floor. Squeaky kept Karly company while Raleigh worked at the mill for three days. He didn't have weekends off like others. So where was she now when he needed her to tell everybody it was okay? He didn't know she wouldn't be there because of her age and because her parents were against it. But it was gonna be all right: the chief said so.

King was asked if he could afford an attorney when he first came before the judge.

"I ain't got no money, if that's what you're askin' Your Honor." He remembered to call the man behind the big bench your honor as Sturm had instructed. It was good. He knew what to do.

Bond was set at fifty thousand after the defense and the prosecution hashed out particulars with the magistrate, and Art knew this would keep the alleged perp out of harm's way. The case was eventually assigned to DeWitt County Judge Tobias Black, a reputable man, and always on the side of the law, who didn't consider King a flight risk when the defense and prosecution agreed on bond. At least that was the deduction Simonds made: Black's reputation was on the line.

The judge warned King not to leave town if he made bail, and asked of the prosecutor:

"Have you applied for a protective order?"

"Protective order taken care of, Your Honor. I know my law. First thing I did."

"Mr. King, do you understand you're not to go near the victim's family, young man?" asked Black.

"Yes, Mr. Sturm here told me that already. I won't go near her."

"Stay away from teen age girls, young man," Black directed again.

Art thought now anybody knows that won't stop a bonafide sex predator. Of course King could be just a fool who didn't have the sense to look for somebody his own age. He could even be a fool who took in an angry little girl who wanted to punish her parents. Art didn't know, but thought bond could be reset later if anything untoward happened. King could have walked out on a five thousand dollar bail, but he had no money which meant he could be held in jail. The trial could be held up for four to six months with King safely off the streets.

* * *

The sheriff was surprised when King was shortly loosed on the streets. Some misguided soul, he later learned, paid the alleged perp's bail! He was gone from custody to run the streets again to do no telling what! Art knew the armadillo, how it moved about at night.

"Any Texan would know what I mean by that statement," he said to his deputy. Bridges grunted that he heard, but wasn't really listening. This move of bail was a troubling situation for the sheriff. He had to face Leona Broughton. Bridges kept shut.

"Trent could well think his case to be open and shut; good for his reputation," Art said, thinking Bridges cared.

Trent cared. What else could King do but accept his judgement when he allegedly was caught red-handed? And, Karly's parents had called off the hunt for their daughter when she returned home from King's house. Trent had learned Leona Broughton told the sheriff she thought Karly was with King the whole time. The hospital records would be subpoenaed and any sign of rape out in the open for the prosecution's use. Even if sex wasn't forced, there was the statutory question. Besides, Trent had forensic findings from King's place.

Considering the law arrived at King's place too late to catch Karly inside the house and it was all circumstantial, forensics had to comb everything there for evidence and testify that Karly was with King at all. The city boys had responsibility for the confession and Trent relaxed as the trial was set. He assumed all was in order since he put the case before the grand jury and King was indicted in rapid fire order. Trent had a reputation as far as Sheriff Simonds knew of doing his best. He hoped Trent had his DNA facts in order.

Chapter 5

Face Off

Three months passed with Raleigh King out and on the street. There had been no more incidents where he was concerned. It was close to the end of the year and Raleigh wanted to spend holidays—Thanksgiving and Christmas—with his mother. He had been allowed to return to his job at the mill and was content. Maybe the bad would go away and he would be watching TV and playing his video games in peace. Ma had promised new ones this Christmas.

Suzie King wanted her boy to be innocent. He was a good son. He was all she had and this Broughton woman was spreading gossip all over town, turning everybody against the only person Suzie had in her life. She cried at night when he wasn't around. Would they take away the only child she would ever have? Raleigh's daddy said they would when she first had him and the "grandpa"rancher wouldn't let him and Suzie marry to give Raleigh a good name.

As soon as the court had allowed Raleigh to leave on bond, he moved back with his mother. He was scared. When Raleigh left one morning for work, Suzie let tears slide down as she choked from the hurt inside. Jerking back where her boy wouldn't see her cry, she shut the door so loud Raleigh turned to see what was wrong. His mother had disappeared – he turned to his ride. All he thought of nowadays was how Karly had lied. Why, when he helped her out?

* * *

All things considered with an anxious, angry town on the city's back and the sheriff's office, Simonds finally saw justice begin. Actually, not all that long what with a back log of cases, interviews of the victim and the perp, lab tests and DNA correlation to look into, motions to dismiss evidence obtained in searching King's home, and rulings by the judge. When Chief Brown revealed to Art early on in the investigation that Karly Young had showered and washed away any evidence, the sheriff dreaded calling Leona. It must've been Karly's parents' idea for the bath. He visited with Brown at city hall first.

"There could've been DNA from kisses, touches, sweat, and her body could've been swabbed," Brown told Art. "Why, they even comb hair in more places than the head to get one with roots for testing. No DNA was found according to hospital records."

"Yeah, I know. What happened to old fashioned circumstance? Did O. J's trial have that much influence on our lives forever?"

"Art, our circumstantial evidence days may be gone," Brown pointed out.

"Nah, not in Texas." He laughed, Brown didn't. Art glanced around the too-cramped office, much like his own. His eyes naturally took in the chief sitting behind the desk with dark circles around his eyes from overwork; lines beginning on a younger-than-Art peace officer and short-handed crew. The dark look didn't do him any favors when it came to being nice to visitors. He sometimes came across as a grouch, but was one of the good ole boys nevertheless. Art sighed, shook hands with Brown and left.

Brown stared at the open door, wishing he could do something for the sheriff. After all, this was Simond's last year in office, but Brown had to think of himself; appointed, not elected to office.

* * *

All minor cases were dispensed the day before King'sfirst appearance, and the court docket cleared for the alleged sex offender's high profile case. Judge Tobias Black wanted one thing on everybody's mind: alleged rape of a juvenile by King, guilty or innocent. The first day there wasn't much done in court as far as litigation. It took the better part of one day to swear in and choose among the hundred and seventy-five people called for jury duty. Art heard later, but doubted from experience that not one exemption statement had been submitted. Dang! This jury was going to be hot.

Noting the unusual turnout and taking that move into account, Judge Black had sworn in the eager crowd: "You and each of you, solemnly swear that you will make true answers to such questions as may be propounded to you by the court, or under its jurisdiction, touching your service and qualifications as a juror, so help you God."

If loudness was an indication of earnest desire to serve, the room echoed in the affirmative.

Neal Sturm was walking around, shuffling through papers, characteristically anxious but not nervous. He was confident from past experience he could represent King if the crowd awaiting jury panel questioning didn't get out of control. This was not the first time an alleged sex offender had appeared in this court, but this had to be a first for the district that this many people in such a small town were interested in serving. Was this a prosecution or persecution? He heard the rumor that Leona Broughton had indeed stirred too many citizens into a frenzy for justice.

Trent led off the questioning of each and every one of the "lucky or unlucky" souls sitting there in the humidity. It seemed redundant to the Sheriff for Trent to ask each and every one if they had been a victim or had anyone in their family who had been a victim, but knew this as necessary procedure. He took particular notice of the prosecutor's spit and polish look, western suit, with the solid black outfit chopped in two at the waist by a big brass buckle. Heck, Art thought, we all like big buckles.

Yet he was concerned that the nature of the case brought out every single summoned citizen. That was unusual in itself, Art thought. Won't be any trouble impaneling enough qualified people from this bunch. Maybe the pregnant lady in the front row would be dismissed first.

Trent had invested at least two hours without a break, asking personal questions of each prospective juror to ascertain how much chance he had of convicting King with what he had: circumstantial evidence. He had already fought the battle of whether there was enough evidence to try the alleged offender. His black hair and smooth face was wet with sweat. Art watched the diligent prosecutor's piercing blue eyes. Women probably thought him a handsome man. Art wasn't impressed with looks. In his opinion, pink-faced men like himself were best looking for the women.

When it was Defense Attorney Neal Sturms' turn and the judge directed him to begin, dang if one of the ladies in the middle of the crowd suddenly stood and asked:

"Your honor, may I address the court?"

Although unusual for anybody to be brash enough to ask such as this in the little county, Judge Black stuttered a second before he answered, "Well, Ma'am, I guess so."

"Your honor," she said, "if you don't allow us a restroom break, you aren't going to have a jury to call." Art was glad she didn't look his way. That remark brought on laughter; tension was abated for now. Art knew the bold woman as a pilgrim from the north, a close friend of Leona Broughton. Would Leona put her friend up to disrupting the court?

"Recess for ten minutes," Black said and an audible, collective sigh filled the room. Some of the women glad-handed the bold lady. Art was glad himself, but never had the nerve to pull something so reckless. He would've just sneaked out. It probably was a first for Black. Art stared at the woman he knew as Laura Rogers.

Talk about nerve! Art liked that in a woman, red haired and all. Good looking woman, and he always wanted a red head. *Seems like we get a lot of types down here anymore looking for a warm place in the sun.* He subconsciously filed her brashness. Experience over the years told him she would be dumped from the panel on peremptory challenge. Both sides had that right for a specific number and this woman was a candidate for that challenge.

For future reference Art paid attention to her dark red hair and deep blue eyes. What would Nora, his wife, think of whathe had in mind? Art was a careful sheriff and often filed things in the back of his mind when actions seemed out of order, especially where women were concerned.

In the case of Leona Broughton, Art learned from her it was grief that sent her south, looking for rest and relaxation. She had lost her husband. The talk was she was loaded with money when she arrived. It was a great laugh around town that Ole Ted took care of her finances. Talk was he had none, but sometimes men hid what they means they had when marrying strangers. Art smiled and turned his attention to the trial at hand.

The sheriff recalled a rumor that King had asked to skip the trial by jury, but Art was positive the defense lawyer, a county-raised boy from Yorktown, would have disagreed. They would make sure the alleged sex offender had his day in court before his peers to cover their own behinds.

King couldn't even afford decent clothes, so he had to settle for whoever the judge appointed to defend him. Sturm was a lawyer everybody in the county knew. He was the only one on the judge's list who could be convinced to take the case, so Art thought.

In reality, Sturm looked forward to defending King, not convinced the young man was guilty after lengthy discussion in the lockup.

Art sat watching, thinking about Judge Black and a jury trial as opposed to a bench trial. If a jury turned King loose, then Tobias Black wouldn't be blamed. The judge couldn't help but know he had a reputation for being soft on offenders involved with teenagers. This was town gossip, all conjecture on the part of the rumor mongers. It was told among law enforcement that Black had a brother who was hung out to dry for getting a teenager pregnant and she yelled rape.

Personally, Art didn't believe a man elected by the citizens would let his family problems influence him when it came to a grown man molesting a teenager. It sure wasn't Black's looks got him elected. The half-balding head, oversized mustache and black-rimmed glasses topping a black robe presented a sinister look.

In the heat of the courtroom, King was sitting bolt upright, innocent-looking just like before with his blonde hair, blue yes, soft lips; baby-faced twenty-seven year old man. Art figured he got his looks and his size from his mother, Suzie. The sheriff could see how a young girl could be fooled into thinking how nice it would be to have a friend like Raleigh, especially if it was going against her parents.

The sheriff wished he hadn't been allowed to witness the jury selection. He had studied one man with a lean face, pencil-thin mustache, glasses, wearing a long-sleeved shirt—unusual in hot Summer time—who had appeared unsettled in his chair. He was one of fifteen selected for final consideration. Art couldn't help but notice the prospective juror prior to final selection in the group as the man changed positions constantly, even putting on dark glasses at on point.

Juror Number 25 had noticed the Sheriff staring at him. He grew more uncomfortable as his head throbbed with an ache that wouldn't let go. He reached up, removed his regular glasses and exchanged them for sun shades. The light was extra bright overhead and his eyes hurt from the headache.

Later he thought better of the move and returned to regular glasses. He was sure his blood pressure was so high from resentment he might have a stroke any second. He didn't want to be there. He tried unsuccessfully to be exempted, but the lady in charge refused to take responsibility fir dismissal prior to selection. He explained why he wouldn't be selected—never was and never would be. He had written a note, presented it, told her, pleaded, but she refused to listen, said it wasn't up to her.

The prospective jurors were shown a short film of why the jury system was used. It was a first for him, being reminded of his obligation and "privilege" to live in a land where juries were allowed to determine the fate of accused.

Not once in all the seven times he had been called and rejected had there been such a push to educate prospective jurors on the reasons why they should serve. Was this new or had it been so long since he was called he hadn't heard? Outward appearance indicated his boredom, not growing resentment as the hours wore on.

The judge grabbed his attention when he explained the case they would be hearing. In fact, when he finished giving the graphic details—an x-rated description—of an alleged child molester of a young boy, rage replaced the resentment.

He knew that armadillo as a boy. Should he say anything yet? Should he leave the room? No, he would surely be asked later during the one-on-one questioning from the judge, the prosecutor, the defense attorney, somebody, if there was a reason why he wouldn't be fair and impartial. Then he could explain wh why he would not be a good selection for this particular trial.

It didn't happen. He was one of the fifteen selected to be questioned and retained or dismissed. The questions weren't asked of him as stringently as the first prospects. For some reason—God alone knew why—he was allowed to barely eke by on a few questions when the process moved on to the next person.

"I think I can be fair," Reggie Cotton had said and wondered where the words came from. He couldn't be fair. He hated the accused already without knowing any facts. Most, in fact, all of the others were questioned at length as to whether they were aware of anything which would prevent fairness. He wished he had been as bold as the woman who asked for restroom privileges in the middle of the original opening. He wished he had been more diligent in obtaining a doctor's slip that he wasn't able to sit in this position very long at a time. His nerves, his senses, all tuned in the child molester sitting there looking innocent.

Yeah! He was as innocent as the pedofile who messed up number twenty-five's childhood, scarred for life incident carried for a lifetime of mental jail sentence for the action of a pervert who was subsequently let off with a few months of punishment. If he had met and talked with Leona Broughton, the man would have known he wasn't the only one who suffered the humiliation of molestation and lived with the haunting for life.

Not aware of anything on Cotton's mind, or even who he was, Art was casually watching the selected twelve sitting there with alternates whisper-quiet when Cotton suddenly burst from his seat, dashed across the room and attempted to rush Raleigh King!

"You need to die devil!" he screamed.

Poor Raleigh, mentally challenged, was so startled he began to cry as he hunched deep down in his seat. Sturm moved to create a protective wall between his client and the crazed juror.

Heck, Art thought, can anything else stupid happen?

The bailiff and two uniformed officers jumped on Cotton in seconds, grabbed his arms, pinned them behind his back and put him down. Art half-rose to assist, but realized he wasn't needed, and after all, he was little more than an observer to the process today. Usually, not too many peace officers were on hand, awaiting their turn as witnesses. The bailiff was trained for such as this. Art would keep his seat and let the court handle the outburst.

Round eyes on the other prospects revealed astonishment that someone could be so quiet-looking and have so much bottled up inside. The whispering jurors watched as Cotton was escorted from the room by officers.

Black, surprised, banged for order, took a long drink of water, knowing this disturbance did his heart no good. Why hadn't this potential problem been taken care of prior to opening? Didn't anybody catch the determination of the fool before court began? Was he going to have to educate the selection committee on what to do when a prospect attempted to be excluded? Dang!

It was time for a recess.

* * *

When the trial was underway Art noticed a strange face in the courtroom sitting in the middle row. He sat head and shoulders over the rest of the onlookers, loose blonde hair falling over large ears; well-dressed man, apparently interested in what was taking place. A colorful fancy tie complemented his attire– a silk suit. Art whispered to Trent and he whispered back:

"The man is a high-dollar lawyer from Houston name of Merriwether, but I don't know what he's doing here. He's reputed to be with a criminal defense team up that way. I don't know who would pay for him to be down here in our county. This case is cut and dried. He was probably just brought in to consult with Sturm on jury selection. It doesn't bother me."

Trent stood, confidence beaming from a smooth face, turned to the jury panel and made his opening statement a call for "guilty on a charge of kidnaping and rape," saying the state could prove their case.

Sturm, not hiding his satisfaction for the chance to defend an alleged sex offender who made the Victoria news, wanted this trial by jury. This case could go national, maybe, and wouldn't that be good for his reputation? Besides, the slow minded man was one of Sturm's "innocents."

Art didn't think about publicity. It wouldn't be foremost on his mind at this point, and the sheriff toyed with the idea he could be completely wrong about Sturm. He had heard that defense lawyers actually relished what they're doing. Well, maybe not relish, maybe more like dedicated.

Sturm called for "dismissal" since all the evidence was "circumstantial," but Black didn't grant his request. Failing that motion, Sturm injected a question on the competency of the alleged offender.

"Your honor, King couldn't even fill out the statement waiving his rights. He doesn't read that well and reading it to him was no help in the matter."

"Do you really want to go through a trial for competency, Counselor?" Black asked. "Hasn't this case gone long enough for you? Do you have a preponderance of evidence to support the allegation King is not competent due to mental retardation? Do you have local mental retardation authority lined up for an Incompetent to Stand Trial motion, or are you just fishing, Counselor? We've already been through this. Defendant is presumed fit to stand trial. What say you, Trent?"

"King's not retarded, just slow," Trent responded. "He holds down a forty-hour work week. King is indeed competent, Your Honor."

Didn't anybody realize King could hear the words they were using; maybe understand they were treating him like a retard for all their fancy words? Art felt sorry for the son of an unlearned, uneducated woman gone bad. The way Trent attached the words to Raleigh in the man's hearing caused even the judge to drop his eyes.

Art's age and loss of hearing was against him as the battle waffled back and forth in voices so soft the aging sheriff couldn't hear a word, but he had caught what Trent countered with: "King is indeed competent." The prosecutor cited his recent investigation, consultation and determinations with a mental health counselor as evidence of competency, who could be witness for the prosecution.

Art thought just because himself and half the town believed King to be half a deck shy didn't mean it was so, but that had to be resolved before a trial was underway. Deeply bored by the slow, drawn-out haggling lawyers do when they're thinking how to word the next question, Art thought he's sick all right, but not like they're arguing "sick."

He forced himself to stay awake, to become more interested as the tension mounted in the courtroom with the possibility King would be found not fit to stand trial, sent to an institution and too soon loosed on the city again.

Black had to hammer more than once to restore order. The crowd was heated up, standing and yelling and shaking their fists at the court. The loudest cries came from a bunch of senior citizens — friends of Leona Broughton.

Trent called upon a known mental health witness, Floyd Birchman. "King has been on medication, something to control his nerves," the witness admitted, "but he's been faithful to go by the rules. He understands he has a chemical imbalance."

Black decided, with expert testimony submitted and King acting like he knew what was going on, the baby-faced man was capable of understanding his charges and could know what the judge, his defense attorney and the prosecution were doing.

"Get on with it, Counselors," ordered Black.

The information had nothing to do with being a sex offender, so Art thought. Their kind just have too many extra hormones desiring little girls and boys. That was the general consensus.

Following the line of questioning, Sturm made a motion King's earlier confession be suppressed. He pointed out the city had fouled up and not read the alleged offender his Miranda rights. Where he obtained the information, Art didn't know.

"Objection!" Trent yelled. "How can he prove this, Your Honor?"

"Your Honor," Sturm said, "We have proof if I may be allowed."

"Allowed," Judge Black said.

Sturm called for the rookie officer—who participated in interrogating King—to be brought to the stand.

Trent objected, saying "Your Honor. All that was taken care of earlier."

Dang! Art almost cussed out loud. What now?

To the chagrin of the prosecution, Sturm could prove his allegation. The young rookie who interrogated King stated emphatically he had read King his rights, which his partner could prove, but when Sturm pressed the issue of the so-called confession tape, the young officer reddened. The judge allowed the video in question opened to the court.

Art knew it wasn't mandatory to tape, but the accused probably would've been taped in a sex case. Apparently nobody made sure Brown's new officer knew how to operate the equipment. He was fresh out of the academy. He shouldn't have been in charge. Dang!

Chief Brown was embarrassed Art knew when he looked at him. Sturm was right. The video was put before the court with the sound totally missing. Miranda rights being read was not on the tape, but earlier testimony had revealed they were read at King's residence, so that part was okay. All that the tape revealed was King sitting there smiling and talking, not signing a confession or giving one out loud. He had a pad in front of him and he could have been doodling on it for all anybody knew.

It would've taken a lip reader to interpret what King was saying on the tape. Dang and double Dang! And this could present the jury with doubt; some might think the officers were covering for each other in testifying as to King's so-called confession.

Brown belatedly realized he had been remiss in going about other business in this high-profile case, but there was just so much time in a day and he was short-handed since the city cut funding. The interrogation was all on the up-and-up, the questioning and the witnessed confession, his officers assured. And why didn't Trent check this out? It was his job to know about these things Brown told himself in retrospect. It was also his job to know and the city's going to mention my duties at the next budget meeting. Adequate law enforcement is a must even in a town of seven thousand plus and the council wasn't addressing the lack of personnel.

Art dared to look at Judge Black and realized the decision weighed heavy. The oft-criticized judge knew his reputation was on the line and there was obvious reluctance on his face and in his voice as he ruled the so-called confession suppressed.

"With no more evidence than what I've heard so far, Mr. Trent," he said, "I don't think you have a case unless you have proof we haven't seen. I'll give you not more than twenty-four hours, Counselor, to present evidence why this man should be tried any further. Court's recessed until that time." He banged the gavel and yelling filled the room as King hurried out.

Black knew how town fever was rising. He knew who to blame. Leona Broughton was doing as much damage as she could even with the sheriff and chief doing everything in their power to keep order. Should he nail her for contempt? No, that would stir a frenzy only the national guard could handle and this town didn't need that kind of publicity. What made him angriest, and he dare not let it show, was that she inadvertently made him and Art Simonds look bad—failing in their duties. She was pushing for contempt and he was just the man to slam her into jail for it. He would hate that: everyone knew she was battling cancer.

* * *

When the news broke that night on the Victoria television station and the next morning in the Victoria paper saying King had left the courtroom again with no conviction as to the Karly Young case, Art had to hire an auxiliary deputy to handle the phone calls. Same thing over at the city offices. The chief really couldn't afford extra help, so they had one of the regular city employees taking calls from parents who were finally noticing the county had sex offenders living in their comfortable town.

Art wondered if the parents took their kids off the internet. When the weekly news in town came out, everybody who never watched the news otherwise put in their two cents worth. Anxiety—better late, better never—was rising.

It was at this point Art realized with the scary situation on their hands, he was relieved not to be in immediate charge, but Brown couldn't do it all. The situation wasn't going away. The town was riled up: "The sex offender's runnin' loose," was one of the yells heard by the sheriff. He and the Chief had no choice but to work together to keep the peace.

Leona didn't know they were discussing her behind her back and if she had, wouldn't care. This time the pedofile was going down if she had to take care of the matter for the law.

Chapter 6

Accused Gone

Late in the evening, near a rundown cabin at Concrete, deep in tangled brush off the blacktop from Hwy 183 a man screamed. He was quickly muzzled before he could draw an audience from neighboring ranch land. The gag was too late, he had passed out. An angry, sheet-clad kidnapper stepped back to survey completed work, then gagged. The other one grunted and turned away. Whimpering and puking wouldn't do the perp any good now.

"Hell," a voice grunted. "Did Karly scream when you raped her, pervert? Shut up!" The voice was lost on deaf ears of an unconscious man.

He couldn't answer with his mouth taped even if he had been alert. Puffed eyes from crying made slits in his face just above a red, swollen nose. The stench of fear rose. He had lost the battle with kidneys and bowels.

Two other kidnappers, one in sheets and the other over-confident in his own outside clothing walked up to the man hanging upside down from a tree limb, blood dripping on his shirt front and into his mouth and nose from the mutilation carried out from above – between spread legs. They cut the rope, jerked him to his feet, and dragged him toward the open door of a neglected cabin. Pistol to his head, they shoved the man through the door. An older man, no sheet to hide him, scurried after the two, checking behind to make sure nobody followed.

"We'll leave him here for today and check up on him tomorrow afternoon," one said and the other nodded. The older man ran out the door, hopping and jumping over fire ant beds to "get the heck out of Dodge," as he put it. The other two took pleasure in his nervous nature.

* * *

Three overhead fans whizzed with dizzying speed from the high ceiling in a packed room the next time court was in session on the Raleigh King case, but they provided little relief. Even with the Air turned up full blast, breathing was hard. Wiping sweat off his face and neck with a bright blue bandana, culturally out of place in the somber setting of a courtroom, Trent nodded as Judge Tobias Black asked if the state was ready. He stepped forward to present his case, but was stopped by Black when the judge observed the defendant was not present.

"Counselor Sturm," Judge Black addressed defense, "Where's your client?"

"Your Honor, sir, I don't know."

"Surprise! Surprise! Surprise! as ole Gomer Pyle would've said." Art whispered to a deputy seated next to him. "Wouldn't you know it? They let a sex pervert out on bail and expected him to come back." The young deputy grinned, but failed to remember who Gomer Pyle was. He refused the sweaty, palm-held jelly beans Art offered. Couldn't the sheriff wait until the trial recessed to feed his sweet tooth, the deputy asked himself.

Sturm admitted he had no idea where his client was. Although a bad situation, it didn't faze the judge. He paused a moment, shuffled a few papers and pronounced King would be tried anyway. The noise level in the courtroom rose. The crowd was furious.

"Where's the pedofile, Mr. Sturm?" one angry man yelled. Black hammered for silence.

"Well, we'll try him in absentia," Black pronounced, and for the jury, that means in the absence of the defendant. Okay with you, Sturm? Okay with you Trent?"

They nodded to proceed—after Sturm asked for and was denied a continuance—and the judge directed the trial to begin. First he had to once again gavel down the mumbling in the crowd about "lettin' a sex pervert loose on the city and "now he's gone no tellin' where." A few onlookers jumped up and ran out to check on their families after believing they were safe with King on trial.

"This is a horse of different color," Art whispered to the deputy. "It probably didn't occur to a one of them good citizens King ain't the only pred-o-file in town," he said using his new word for predator-pedofile types. The sheriff popped in a jelly bean, chewed and swallowed. The deputy thought he might get sick and not from the heat.

Trent was quiet. Art decided he must've assumed King would be found guilty due to absence, then picked up later. The prosecutor aggravated Simonds by calling his first witness to be Deputy Bridges who took the phone tip about King having Karly in his place for three days. Why didn't Trent call on the city first? Art couldn't figure. They were primary, after all. Bridges took the stand to testify about finding evidence Karly had been at King's place.

Puffed up by the attention centered on him, Bridges was glad to tell it like he saw when he accompanied the city boys to search King's place. It was his chance to shine before the election later in the year. Trent being of the same politics could've been accused of doing his friend a favor.

"Sir, she wasn't there when we busted in," Bridges asserted.

"Busted in, Bridges? Did you mean to say when you all knocked and entered? And did the city have a proper search warrant for going into King's house?"

"Yes. We wouldn't have entered if we didn't, Sir."

"Well, where was Karly Young?" asked Trent.

"We followed up on a tip she was back home with her parents, but the alleged victim had been at King's place for three days, again accordin' to her parents. We're sure she holed up in a bedroom there, what with food wrappin's all around the floor, a blanket and pillow on the floor," he said, and Trent let him ramble. "He let us in without trouble, sayin' Karly had gone home to take the beating her parents had promised days before she knocked on Raleigh's door. He said 'I told her she wasn't supposed to be here, but she said it would be all right, said she was scared. I know about scared so I brought her on into my house.' "

"Hearsay," Sturm objected. Black warned Trent with a look that said don't lead the witness, but motioned for Bridges to continue. Bridges was eager to oblige.

"King claimed she wanted to be there. We believe a thirteen year old don't know better than to go home with somebody they know, and 'specially when there's a pup involved." The only thing he left out was who gave his department a tip on Karly's whereabouts.

"Objection!" Sturm yelled, followed by "Not pertinent! Your honor, would you instruct the witness to stick to the question and leave out his beliefs and dogs?" Art felt tension—rampant in the courtroom—was effecting even the defense. He was getting loud.

Black scowled at Bridges in a special way he had. His heavy brows overshadowed the sharp, beady eyes and fit in well with a little beard jutting out from his chin. The brows made him look more menacing than the Brahman bull Bridges encountered earlier in the year. He closed up.

Sturm, during cross exam asked, "Would it be fair, Deputy, to say you didn't see her there being fed and playing with a dog?" Bridges had to admit he had not. He looked at Art, clammed up and was turned loose with Sturm asking for the right to recall.

City Officer Dan Thomas, the next witness Trent called up, related his department's careful handling of the arrest of Raleigh King verifying Bridges' account.

By this time half-asleep Art was thinking about anything but the trial. He missed a lot of the back and forth questions, the hem-hawing around, and didn't care. He had to stop eating them dang good tacos at the DQ. Once in awhile, a noise would jerk him back to the proceedings, but mostly he was bored, having to sit through so many lawyers arguing cases in his years as sheriff. His hearing was failing, something he would never admit to, and his opinion was the sound system in the courtroom wasn't geared for letting onlookers with hearing problems know what was said, just for recording all the proceedings.

Art glanced sideways at the jury. They were just as bored as he and one failed to cover a yawn. Art looked to see if either lawyer noticed. They didn't. People should be awake in consideration of a man's rights, Art thought. They made up their minds long ago.

Sturm had one more question for the city officer: "How was the warrant obtained to search King's house? Did you have probable cause to bust into a man's home the way Deputy Bridges described?"

Thomas nodded his head, but spoke up when reminded by the judge, "Yes Sir, we did. Trent ordered it, but we didn't bust in, we knocked."

"And Trent being...?"

"The prosecutor, Sir," Thomas responded, and glanced at Trent as if to ask if he was doing everything right as they rehearsed.

Sturm indicated his questions were finished with the local officer, but then recalled Bridges for cross stating rather than asking: "If Karly indeed was in King's house, she was there voluntarily." He banged on the table he stood
behind to question Bridges. The jury jerked awake.

"Leading the witness," Trent interrupted.

Did Sturm make a mistake in stating that Karly indeed was in King's house or did he do it on purpose? Art couldn't tell about lawyers. Bridges didn't catch it. Said he didn't know. Art looked at Trent and he was grinning big. Art wondered if the smug prosecution was thinking Sturm cut his client's throat. He didn't deny her visit to King's house. He had something up his sleeve for sure.

Then Sturm had to be brought down by the judge for putting words in Bridges' mouth:

"Oh, I'm sure, sir, if you could tell she had been there, you could tell if she was held against her will, Deputy."

Black instructed Sturm to ask a question or move on.

As soon as Sturm withdrew the statement, he asked, "Was the door locked?"

Art noted that Bridges was sweating. Art also noted that Bridges—Art's token black deputy-turned-excellent-law man, not a great witness—didn't catch onto the possibility Sturm had cut his own defense down to size saying things which helped Trent in his prosecution, or did he?

Over-confident from his role in the arrest of King, the deputy admitted again nobody saw Karly in the house with King, and started to say "King confessed," but Sturm cut him off with:

"Just answer the question."

None of the lengthy testimony given in the courtroom

mattered, Art decided, when it came to a witness who wasn't there. She had been subpoenaed, but no surprise, Tom and Sue Young had refused to allow the prosecution to put Karly on the stand to testify. She was too delicate, they said. An angry Leona told Art that bit of news right before the trial. Now that's what Simonds called overkill. There was nothing delicate about Karly Young. She'd more likely tear King's head off than not. Simonds informed Leona they had no choice. Karly would be made to testify. Period.

Judge Black ordered Trent to bring in his witness Miss Young the next day or forget the case.

* * *

Leona Broughton attempted to hold Art's eyes in the hostile court room when he dared glance her way, but he turned, flinching from the ice in her face. It was warming up in the courtroom, almost as hot as the hundred three degrees outside, but Art bet himself Leona wasn't warm. He had chosen the wrong seat, by an unshaded window. He swiped at his face and neck with a brown bandana. Nora would never approve of a brown bandana on an important day like this, his mind propelled him into thinking. But his wife had died. She wouldn't know.

Leona frowned, knowing she had to take care of things on her own. Art Simonds, the city and the prosecutor let King get away with raping her granddaughter just like she knew they would. She had promised herself that anyone who touched her kin would suffer the ultimate. She turned her attention back to the trial and smiled. She was angry that Tim and Sue were hiding from the entire process. Good gosh, it was Tim's daughter, for crying out loud.

Leona didn't expect Sue or her parents, the pseudo aristocrats, to be anywhere near, but her own son, Karly's daddy, what the heck did he mean? If Karly's momma was alive, she'd be on the scene. In fact, if she was alive this situation never would have occurred. Even in darkest times she had cared where Karly spent time.

Art saw Leona's twisted face as she looked his way. He felt apprehensive.

She motioned and Art followed her outside the courtroom.

"What's happening, Sheriff? Why is Trent getting riled up and not doing his job?"

"Leonnie, I think he's doin' the best he can. Just maybe, mind you I'm saying just maybe it's stickin' in his craw that he lost a case of two homosexuals killing another one of them to Sturm and nobody took a fall."

"Whatever. All he has to do is his job," she offered, looking away.

"Leonnie, listen to yourself. All he has to go on is circumstantial evidence and your Karly needs to step forward, rather her parents need to push her for testifyin'. It's Raleigh King's word against hers with no DNA to go on, thanks to your son and his wife."

She turned and stomped back into the courtroom.

* * *

Off Highway 183 a hunter looking into constructing a deer blind walked up to a half-burned cabin on the Broughton property. He knew there'd been a report of smoke in the area, but apparently neighbors had extinguished whatever caused the fire. This was not a time to be burning anything with the dry spell, but since it was taken care of he would just look inside and see what was left. He looked around, no one was in sight so he stepped into the charred building.

"Oh heck!" he mouthed, but no sound came out. He jerked out a cell phone and dialed the sheriff's office where he talked to Deputy Bridges.

"Be right there! Don't leave and secure the scene." Bridges instructed.

* * *

At the courthouse Trent called in subpoenaed hospital personnel to the stand one by one on Karly's condition and possible rape when she came into the hospital. He knew they would have to have medical secrets pulled from them without parental consent of the victim. But, maybe, just maybe, with them appearing for the prosecution, it would impress the jury, Art thought.

The sheriff dozed again during the testimony thinking it was useless. It wasn't unusual for him to fall asleep any more.

It was time to retire. Sixty years of age bore on his mind. It was time to get out of this rat race. Trent could ask questions as to Karly's condition when her parents brought her into the hospital, but the unwilling witness didn't have to answer, Art thought, but didn't know for sure. If one didn't answer questions to suit Trent, it could be assumed by the jury Karly wasn't raped.

"She apparently had sex with someone," rape crisis nurse Janet Lindsay admitted, "but she wouldn't admit it, and she wouldn't say who. She had been bathed thoroughly and we couldn't get DNA from anything on her." Lindsay wondered what the prosecutor expected of her since there was no evidence of actual rape, just sex. It wasn't the girl's first time, but it wasn't Janet's place to inform the court of this.

"No more questions," Trent said and turned the nurse over to Sturm.

The defense attorney walked slowly toward the witness asking, "Did you see any evidence of forced penetration?" Lindsay said "No." What else could she do?

"Did she admit she was raped?" he asked, and again the nurse said no.

"Asked and answered," Trent complained and Black looked at Sturm.

"That's all the questions I have, your honor," Sturm said. The judge dismissed the witness.

Art, along with Leona, had already grown concerned for the case when Tom and Sue Young fought against sending King to prison on Karly's testimony. It was their choice. The state couldn't try an alleged offender without her setting there in person, Art thought. I don't blame Karly's parents in a way, because everybody knows how reputations can be ruined. The state would call her anyway.

None of Karly's family but Leona and the girls's father attended. Karly's step-grandparents, the Clements, kept a safe distance from the ugliness of a trial involving their daughter's problem step-child. Art wished Leona hadn't shown today. If he had this God thing right, God forgives, the people don't, and I'm sure Leona would be one who wouldn't. Anyway, Karly'll have hard enough time living down whatever was true or untrue.

Right off the bat, Sturm objected to Trent when he recalled the city officer, asking "Is it your testimony King made a confession. He answered "yes," before Judge Black ruled, and Trent had no more questions. He turned King over to the defense.

Strum walked up and looked the officer straight in the eyes. He stood for a moment and then pointedly asked: "Would it be fair to say a confession was elicited from King by your department offering him leniency?" He had to bring up another reason to throw the confession out, and when Art looked at Police Chief Richard Brown, he knew Sturm was wrong. The sheriff hoped Trent had an answer for that, but he didn't. Dang!

"No Sir, we didn't offer him leniency," the officer answered. "We taped it, but since this was a serious sex offense charge with a thirteen year old, I did and you know it was suppressed earlier because it was faulty. It ain't mandated, just used for clarifyin' a perp's own words."

Sturm asked the judge to address the witness about bringing up the confession and calling the accused a perp when he was an alleged perpetrator. Black admonished the officer and instructed the jury to disregard the mention of a confession. Sturm wasn't done.

"Officer, wasn't this King's first alleged offense?" he asked and looked the jury straight in the eyes, not letting the officer answer. He turned his back and walked away.

Trent asked for redress, jumped up and asked "Isn't King a known sex offender, registered here in town as mandated by Megan's Law?"

"Yes," Thomas answered, "he's on the list accordin' to records and my computer," but Sturm didn't want to hear that and objected, asking the judge to order the jury to ignore the officer's testimony on sex offender status.

Black asserted "Counselor, you brought up the subject."

Risk assessment levels were not mentioned, but Art knew them by heart: low, medium and high; high posing the most serious danger, a continuing danger. King was surely low risk.

Pulling his thoughts together, Art told himself maybe Sturm was winning but Black instructed the officer to state a simple "yes, or no, with no explanation as to how he knew." Black instructed the jury to disregard mention of a computer list. Something about not using past offenses if it didn't prove to be related to this case.

Art had to give Trent credit for guts. He stared directly at Black's and out of order busted out with "What about Moral Turpitude, Judge? Don't it hold water in this court King allegedly committed a sexual act on a child and is a listed sex offender? How about his past record? Are you going to let Counsel get away with that?"

Black hammered on the bench. "You're treading on dangerous ground, Trent. One more and I'll cite you for contempt." He instructed the jury to "disregard." Toby was in control and would let the world know.

Sturm jumped on Black's threat and moved to strike the past record part.

"Approach," Black called. Both attorneys stepped up. Art felt sicker. Black explained, loud enough for the entire courtroom to hear:

"Sturm, you introduced the record by asking about this being his first offense."

Art knew his department believed the girl who got King in trouble years ago placing him on the offender list should've been an issue, but he would wait and see.

Black said she was fourteen just like Karly. He was off a little on the age. Karly was barely thirteen. Art thought maybe the judge didn't take time to review the case sufficiently to know how old she was, or could be all this monkey business was getting to Black the same as himself and the rest of the onlookers. The judge appeared tired.

He was tired. Doc told him to get off the bench or die in his robe some day when things were out of order and his temper on the rise. Black unconsciously placed a hand on his chest , not that anyone would notice, and felt heat under the robe. Nothing was amiss at the moment.

Sturm pointed out since King was only seventeen at the time he was labeled a sex offender, Karly's case had nothing to do with the past. Black agreed; he must have reviewed something,

Art thought. Trent just stood there. Couldn't he come up with anything? An objection, maybe. Dang!Art stifled another cussing spell.

Then Sturm appeared to lose it and pointed out just as loud as Black: "King was only three years older than the girl in the first case," and the two lawyers ran around the difference in victims for several minutes. It was getting hotter.

The judge was silent and on went Sturm with his lengthy explanation as to how moral turpitude didn't fit. Art was not educated on court procedure enough, but he didn't think Black either a stupid man or immoral. He looked over his shoulder at Leona. Ice froze his gaze and he hoped she wasn't thinking what he thought she would be thinking right about here.

"That'll be enough, counselor," Black said, "you brought this in, Sturm, now live with it." He waved the two back to their tables.

Was that a smirk on Trent's face? Well, he hadn't won yet. No matter that he called in the mental health professional from San Antonio, Floyd Birchman, a counselor who serviced Cuero patients periodically, to testify as to a sex offender leaning toward young girls, hoping to at least push for getting King off the streets by institutionalizing him. That move led nowhere. He had already been judged competent to stand trial, but maybe Trent thought the ruling bore repeating.

Whatever happened to the punishment fitting the crime, Art didn't know, not being a lawyer and he didn't have as much training as is demanded in the modern day law enforcement world. One of the reasons he wasn't running again for sheriff was because the state raised the standards for law enforcers as well as appointed criminal lawyers. He was flabbergasted thinking this defense lawyer knew what he was doing: he would defend King to the end.

Art came into law enforcement when it wasn't necessary to attend the academy to do the job. Common sense and insight kept him going all these years. It was time to retire.

Chapter 7

Victim to the Stand

For Art, the defense for King went south from the time Sturm questioned whether Raleigh was a bonafide sex offender just because he and an underage girl became too friendly when they were teenagers. How many of the jurors had fallen for a teenager in their day? Art looked at Leona Broughton in the courtroom and could see red creeping up her neck. He thought again of what could've happened to King for him to not show up. Where was Leona Broughton all that time and would she follow through on the threat everybody in Cuero had heard from her bitter lips? She hadn't recovered from the meltdown at Port Lavaca, had she?

This brought to mind for the sheriff that Sturm couldn't call King to testify in his own behalf when the judge asked him if he had a witness. In his client's place, Sturm did call two women Trent knew about, but would Trent put much stock in them as witnesses, to testify that King was not a violent date and they had fun with him?

Next, Sturm called in the cotton mill manager concerning King's work habits and asked, "Did he ever have trouble working with young girls in your industry?"

"No," the manager answered. "Raleigh just did his job and went home each shift, as far as I knew, stopping off at a fast food place for his evening meal. I had no trouble with King and heard of none."

King still hadn't put in an appearance. The public defender looked at Chief Brown who shook his head and shrugged his shoulders. Sturm asked for more time.

Trent was positive this turn of events should help. He questioned the girls after Sturm was through, but it appeared to Art he just let everybody know he was doing his duty. They stuck to their stories.

Things were heating up for Sturm. He shuffled a few papers and asked for a recess to find his client. "I'm sure something happened to him, Your Honor," he pleaded. "He's innocent and he assured me he would be here on time."

"You have until tomorrow, Strum," Judge Black said and recessed for the day. Apparently he wanted to give King the biggest benefit of a doubt he judicially could.

Sturm turned around and whispered something to the Chief, who just shook his head and then nodded. Art guessed he was agreeing to find King. For a small county defense lawyer, the alleged disappearance of King didn't help.

Art wondered if the judge should allow the defense additional time when the defendant failed to show. The sheriff rose to leave the courtroom and Leona beat him out the door. He wanted to talk to her. She was ahead of a furious crowd, yelling about a pervert loose on the town and it was all the judge's fault for granting bail. Anxiety was in the air, but Art wondered how long before they went back to TV and computers with no thought of what their children were doing. He bet himself any perverts out there watching the trial results were overjoyed.

Simonds stopped the chief of police and asked,

"Did you check Raleigh's mother's house? If I remember the times we picked him up and turned him loose, that's where he always headed. Somebody said he went there when he was turned loose on bail."

"Yeah," Brown answered. "It was the second place we looked. The first was where he lived when y'all looked for Young's daughter, Karly. He wasn't there. Ms. King let us look all through her house and out back in a shed. He'll turn up somewhere, someday and then we'll have him for jumping bail. Maybe we can bring him in on harboring a runaway."

Brown did not like Art questioning him on the search. After all he was the one in charge.

* * *

The next morning found Sturm telling the judge King couldn't be found, and Black said "We'll try him anyway as I told you counselors earlier, but if he isn't here by noon, it's over. Maybe call a mistrial."

He sure wasn't going to let this case lie. It was too high profile, even for this little town. Having a Houston lawyer sitting in the courtroom, even in back, was the same as asking for notoriety. Black was just as interested in this case being done properly as the rest of the town. The room was full of inquisitive reporters. Black had barred the cameras, but he was positioned so his best side would show in case one was slipped into the room.

Suddenly Sturm realized he might lose. He grimaced at his associate who thought this was not a good thing – to allow Trent to see any emotion.

"Clean up your face, Neal," Brad Jones whispered. Art heard him say "You look weak."

Sturm asked for a brief recess.

Black asked "Why? You just got here."

"Your honor, Sir, I need to consult with Attorney Gerald Merriwether sitting in the third row, to clarify my next move. It'll only take a few minutes."

"And he is?"

"He's a defense attorney from Houston sitting in on this case, Judge, and I need to consult with him."

"All right, but move along, Counselor!"

As Black peered at the third row, Sturm dropped a handful of papers, throwing the judge off guard and the crowd burst out laughing. Black had to call for order, but he allowed a recess. "I've seen shenanigans in court, but this? " he whispered to the court reporter.

Black well knew the gossip and rumors about him being soft on sex offenders. It just wasn't true. He witnessed the injustice of his brother's young love affair, but it only made him cautious concerning young boys, not twenty-seven year olds. He hoped his last year on the bench wouldn't be a disastrous one. His heart wasn't in good shape; he tried to not get excited.

Art thought, what's Sturm up to? Why does he need a Houston lawyer to help win his case for King? He looked at the defense attorney and realized this was the second time he had to admit to himself he was prejudiced against long hair like Sturm wore, even tied back. Art reckoned to himself that he, a sheriff, must be a red neck like some people said. Sturm's call for a brief recess wasn't anything like when Laura Rogers called for a restroom break during jury questioning. Dang!

When court reconvened, Houston lawyer Merriwether, a sharp-faced English blood, had seated himself directly behind Sturm. He whispered something in Sturm's ear. The defense attorney turned to his assistant, whispered and Jones left to bring in Suzie King, Raleigh's mother. She was dolled up for the trial and trailed in like she was somebody. Everybody in town knew her for what she had done years ago. Nowadays it wouldn't matter.

Trent objected. He hadn't been informed of this witness but Black allowed her anyway.

"I don't see how it could affect this case, the way things are going," the tired judge said.

Sturm had accomplished what he wanted to do: halt the proceedings long enough for Trent to get blind-sided. What the prosecutor had called for and now lost, was that King should be considered at least a "medium risk," and put away where he couldn't get to any more girls.

Where was Trent's mind at this point? Art asked himself, and decided he, himself, wouldn't make a good prosecutor since he had to admit to prejudice towards people who are different.

"Hi, Ms. King," Sturm said, smiling like a cat licking up cream. "Don't be nervous, I'm just putting a few questions before the jury for them to consider. My first question is how old was your son when the sex offender status was attached?"

"Barely seventeen," she replied, smiling like she wasn't sure if she should.

"And why was he branded with a sex offender status, Ms. King?

"What exactly does branded mean?"

"The name burned onto your son when he was seventeen for having a fourteen year old girl friend with whom he had relations?"

"Oh, the court said he was guilty of statutory rape. You know, like when young lovers get caught," she said, and Art could see where King got his brains.

He thought of the way she had her illegitimate son, Raleigh, and wondered if anybody yelled "statutory" back then.

On cross, Trent tried to recoup his loss by stating, not

asking: "Your son is a lot older than seventeen now."

Sturm objected "Your honor, is prosecution asking a question?"

In spite of the judge's warning look, Trent insisted, "He's a heck of a lot more than seventeen years old now, and a heck of a lot more than three years older than Karly."

The second statement caused Black to strongly instruct Trent to ask a question or move on.

King's past sex offense could rule out what they called "low risk" as far as Art was concerned, and if he remembered his law, this would be no low risk crime like the first, but Sturm objected to Trent putting words in Ms. King's mouth.

"Leading the witness," he said. The judge sustained and Trent let it slide.

Dang! Art cussed silently. Any minute he would explode.

Leona was right about defense attorneys, he thought. Get 'em off no matter what, but do it within the law. Art didn't feel any less sick that it was their job, their assignment for a fair trial.

Sturm again made a motion for not entering King's past record of sex offense, and Trent, without sufficient belief in King's guilt, faded. He had allowed Ms. King to step down, asking to recall if needed. Then he half-heartedly recalled the mental health professional, Birchman, to the stand and after getting nowhere, asked:

"Is it possible King will commit future crimes toward young girls, given his record and become more medium risk than low risk?" Before he could answer, Trent asked "Would you, could you, Mr. Beachman, recommend King be given some kind of treatment to deter future sex crimes before he becomes a higher risk to the community?"

The politically savvy mental health counselor from San Antonio sat weighing his answer, and then refused to take the chance answering a question that would put him on the spot. He knew about law suits. Floyd turned to the judge and Black dismissed him.

Trent just plain disappointed Art. He thought Trent would have been better off if the judge hadn't appointed a defender for

King and it had been a bench trial.

Black instructed the jury to disregard Trent's question of recommended punishment by a mental health counselor, as he, the judge would decide punishment, if any.

Sturm recalled Ms. King long enough to ask: "To your knowledge, if your son had Karly Young at his place, would he have used force, or would she have to be compliant?"

Leona hissed! Black shot her a warning glance and she covered her mouth. Must have bit her tongue when Sturm had the nerve to ask, Art thought. Sturm was fishing, and Art was asking himself what kind of attorney would open himself up to admitting that King had relations with Karly when he asked the question, because he stressed at the beginning his client was innocent. Ms. King didn't know what the word compliant meant, but she nodded and Black ordered her to speak up.

"Sir, I don't believe I know the meanin' of that word compliant."

"That means the teenage girl would willingly let your son have his way with her," Sturm explained.

"I don't know, sir, because Raleigh, he didn't live with me. When I visited him at the jail, he told me Karly wanted to stay at his place, that she was afraid to go home. Raleigh, well, he's always good to people. He let her stay, he said, and he never lied to me. He's such a good-lookin' boy, he don't need to force girls."

"Hearsay!" yelled Trent. Black stared down at him.

Sturm had opened up a keg of worms for the jury to ponder, Art thought. If Karly Young wasn't there, why ask such a question? What exactly did Sturm have up his sleeve?

Then Sturm asked: "Why do you think your son's accuser failed to appear in court to face him if he indeed violated her? Are you ashamed of Raleigh, Ms. King?"

She shook her head, tears oozing from squinched up eyes, No need to answer, she wasn't an expert on why Karly wasn't present. She just knew who stirred up the town against Raleigh — Leona Broughton and *that witch will get hers* raced through her mind. Ms. King sat waiting while the lawyers approached Black for a sidebar.

Whatever they said, Art couldn't hear, but Ms. King was dismissed from the witness chair. He watched her looking over the crowd toward a stranger, a cowboy peering intently at her as walked by. The stranger dropped his gaze and Susie left.

Defense called for hospital records to be ruled out too since the prosecutor had not produced an eye witness, and no testimony from personnel that Karly had been raped, just that she had sex. Karly's parents had already helped that along the day before by throwing a fit against any health counselor, or a doctor, reporting her condition after the incident. Art had a thought on that.

Black didn't go along with the motion. "The records are in," he said.

Art hadn't heard what the records reported, but if they were in, Trent could use them later. The sheriff's office did their part, and the city too, Art thought, but then there's a burr under the saddle for Sturm with King missing. It was almost noon. The jury shouldn't have any trouble.

Trent played his ace in the hole.

"Karly Young to the stand, please," he ordered and looked to the bailiff.

She came in the room stone-faced, Art saw, just like the grandmother she hated, or appeared to hate.

"Do you swear to tell the truth?"

She nodded and was asked to speak up. "I do."

Right off, Trent asked the question on everyone's mind: "Were you raped by Raleigh King when you stayed in his house three days?"

"I - I don't remember," she stuttered, and Art noticed her looking to the back of the room where a teenage boy sat with a man presumed to be his father. Did they allow kids in here?

Trent was taken aback by her answer. She had been easy to work with in the examining room. What was up now? Would he have to subpoena her parents in this matter? He decided he would if she kept up this charade.

"Karly, don't be frightened. King is not present and can do nothing to you here. Just answer the question as you told the hospital authorities and your parents, please."

"You said I could answer the truth, Mr. Trent, and that's the truth," she stated defiantly.

Trent asked for a moment to consult with his associate and Black allowed, but admonished:

"Get on with it, Mr. Trent. Is she going to testify or not?"

"Okay, Karly," Trent said softly. "I want you to tell the truth. You're under oath. Did Raleigh King rape you?"

"Yes! Yes, he did," she answered a little too loud.

The courtroom became a noise hole. Black hammered for silence, threatening to empty the room.

Trent persisted.

"Karly, did he hold you against your will?"

"Yes! He dragged me into his house and I screamed and screamed and he wouldn't let me out. It's the truth, I swear."

"How did you get away, Karly, and run home to your parents?"

"He went to work and forgot to lock the door. I ran as fast as I could."

"Okay, Karly. Thanks. Judge, I'm done with this witness."

"Is the defense ready?" Black asked.

Sturm approached Karly with a smile. She didn't return his lead.

"Were you really raped, or did you just let him have his way?" Sturm asked, followed by:

"Objection!" on Trent's part. Black said, "You opened this up, Trent."

"Yes, I was raped," Karly insisted, allowing tears to run down her cheeks and a good sized chin trembling to enhance the effect. She looked especially stringy today Art saw.

"Why didn't you try to escape sooner?"

"I couldn't. He kept me locked in."

"Did you hear Ms. King testify that her son told her you wanted to stay, hidden from your parents?"

"Hearsay, your honor," prosecution objected.

"Sturm, watch yourself," Black admonished the defense.

"Did you have trouble with your parents on the day you disappeared, Karly?"

"Well, yes, but that had nothin' to do with Raleigh. He liked what he saw and grabbed me."

Sturm paused. Then:

"So you say, Karly, so you say. But he knew he couldn't have teenagers around or he would go straight to jail as a registered sex offender. Did he not mention that to you when you asked to stay at his house?"

"I didn't ask! I didn't," Karly cried out and the courtroom buzzed until Black rapped three times.

"I'll clear this courtroom with another outburst," he promised.

Sturm turned back to grilling the uncomfortable teen. "What if we don't believe you?"

"Daddy! Stop him! He's making me cry!"

Tim Young dropped his gaze.

"I think we've had enough, Counselor," Black said. "You may step down, Miss Young."

Karly rushed to her father's side. He slid an arm around her. She whispered and Tim Young pressed a finger across his lips. Karly smiled into his chest after ducking her head where the court people couldn't see.

Art saw. He sat with head bowed. He'd been right all along. The girl had gone willingly to Raleigh's house without a thought in her head of the sex offender not being "allowed." She was selfish through and through. Any fool could see that, but would the jury?

Being experienced with thirty years of law enforcement, Art sat thinking if Karly Young turned up pregnant, what then? There would be another illegitimate King born unless he missed his guess. But then, he thought, there's always abortion. Oh heck, that would bring on a protest meeting for pro-lifers who had a way of infiltrating a town. Imagine facing Leona after a protest march. Dang! Thirteen years old! Art was glad his term was ending.

Before things worsened, Trent called a surprise witness, a town citizen to testify that he lived next door to King.

"Sir, I ask what did you see on the day Karly Young disappeared?"

"I seen Raleigh reach out and pull the girl into the house," he stated with a know-it-all smile. Sturm objected, but was overruled. He'd had his surprise, it was Trent's turn. Why the helpful neighbor hadn't come in sooner and told the city, Art didn't know.

Sturm said, "One question." He stared at the witness for a minute and then asked: "Didn't you have to work that evening? We checked. You were on the afternoon shift that particular day, weren't you?"

Raleigh King's neighbor said nothing. Was he caught?

"Your honor, I have no more questions for this witness," Sturm said, disdain dragging down the corners of his mouth.

The confused neighbor, expecting to shine with his eager witness of Raleigh King's actions, looked around the room for confirmation from the on-lookers that he had done right, then at the judge, who advised him to step down. He did so, smiling at the prosecutor as he passed. Trent ignored him.

Black recessed for lunch and apparently forgot he had given Sturm only until noon to get King into court. Art wondered if he forgot, or just wanted to give Sturm more time. Trials shouldn't go that way. Why wasn't Trent calling him on that?

Art hurried to the side of Chief Brown and asked why there weren't any more neighbors who saw the so-called abduction take place.

"We weren't sure that one did, Art, but we took the chance and we're taking no more."

Chapter 8

Defendant Found

That afternoon—following Sturm's and Trent's summations, one asking for "not guilty due to reasonable doubt," and the other pleading "guilty for kidnaping; at least statutory rape,"—the jury was instructed to consider all the facts. King still hadn't been found. Art remembered how Judge Black paid attention to every thing said in the courtroom. The sheriff couldn't, but then Art was not trained for listening to court cases.

The jury wasn't out long. They marched in silent, bland faces belying the fact they were called upon to decide a young man's future to announce. The foreman nodded at the judge as he handed a slip of paper to the bailiff.

Outside in the car lot a voice yelled into the crowd: "The jury's in!"

Leona Broughton and her loyal companions hurried up the steps into the building from where they had been talking, whispering as they ploughed into the courtroom of the DeWitt County Courthouse. Anxiety almost overtook Leona as she slumped down in the nearest seat. It had been a long day, with the alleged sex offender defendant failing to show for his trial. He was tried in-absentia. Deep furrows aged an already older face, but there was something else there, Art told himself. That couldn't be a gleam of satisfaction.

"Laura, what do you think they'll find?" Leona asked her best friend.

"What can they find? He's guilty as sin," Laura said. She unexpectedly laughed. Three heads turned her way and stared at the sound.

Leona shushed her, placing a hand over her own fast grin. The action was not unnoticed.

Carlton Smith and three other men Art knew from the local senior center sat quietly, white-faced like they were expecting any moment to be yelled at and arrested just for knowing Leona Broughton and her loud mouth.

Disquieting questions echoed throughout Smith's nervous system, causing sweat beads to form, run down and drip into his eyebrows. He dropped his head, turned sideways to look at Laura Rogers and Leona as they sat statue-still. *They're sittin' there like full of innocence and all. Dang women!*

Those ladies were pinched up inside, hoping the verdict was "guilty."

"Come to order," Judge Black said, banging his infernal gavel. Sheriff Simonds jerked to attention in spite of himself. He was anxiously awaiting the outcome of so quick a verdict. The jury hadn't been out three hours. Raleigh King didn't stand a chance of being found innocent. If there had been reasonable doubt as Defense Attorney Sturm requested, the jury of five women and seven men would have been at odds longer than three hours.

The twelve member jury, faces set in granite, sat down and awaited the order to release their findings.

"Mr. Foreman, have you reached a verdict?" Black asked.

"Yes, Your Honor, we have," he said, standing and holding a paper of which the judge had a copy.

"What is that verdict, Mr. Foreman?"

* * *

Bam! The foreman was interrupted before he could open his mouth. A crashing noise from the rear of the room resounded through the high-ceilinged courtroom like a cannon in Art's ears. Double doors flew open!

The foreman's mouth gaped and the startled juror said nothing. All heads turned in the direction of the noise as a sweaty-faced Bridges rushed forward, hat in hand.

Deputy Bridges leaned against the railing surrounding the prosecution's table, whispered for attention, said something in the startled man's ear, and District Attorney Terrence Trent jumped up to address the judge.

"Your honor, there's been a development!" He said louder than he needed. "Permission to approach?"

"This is highly unusual, Trent," Black responded, "but both of you approach," he added, motioning for Sturm.

"Approach," Black repeated as Sturm hesitated. Black

turned to the jury and said, "Y'all can sit down," pointing his gavel straight at the foreman waiting to tell the findings of the jury. Black was tired, he was woozy and he wanted this to end.

The attorneys stood close to the judge's bench, Trent whispering. Black, who had leaned forward—hand cupped over the microphone in front of him—jerked backwards. He waved the lawyers to their tables, sat silent for anxious minutes as the murmuring in the room grew. Black looked at the jury, stuffed the findings in a folder and announced:

"Case dismissed due to the death of the defendant."

The announcement brought on a roar from the crowd. Black ignored them, wiping sweat from his forehead with a white handkerchief. Then he pounded the gavel for order and said, "Members of the jury, you're dismissed and can go home with the court's appreciation of your time and effort. The bailiff will escort you out."

The perplexed panel rose with the foreman and stood looking at each other, wondering, strongly desiring, but not daring, to ask questions. Members of the press, radio, news rags, and television fled the scene, ready to report the latest happening to editors. Art watched Carlton Smith and his Texas sun-burned buddies follow each other out the door. Only one news reporter remained to question Trent.

He wasn't the only curious man on the scene. Art Simonds had to know.

"Trent, hold up! What's going on?"

The flustered prosecutor turned and whispered, "Raleigh King's body was discovered in Leona Broughton's half-burned cabin at Concrete just two hours ago! A hunter called it in to your office and Bridges sped to the scene – sirens blazing I imagine – to verify. It was King all right, Bridges said. He was not only dead, but mutilated. That's why he failed to appear. Know anything about who might have done this, Art? Anyone who could castrate a young man?"

Simonds couldn't move. Finally, he thought to ask "Did the JP get involved right away?" No answer. Art turned to look at Leona, saw she was gone, then hurried toward the back. He wanted to speak with her before anybody else did. She wasn't in the room or the hall. Neither was Laura Rogers and Ole Man Smith or his stone-faced buddies. Art rushed out the door to prevent her from leaving before he had a chance to ask.

He didn't make it. She was swallowed up in the rush of people pushing and shoving; a reporter and cameraman leading the parade out the doors and out into a screaming crowd on the courthouse lawn. A third reporter who stayed behind to question Trent came pushing past. He had the scoop and by morning every camera in Texas would be trained on the little town.

Jury members were whispering about why? Nobody had the gumption to tell them anything else. They ambled out, grumbling.

Art had returned to the courtroom; he just sat there. Trent turned away from the bench, noting that Art had wandered back inside. Trent wondered aloud if Leona Broughton could have anything to do with King's death.

"Great horn toads! No!" Art quickly responded. His old friend wouldn't kill. "I'm wonderin' how somebody thought to look at the Broughton cabin for King."

"Oh, your deputy said there was a fire and a neighbor reported it, but nobody looked inside the cabin until morning. That's when he discovered the body. Now we have no alleged sex offender and the town has no justice," Trent said, "and Leona has no satisfaction of seeing her granddaughter's alleged perp sent to jail or at least to an institution. My case has gone to you know where in a hand-basket. What must all the other so-called registered sex offenders be thinking about now? What a good town to live in?"

"No need for sarcasm, Trent," Art said. He knew this occurrence would never leave his mind.

Sturm, watching carefully, realized he had not really lost a case, just a client. This would not go down in history as a defense case lost. When he turned to look over his shoulder at Merriwether, the esteemed gentleman had left the building.

Art watched Bridges talking to the city chief, who looked at Ms. King and motioned her to his side. The sheriff wondered why she hadn't left the courtroom. She let out a scream! Art jumped and wondered out loud "What did they say to her?"

He kept watching as Ms. King turned and searched through tear-filled eyes to the back of the room where a long drink of water sat staring at her. He was an ugly-looking cuss with a pocked-up face and slicked back hair.

Art wondered who the man could be and how he was interested in this case, noticing the unblinking, blank stare during the trial. Was he curious or did he have a personal interest? The sheriff didn't know. It wasn't unusual for him to not know everybody in the county by looks, unless they had been arrested.

The stranger stood and left, Ms. King staring and reaching out to him, apparently trying to tell him something he didn't wait to hear. He was oblivious to her cries.

* * *

Simond's mind replayed the way Leona Broughton had not only showed up in court at the beginning of the trial against her son's orders, but had booed the judge out loud when he granted bail for King before Black could leave the room, asking him out loud if he was a sex offender himself to let the man off easy. Man, she was plucky! She was lucky Black didn't hold her in contempt. Maybe he had compassion.

He had ordered her out of the courtroom with a dismayed sheriff having to apologize for escorting her. Black left before Leona could say anything, leaving anybody who wanted to, and was brave enough, to explain details to the aggravated woman.

That job had fallen on Art, and he said, "You have to go, Ma'am, or keep quiet. You cain't yell at a judge that way. I'll tell you about it if you wait out in the hall." The way she had looked, he didn't know if she would leave quietly, but she smiled and left.

Today, he hoped Suzie King had left the building not knowing what Leona might do or say.

That fair-skinned lady and mother of Raleigh King had indeed left the building, glaring at Leona with all the venom she could muster. The crazy old grandma was busy stirring up all kinds of gossip about Raleigh and that was what got him killed if indeed he was dead. Suzie King knew who needed to die and it wasn't her baby.

* * *

Meanwhile Sturm was shaking hands with Trent the way lawyers do, and Art was just shaking his head. At this point he knew nothing. If it had been his case, he thought, he would've found a way to pin something else on King, like harboring a runaway to keep him in jail, but seems like this was dumped on the city due to property lines.

Art also thought King believed he wouldn't be held, predators like him looking for teens on the internet rarely were, and if they were, they got a slap on the wrist in a lot of courts, because parents didn't want the stigma and wouldn't press for justice. Art knew why Judge Black seemed lenient, but Leona didn't. She needed to know. Art found her outside talking to the four shining knights from the senior center and Laura.

"Give me time," she said, jerking Art's thoughts her way. "I'll find out why Judge Black was so easy-going on this mal-adjusted crud." She turned to Art and said, " He dismissed the case, Art, he dismissed the case."

"You don't have to investigate, Leonnie. I'll tell you myself. But first, you need to remember they found our alleged pervert dead in your cabin. Wonder who took him there?"

She didn't blink; just stood there. Art was flustered. She had no reaction to the news, so he swallowed and saw a way out.

"Leonnie, I've already told you over coffee why Black is rumored to be soft on sex offenders. Right now, I have to high tail it out to your cabin and gather what evidence Bridges might've missed. It's my responsibility."

She turned her back and waved an arm in the air, dismissing the sheriff.

Art knew he had to get to Concrete and make sure Bridges was taking care of matters, not grandstanding for the other peace officers who might already be on the scene. This was no time for standing around jawing with a willful woman. He would tell her what she wanted, but did not need to know until tomorrow.

"Oh heck, come back. I'll fill you in for five minutes, no more."

She turned, not smiling, but ready to hear his feeble excuses.

"When Toby was young, his seventeen year old brother got a teenager pregnant. She yelled rape to save herself and her folks pushed for statutory. He didn't serve time, but he was branded, so the entire family moved out here to DeWitt County from Houston, and sent Toby off to school in San Antone. Folks here never knew anything about his brother. I just happened to learn through the system."

He stopped to catch whether the aggravated old lady was listening. She turned back to face him so he continued his explanation of Judge Black.

"I kept my mouth shut all these years because I believe too many boys get branded when they get caught up in young love. Maybe I'll change my mind some day, but that ain't why the trial ended, because of a soft judge. As I said, King was found dead in your cabin over at Concrete this mornin', accordin' to Bridges. Is that a coincidence?"

Leona stared at Art for what seemed five minutes, never tearing her eyes away, still not blinking. He did. She smiled, mumbled something like "Isn't that too bad?"

Dang, did she already know about King? He couldn't read her face. He hoped she hadn't done anything. He felt queasy, recalling Leona's idea of how to take care of sex offenders.

Art didn't linger after attempting to read Leona's face. He hurried to find his deputy and fill in the blanks.

"Bridges!" he shouted as he saw Tom leaving with Trent.

Bridges stopped. He was uncertain for a moment, then reached Art's side unsmiling. His light brown complexion reddened as he realized the trouble he was in. He forced a Stetson over short-cropped hair and straightened to his full six-feet three inches.

"Art, it's out of our hands. The Justice of the Peace already called on the Texas Ranger to be aware of what's happening. She looked at the body long enough for me to identify King, then did what she had to."

"And you didn't see fit to tell me first, your boss? What's goin' on Tom? This ain't your call to tell Trent instead of me. I decide who gets called and who is in on a case, not a deputy."

"You're right, Art. I was caught up in the excitement of findin' King and wasn't thinkin' about who to tell. I know the drill, dang right I know the drill."

"I think you protest too much Bridges, but knowin' who's cabin it was where King's body was discovered, I realize why you wouldn't come to me first." Leona Broughton and Art went back further than he did with Bridges. It was too close to an election for Bridges to be thinking anything but future and Art was almost the past. He'd be elected and assume office in January, 2005. Too bad, Art would have supported Bridges all the way in the campaign. Now he was uncertain.

The sheriff left his chief deputy standing and staring. He sought to find the justice of the peace, to find out for himself if and why he had been left out of the call for the rangers. Being tied up in court watching was no excuse for negligence in the pecking order.

He pointed to his vehicle and Bridges got the message. Lights and siren on, the two headed for the murder scene to claim responsibility for the secured sight.

No where to park, Art just headed into the brush, cutting down somebody's yellow tape. He hoped it was Bridges who had the goose sense to put it up. Even then, there was no place to park. He stopped short of running down a reporter and stepped out to greet the deputy Bridges left in charge.

"What do we have here, Gomez? You keeping a hold on things?" he asked the young deputy.

"Yes Sir," Gomez eagerly responded. "This here's the biggest thing to happen since I was sworn in, Sheriff. I was proud to hold on here while Bridges let the court know where King was all this time. It beats lookin' for a lost bull."

Art was angry, but kept it inside. Bridges had no business leaving a rookie in charge just so he could grandstand at the courthouse before Trent. If Tom wanted to be sheriff that bad, well, maybe it would be best to ignore his anger and investigate the scene.

"Howdy boys," he said to the other peace officers. "Everything under control?"

"Sheriff, about time you got here. Where've you been?" a

state police officer asked.

"Long story, but I was at the courthouse watching a trial without any defendant. I guess you know by now where the defendant was."

"No matter, you're here now so let's get this crime scene further secured. Sorensen is havin' kittens from all the tramplin' around. She's takin' charge of callin' in the medical examiner. I don't care who does what. Have you, well no, you haven't," he said answering his own question. "Do you want to inspect the body and the cabin before Sorensen orders him moved?"

"Dang right, I do. Bridges should've called me out of court before anybody else. Don't know what's got into my best deputy."

"Could be he needs points for election in November, huh?"

"Yeah, that could be it, but I hope not. He'll make a good sheriff. I trained him," Art said of the first black man who could win the job.

Art wasn't ready for the sight of young Raleigh King dead and stinking. His mouth was taped, his hands taped, and his body half burned. Unmistakable: it was the son of Suzie King, her pride and joy, probably innocent and killed for nothing. Art felt a tear slide down his cheek and angrily swiped it away with a tough fist.

An hour here was more than he could take. He needed a fix. He set Bridges in charge and headed to the DQ, for tacos. This was no time for office jelly beans. He didn't want to believe Leona had done the unthinkable? It wasn't retirement time yet.

* * *

Two days later, Art ran into Toby Black

"Off the record, Art, what do you think about the trial? King didn't want a jury trial, but by golly he got it, not that it means anything now. Heck, I didn't want the blame if he was set free. His defense had all the cards. I think Sturm did a good job on the defense. I'm not convinced Raleigh King was ever guilty. I can only go by the law. I guess the reporter from Victoria will give me the business, but I can't worry about what people think. Anyhow, there was reasonable doubt about that girl. How do we know she didn't lie about her age and lead him on? Heck, maybe there was nothing involved. Her parents were ashamed, and my hands were tied. It doesn't mean a thing now with King dead."

"No Sir, Toby, it don't," Art answered, holding balled fists against his sides. He had no reason, he just felt like Leona deserved justice and it hadn't been served unless King paid the price. Art wasn't done raking Judge Black, but it could wait until his term of sheriff was up later this year.

"But whatever happened to statutory rape in these little girl cases, Toby? That gone out the window with Moral Turpitude? Couldn't he have been labeled guilty for the family's sake even though he's dead?" Of course, his questions were out of order, seeing as how they had no perp.

"Whatever happened to your court room manners, Simonds? Your friend Leona Broughton couldn't keep her mouth shut! If she hadn't been useful to me the last time I was up for election, she would have set behind bars for contempt."

"If you knew about her meltdown the third day of her granddaughter's disappearance, you would at least have sympathy, Toby. We had to bring her back from almost an unconscious state on the beach at Port Lavaca. She didn't even remember gettin' there— that's the state she was in. She could've killed at that time. You've undoubtably heard her story of molestation when she was young and nothin' done to salve over her wounds. What if it was your own granddaughter disappeared, Toby? Think!"

"I can't control a courtroom situation with a mouth like that stirring the citizens into a frenzy, Art. You know that. Now why don't we just part friends and let people like this King and his mother live their kind of lives away from the good citizens?"

"Toby, you don't know the half of a mind like Leonnie's. I've seen more of the seamy side of life than you'll ever experience. Get out among 'em, Black, before you get too high and mighty sittin' up there on your judgement seat. You ain't God."

"What's gotten into you , Sheriff? I've never seen this side of you. You aren't in love with that old lady, are you?"

"Heck no. She's older than dirt, Judge. I guess I'm just into her hurt and pain of the way girls in her day were treated when some dang pervert stifled their childhood and nobody understood. Maybe you don't understand either, Toby. I've got to go."

Black turned and walked away. Art was sorry he felt it necessary to attack the judge. Toby never did anything to me, he thought. Art suddenly felt sorrow for both the judge and for Leona; sorry for their young days of family trauma, and sorry for the effect on their older years.

The comfort of his office loomed in his mind and he turned to hide for a nap.

Chapter 9

Creating Hostility

News bled through town about King's death like a leaky gas main, and a few days later, a group of mixed heritage senior citizens sat with Art in the local center talking about how "the bastard who took Karly didn't get away with it. Somebody took care of him anyway."

The sheriff's in-built alarm told him he should've stayed away, but he dropped in now and then to keep a foot in the door of this rumor mill. The lunch was good, but that bunch was holding a branding iron right to his face for not making sure King got to trial.

"He wouldn't have disappeared," one of them said, "if he'd been kept in jail. He should've been made to face the community," they said, "but he got what was comin' to him. Don't he know better than to mess with Texans?"

Art felt the heat of their attack and could have held up for himself since his department did it's duty, but why? He turned to the loud mouth and stared at Carlton Smith.

"Everybody knowed who his paw was, even though he never claimed the fatherless maverick," Ole Man Smith was saying, "he showed up at the courthouse, I heard. Anyhow, King did show up to work the day he got out on bail," he added, "but then the manager never saw him again."

An old woman, probably in her eighties, but very alert wondered how Smith could label somebody illegitimate. "You know him personally?" she asked.

"Don't have to," Smith answered and laughed. "I know his mother and she's never been married. Got pregnant by a big rancher's son, so they say, and they ain't claimin' him. Rumor is Raleigh's ma was paid a handsome sum to keep shut up."

"How do we know you ain't a pervert, Smith?" the old woman persisted. "You with them tiny bright blue eyes and half-bald skull and your teeth showin' every time a woman walks in the door. Wouldn't be the first man to keep quiet."

Smith didn't answer, just sat with folded arms, a know-it-all smirk pasted on his sun-aged face. He pushed back an ancient small-brimmed western hat revealing a nickel-sized mole on his balding head right where it was noticeable and ugly. Beady eyes enlarged as he pulled off his thick glasses revealing moles underneath the ear pieces.

Art realized he must be near sighted. Coupled with an almost boneless nose—rumor had it his own father broke it when he was young and didn't seek medical care—Smith was a different man than the one who sat for days in a hot courtroom. He turned and smiled at his Tex-Mex friends sitting to his left. The smile lifted his face into a beautiful smile rarely revealed due to sagging jaws. His friends lifted their tea glasses and smiled back.

Art didn't like the tone of the conversation. Were people turning against each other over this murder? Was his county becoming incensed enough to take the law into their own hands? Nah. This was just talk. Smith was too loud and his face was red with passion of the moment. What was his problem? Art turned around to watch Leona.

She was sitting where she heard every word. Art could feel her mind grinding, see her lids batting, eyes sweeping back and forth like windshield wipers, remembering how it had been with her. She had to be bordering on rage, maybe insanity by now. She once told Art over a cup of coffee that fifty-nine years ago her molester was sentenced to only one year in prison and was released on good behavior after nine months. She told him often enough how she could never understand why somebody didn't just castrate every one of them.

Art bet everybody in town knew the story. She began telling her story after Ted died. Art didn't pity her, but he disliked having to hear the tired story, so old nobody listened anymore. He thought nobody listened until Smith came up with his statement that King got what was coming to him.

"That's the way it goes," Leona said loudly, breathing hard. Something was growing inside her and Art didn't like the looks of it, but she hadn't done anything he knew of to get even for her own years of suffering. He tried to relax and sip coffee; he wasn't interested in her stories.

Out of control, Leona yelled at the crowd, misty red eyes popping, and worse than Art had ever seen her act: "Me sentenced to fifty-nine years of hell and condemnation from relatives, and my molester got off free! I should have pulled the trigger when I was twelve and my cousin and I had that ess-o-bee in our sites. If my cousin Jim hadn't snatched the gun away, that dirty-crotch ess-o-bee wouldn't have been free long. I vowed right then and there if I ever had a child or grandchild molested, the perp wouldn't live to go to trial."

She paused to wipe her eyes and Art couldn't tell if it was real or for show.

"Couldn't get my hands on King before the trial," she said, but I thought with the law nowadays, he would surely get his. Nothing happened to any of my kin all these years, thank God, so why did it have to be my hardest to love granddaughter when it did? Still, this shouldn't happen to any girl. It was time somebody did something."

Several seniors, including Smith and his buddies, slid over to reassure Leona they understood but she waved them away, tears running down her cheeks, nose dripping. She picked up her cell phone from the table. Tension was mounting and she was the leader. It was her, Art was sure, hammered in the idea King got away with rape, inciting citizens into a fury.

The bunch who had surrounded Leona stared holes through Art and he mulled over whether he should hang his hat here anymore until the town settled down. Dang, it wasn't his fault the judge let Raleigh out on Bond. If they wanted to blame somebody they should go see Sturm, King's defense attorney. Art made himself hear what Leona was saying on the phone.

"Laura?" she spoke into the mouthpiece and Art listened to the rise of anger in her voice. Chin trembling, she was telling her friend all about the talk at the center. He edged closer. It was the only way he ever knew half of what was on her mind. Thank God for cell phones, he thought.

"I remember Ted telling me about a case a few years ago before Art was sheriff," Leona was saying, " when a young man received a light sentence for raping a well-known Cuero man's daughter."

Was she trying to tell Laura something Art ought to know? His hackles rose. His mind shifted to warmer thoughts of the red head. He would have to invite her out to lunch one day and find out her end of the conversation. He heard Leona tell Laura the story over again on the phone from right there in the center and like true best friends she filled Laura in on the conversation by Ole Man Smith. Then she shared her opinion the monster got what he deserved. It wasn't talked about that King had been castrated, so how could she and Smith know he got what he deserved? Art felt sick and had to refrain from dropping a hand down to protect his own tools right there in public.

Leona renewed her conversation with Laura, talking about the town leader's daughter, saying "No body did a thing when the man's body was found at the river, face down in the mud after he got out of prison, Ted said." Leona retold the old story while Laura listened. "It was justice pure and simple. It could be what's needed in this town to get perverts off the streets. Probably the girl's father took the law into his own hands. It's what we need here now."

Art mumbled, without raising his head, "Good for her daddy." His thoughts didn't stop there. Leona's age was against her. Her relatives to hear her tell it over and over, condemned her, not the man who screwed up her life. If the listeners heard it once, they heard it ten times how she spent all those years in a self-imposed mental prison. Art felt pity.

"Karly doesn't have the foggiest of what she'll be going through from here on in," Leona told Laura. Art guessed she didn't care if the whole center was listening to her phone conversation. "Nobody should have to be sentenced to a lifetime of memories and heartache for a man's crime, and suffer humiliation, too."

The tears had been replaced by anger. Revenge-edged words dripped from her lips. Art thought about the beach in Port Lavaca and asked himself: is this the same woman I brought back from there? He didn't get to hear anymore because he was interrupted by Smith.

"Well, what can you do about men like King, Sheriff?" he shot straight at Art, not caring what he was doing and not caring if Art heard Leona tell Laura what ought to be done to all the perverts in Cuero and surrounding county. He too knew this story by heart after all these years. Every time a sex story came out in the news, Leona was upset all over again.

"It's almost out of my hands now, Smith, as of January. The Rangers will follow through and I, along with Brown who will still be chief and be watchin' the action. I thought Leona had forgiven her monster," Art said, but Smith came back:

"She'll never forget. We're not goin' to forget this time either."

Was that a threat? Smith got up and motioned two or three men to follow him. Now What?

Leona clicked her phone shut as Art watched. He planned right then to call Laura and try to discuss this particular conversation. He watched Leona scrape back a cheap chair, leaving her lunch untouched. Art had to admit he was uneasy, like he had lost control. Again he could see wheels grinding. She had a lot to think about. Should she find out from Art what went on with King meandering around town, or let it lay?

Art decided it wouldn't hurt to tell her what he knew. King was set free to capture and mess up other girls' lives, but with the threat over, maybe the town would calm down and Art could drink coffee in peace. No telling how many King had already ruined and their parents wouldn't allow it to be known. Well, they didn't have a chance to find him in the river like that story Leona told, Art thought and hid the smile working through his mustache.

* * *

"Now, Leona, let this drop," Art pleaded the next day when she flagged him down just short of escaping into the county jail. "You should've known they'd let him out on bail. It don't matter anymore. He won't hurt anybody else. I don't know what the jury was gonna say. They should've give him somethin', but the jury didn't have a chance to tell us what they decided. I asked a few questions of the cotton mill manager downtown. He admitted King didn't show for work the next day, so I thought he prob'bly left the state. Good riddance. Maybe there won't be a next time in this town since King got his. Maybe the perverts will think twice."

All this conjecture on the sheriff's part was to keep Leona from talking. She protested too much when it didn't mean anything. What was she trying to do? He sucked in his gut, thinking maybe he wouldn't be bothered with trash like King again with word out all over town that sex offenders in the local neighborhoods could wind up dead. He looked at Leona who stared straight through him.

"Simonds, I don't have the slightest idea what you just said, or if we'll see somebody like King again. I just know in this county even a murderer can get away with crime and I'm not blaming you," she reminded me. "It's the slick lawyer from Yorktown, you know, with the destroy-all-the-girls attitude. My God, asking for a recess so he could put Suzie King on the stand and outwit Trent. Why didn't Black call him down for that?"

She didn't wait for an answer – appearing to not want input.

"I tell you something else, I'll remember every face on that jury and hell will freeze over before I speak to a one of them again. They probably would've found him not guilty since it wasn't their kin. Remember when a jury with guts would've forgotten the part about the city maybe offering King leniency or the confession wasn't audible?"

"Yes, Ma'am, I reckon they did years ago, but that's changed. Too much of that new political correctness goin' around, even here in Texas. He didn't kill her so there's a question. You know even if he managed to hurt Karly, King might've gotten away with it. We once had a district attorney who failed to get a jury to convict a murderer who was witnessed to by three people a few years ago. The local law messed it up and he didn't have anything but circumstantial evidence. Don't you remember Trent's first case when two gays allegedly killed a third one and abandoned his body in a rental house for days until neighbors complained about the odor? Does that not tell you anything about experience?"

In case she didn't recall, Art reminded her.

"The judge even asked Trent if he wanted to object to the defense's line of questioning in that murder case. Trent just shrugged his shoulders and shook his head. He didn't know back then how to get them convicted, but I'm sure he's wised up some since. We even hauled in a Huntsville inmate for a witness against the two homos and prosecution didn't even call him to the stand after usin' tax payer funds to get him here. The Rangers didn't find enough evidence to support the claim that one of them killed the third man. The prosecutor tried the two anyway and one wound up puttin' the whole thing on the other. It didn't fly. The only way the case would've been settled was if one pled out. Now that I think of it, Sturm won that case and maybe Trent's trying to get best him ever since."

Leona refused to answer. She was tired of talk. Especially the past failures of townspeople which didn't matter here anyway. Action was the only thing on her mind and she would see to it that the town was aware of all the sex offenders on the internet and living close. Wish I may, wish I might, she remembered from childhood, but it won't get done unless I take charge. If only I wasn't so old, she thought. I could rouse these old men into doing my bidding.

"What did you say, Art? I wasn't listening," she said, numbed by boredom.

"I recall seein' you talkin' to the judge after the gays were let go of the killin'," Art was saying. "What did he say?"

When she was silent, he popped the killer question: "Did you vote for him? Did you vote for Judge Black?"

"Well, let me know if you ever find any more perverts," she said, ignoring his questions. "I'll be waiting to hear from you." *If that young whippersnapper thinks I'm going to listen to him anymore....*

Art knew she voted for the judge or she would've agreed with him. The judge's politics were the same as hers, and the same as the President's. He watched Leona pull out her cell phone. If it wasn't for her phone he wouldn't know much of what she was up to. He heard her ask, "Laura?"

Laurie, as Art called her, was a Yankee just like Leona, except she'd been in Texas a lot longer. Married a cowboy named Rogers, still running a ranch of sorts over on the west side of the county inherited from her late husband. To Art's way of thinking she was strong as a man, and Leona always seemed weak, not doing anything that took more than pecking at a typewriter. One had the education, the other one made the money.

"Hey, Laura," he heard her say as she walked toward the door. "Wanna have lunch? I'm buying. We'll go for another ride."

* * *

The town quieted down, but peace didn't last a June frost.

"Sheriff!" shouted a harsh voice. It could only be—

He hurried into his office, shut the door and turned the handle. Leona didn't follow. As soon as Art felt her presence leave the building, he slipped out for tacos at the DQ—his favorite local law enforcement gathering place.

Growing weary of the crazy talk in the fast food establishment about King and guessing who killed him, Art feigned business to be taken care of, retraced his steps to the office to sit in his old leather chair and think. He was upset with the townspeople and their lack of concern that King had been murdered without benefit of a guilty verdict.

The office loomed as a forbidden hole. He walked out to his vehicle, took off and drove until he came to Five-Mile Roadside Park where a concrete picnic table with benches lured him into the sunshine. He had stopped momentarily to relieve himself, but the table looked warm, felt warm to the touch and proved to be inviting. He pealed off his denim jacket, rolled it up to prop his head on, removed his hat and laid back to stare into the trees meditating about the events crowding his life just now. Art dropped off into familiar nap time.

An hour later in the half-darkness, and somewhat chilled, the tired law man woke, rolled over and dropped his arm over the side. Dang, he was stiff. Crazy thing to do, fall asleep on a cold slab of concrete alongside the highway. He remembered a time when tables were wood.

Ck-ck-ck-ck-ck! Unmistakable! Rattlesnakes! Art opened his eyes to more rattlers than he had seen in a lifetime crawling around after he disturbed them by moving. The entire slab of concrete below was alive with snakes. *Oh help me Lord*! What the cornbread, cotton-picking heck was he gonna do? He swore one of them was looking him in the eyes, daring him to move. Dang!

Trying not to make any kind of sound, he slowly pulled himself erect, watching every move of the slithering snakes asking himself shouldn't they be lying still in this cool air? No. Not for a lowly sheriff, he told himself. He looked up and down the highway. Not a headlight in sight. This was one predicament a lone star-wearing sheriff would have to get out of without assistance.

Tensing his body for the biggest leap he would ever make in his life, and at his age, Art sprung from the table far enough out that he hit the ground running. From there to his vehicle took one second. He didn't look back, just slammed the door and pealed out into the highway, grateful to be alive. Dang!

* * *

The next day his office seemed like the place to be except for going down to a Mexican cafe on Esplanade. He tried out their tacos, washed them down with unsweetened tea, and fled to the office when he saw Leona coming. He didn't want to talk with her and relied on the automatic door lock. He had left orders she wasn't to come in unless he instructed. He fell asleep.

Chapter 10

Unlikely Witness

The door flew open! Dang if he didn't leave it unlocked again, he was a broom-tailed maverick. Surprise. This time, it wasn't Leona. It was Carlton "Ole Man" Smith. He didn't wait for an invite, just plopped down and started telling Art a strange tale about being out in the woods over by Concrete where Leona Broughton's cabin was located and had seen some "odd goin's on."

"And....." Art encouraged.

"I was out for a drive, lost for a time, maybe even disoriented; had to pull into the old Stage Coach Inn drive and back out to find my way back to the highway. Just then I witnessed two hell-for-leather hikers plowin' through overgrown weeds, slappin' limbs outta the way right towards Leona Broughton's cabin. They was wearin' hoods, or sheets over their heads, hats pulled down to keep the cover from droppin' off and showin' their faces." He waited for Art to react, took off his glasses revealing beady, near-sighted eyes.

Art was silent long enough to think about what he heard. He knew of the historic stage coach inn. He had taken Nora out there when they first married. It was built in the late 1800s. A sturdy two story building of unique stone, brought in from St. Louis if he wasn't mistaken. He wondered what Smith was doing in Concrete. It was a long way from Cuero for a man of Smith's age to just be driving by. And where did he get words like "being disoriented?" It was way out of his vocabulary.

The entry way to the cabin had long ago grown over with weeds. Why would anybody plough through them for any reason? Well, the law and himself had ploughed in when King's body was discovered. The last time Art had been there before the killing he noted that the cabin was a run-down, tin-roofed, neglected building. The old fireplace was falling in. One of the windows was boarded up. Ted Broughton deserted it when he moved out into Leona's two-story historical house on Esplanade.

Art perked up when Smith said jerked him back to the subject at hand:

"They had a gun and had it aimed on a blond-headed man, and he was stumblin' along chokin' and cryin' with his mouth taped shut. I could swear the front of his pants was wet. Maybe he peed on his self. Maybe he had been cut. The spot was red-lookin' and it could've been blood. Didn't they say he'd been mutilated? Well, yore prob'ly wonderin' why I didn't come see you until news got out about what happened up there, Sheriff. Maybe you're wonderin' why I didn't try to save that victim in trouble."

"Yeah, but I'm more interested in how you came by that expression, hell-for-leather, Smith," Art said to give himself time to relax. "You ain't been hangin' around them bikers again?" Before Smith could answer, Art asked "Could you see faces in this incident?"

"No, they was dressed in sheets tied around the waist, but their jeans showed down to their boot tops. They had hoods on to hide their faces," Smith answered. "I couldn't see no hair stickin' out, but I already told you that, Art."

He related they didn't have a car, or at least one he could see. The way Art heard Smith's story they didn't look down at, or try to get rid of grass burrs clinging to their boots, jeans and sheets. And they stepped wide of the fire ant hills too, he said. What Smith said told the sheriff they were familiar with life in Texas, not tourists.

"I watched the two drag the third one up on the cabin porch and open the door," Smith rambled on. "It wasn't locked. They didn't rush in, just peeked into the darkness. It could've been filled with varmints like snakes, fire ants, skinks, scorpions, whatever. I couldn't see real well, and I thought the shorter of the two had a club, but it turned out to be a flashlight. They both had on gloves and I couldn't see the color of their skin. Could've been white, black or Mescans." Smith certainly did recall the conversation, it seemed. How did he hear it so well? Art didn't know. The old buzzard wore two hearing aids, but then this was a story. Smith continued:

" 'Let's put our company in here,' the light holder said, and the other laughed like a hyena. I edged closer from my tree to listen."

Word for word, Smith quoted to Art how it all went down. Boy is he ever a story teller, Art thought. Worse than a liar, but what was he doing here telling me some weird tale? Smith hurried on with his nightmarish version of a killing:

" 'Where's he gonna go?' the tall one asked. Can't do any harm tied up here and especially in chains. Let's leave him enough stretch to use that old pot in the corner?' Now, Art, that weren't no southerner to my way of thinkin'. Their voices was low, you know like women talk," Smith said, "and not once did I hear 'em talkin' like us."

" 'He has something left to go with,' the tall one said and laughed. 'After all, we only took off his sac and half his tool, but we better check it out once in awhile. And we bandaged him up right nice, medication and all.' "

It was right here that Art felt pity for Raleigh King. What if he had been totally innocent? No one would ever know. How he must have suffered, more than enough for Karly Young's say-so, and more than enough for Leona Broughton. Smith jerked Art back to the story.

" ' If we feed him every day, he'll need to use the pot,' the short one said. 'It's probably empty. I'll lift the lid and look,' he said, and stepped that way, light shinin' across the cabin floor. He couldn't see, I guess, 'cause he yelled 'Darn!' The light fell on the floor. I guess he snagged a toe and tripped over the pot, but nothin' spilled out. I could see it was empty. And there weren't no fire built in the fireplace. It was fallin' in and dangerous. I somehow was outside and had to hurry 'round to a broken window so's I could see what was goin' on inside. I could hear, and I could see through the cracks in the boards," Smith said.

He interrupted his story-telling to say, "These ole board and batten cabins are good for that. Anyway, them two tortured that man at least an hour, lettin' him try to scream through a taped-up mouth. I left the window when they quit, thinkin' I didn't want to get caught and be next."

"Funny how things can go. Curiosity got the best of me and

I sneaked back to see what was happenin' after they didn't come out. They couldn't hear me; it had rained for once and the ground was wet. They were talkin' again. The tall one said, 'Okay, I'll check our boarder,' and clomped over to where they dumped the man on the floor."

Smith stopped and waited to see if Art was shocked. Art didn't let it show, but he judged the old man had a dream, not an actual witness of murder for sure now. There was no rain at the time of Raleigh's trial.

"Then reachin' down to check on whoever it was, the tall one yelled 'I can't tell if he's still breathin'!' "

"Art, again I say it sounded like a woman, anyway somebody with more education than I got, but I cain't be sure what with the hat and coat and jeans. I saw from the light the pot-checker shined over that way that fire ants had a mound right where they dumped him. Now you know that they'd fill up his eyes, nose and mouth, but I ain't sure that's what happened. Then the tall one asked, 'Did you loosen the rope around his neck?' "

" 'Yes,' the short one said, 'but I didn't think he'd bleed to death by now.' "

"My gyawd, Art, I think that was a dead man! The short one said 'it's been four hours now. Remember we castrated him hangin' upside down, blood runnin' down into his mouth and nose. We didn't tape his mouth right, you old fool. He must've smothered. We weren't going to kill him, you said, just teach him a lesson.' "

" 'That's how Mama killed chickens, hung them up by the feet, wings flapping, slit their throats and let the blood drip' the tall one said, laughin' that crazy way again, and then said 'but like you said, we didn't mean for him to die. What would be the point if he died and got out of his misery?' Then, Art, he pointed out to the other how his mother stuck a knife blade through the roof of their mouth to kill 'em so they wouldn't suffer. 'But I think perverts ought to suffer,' he said. He didn't stop there," Smith said. "He said the man was no better than a chicken, stealin' little girls and doin' things to 'em. 'We didn't slit his throat,' he said, 'so he should've lived, even without his you-know-what.' "

Smith shook his head as if to clear it, almost lost his coke-bottle glasses and continued recounting the facts of his adventure. At that point, Art should've asked him what he was doing in Concrete, even if it was imagined. He knew Smith didn't live there, and Smith knew better than to trespass. Trespassing gets you shot in Texas, but he guessed not in a tale like this one. Smith also forgot the man's hands were tied so how could he use the pot if needed?

" 'He maybe suffocated,' the short one said." Smith was almost whispering their words now. " 'He wouldn't want to live with no tools left down there, anyway,' they said and laughed. 'That's what he's all about, usin' them tools,' they said. The short one yelled, 'Oh, my God! What do we do now, you crazy old fool?' "

" Now Art, that's what was said, and I stayed glued to the crack and heard the rest. I couldn't leave, don'tcha see?"

Smith automatically reached down to protect his old tools. Art nudged his arm to continue the story. He shook off the sheriff's hand and rose like he might leave if Art didn't have patience.

" 'Bury the pervert, what else?' the tall one said, Sheriff, and then said, 'We're gonna die for this anyway if we're caught. Did too much talkin' the other day. They'll tell. They're all gossips anyway. Best hide the evidence, don't you think? Do you think he suffered, even if the fire ants didn't get a chance to crawl around inside his mouth and nose?' "

"Sheriff, the tall one laughed out loud like a maniac ever time one of 'em said anything. What kind of people was they, Art? Was they insane? And, how did they get out there in the woods? I didn't see no car." He'd said that once already.

"Hey, I don't know," Art said when he could get in a word. "What would they need with a car if indeed this was just your imagination. Besides I don't want to think about fire ants." Art's skin was crawling by now, and starting to burn, but Smith wasn't done.

"Wasn't there a bed or something in the cabin, Smith?"

"Sheriff there was no furnishings in that old cabin. I would have noticed if there was. Broughton abandoned it afore he died, dont'cha know? Everybody knows that."

Art stared. Smith ducked his head, not done with his far-out tale. "Art, the short one was gettin' grumpy and said 'This was yore idea. You bury him. Well, really, what am I thinking? You can't do that, you're not strong enough when it comes down to it. You weren't strong enough to pulley him alive upside down onto the tree limb where we could cut him.' The cohort looked up at a pulley still hangin' on the rafter and sighed so heavy I could hear it through the cracks" Smith said. " 'Now you know the roof wouldn't have held that body,'" the first one said when the rafter was pointed out. 'Why do you think we used a tree?'"

"Where did you come up with the word cohort?" Art asked Smith. He thought the old man must be watching too much TV.

"Same place you came up with that new name for sex offenders, Pred-o-file, Art. Leonnie told us all bout your new name for them perverts. We like it."

Smith looked feeble to the sheriff, maybe not so alert, but he recalled the exact words the two were saying at the death scene if it was true. He ignored Smith's referral to the new name Art tacked onto perverts. He needed the rest of the story. It sounded plausible for a murder. "Well, what happened next?" he pressed.

"Why Art, the short one said 'Guess I'll have to help, I'm in this up to my eyeballs.' "

" 'I have a better idea,' the tall one said. 'Let's burn the cabin.' Art, that was when I felt myself driftin' away from the cabin. I didn't really care who they burned. I heard too much talk about a pervert, and then this Raleigh King turns up dead. He got what was comin' to him, way I figure it."

"Well don't leave me hangin' Smith, just who were these killers at the cabin?"

"I ain't sure. Like I said, I was scared and I ain't told a soul about this but you, Art."

Art asked himself what's wrong with this picture? Where did he come up with this stuff?

"Keep it that way, Smith," the sheriff instructed, "but I need to be sure you actually witnessed a crime. Your tale is fishysoundin' at best. I wouldn't tell this to anybody else."

Art hoped that would stop him from talking around town and he knew the department might need this info later.

"Chief Richard Brown and Deputy Bridges will handle things," Art said. "I cain't stay out of it. Cuero is in my territory, so to speak. All the county is." Simonds showed him the door still wondering what he was doing at the Broughton cabin. He puzzled over why Smith went out of his way to tell the outlandish tale. Dang!

* * *

Art fell asleep, awoke with a jerk and asked himself: Was that a crazy dang dream! He shook his head, reached for cold coffee, set it down, stood and walked outside for a breath of air. *Sleeping too much lately. Time to retire.* The fire Smith mentioned in his story, one Art had already heard about, was undoubtedly brought on by Trent telling Art about the cabin fire leading to the finding of King's body. Dreaming that Smith was actually here? Confusing to say the least. Nah. This was no dream. Smith actually sat in my office and told me this outlandish tale.

Chapter 11

Art Investigates

Later in the week Art knew more trouble. Another girl was reported missing and the town was up in arms. Did they think just because Raleigh King was gone that there were no more predators in the town? Showed how much sense parents have allowing kids loose with no supervision.

Art found Chief Brown at Alfred's barber shop on South Esplanade.

"Now what?" Brown asked out loud.

Did Simonds have to confer with him every other day? Between the sheriff and Leona Broughton a man couldn't get in any nap time in his favorite barber chair. He put on his glasses. It didn't help.

"Well, looks like the town's in an uproar and we wondered if you need any help, Chief," Art said. "If we have another girl missing as I heard, and she's from the town here. We need to find her before the citizens get up in arms. We're not beyond vigilante tactics, Chief. King's death ought to tell you that."

"I have my men lookin' and that's about all we can do after the Amber Alert and other things we do when a girl is missin' for more than twenty-four hours. What do you want us to do?"

"I want us to be on the alert for anything suspicious. Remember what happened to the last sex offender? Want us to get a reputation for lawlessness?" Art was perplexed. He thought Brown would be alarmed and glad to have help. Didn't they always work together?

Brown was alert, but until something else happened he would remain calm and expectant.

Art recalled that he—unlike Brown— had visited the senior center; knew things were getting out of hand with the old codgers, with Leona Broughton, and her friend Laura. The county was bordering on chaos, an ominous rumble throughout and Art couldn't ignore the warnings. This sex sex offender thing could be the town's undoing, he thought, if it wasn't squelched pretty doggone soon. Art wanted to look into things and called the only suspect he had in the King murder. Bridges had described the mutilation Art left to others to view, but he knew only Leona had promised that kind of death for "anybody fool enough to bother her kin."

"Goodbye Chief," he said. Brown waved. Alfred was silent.

* * *

"Leona? Good mornin' Ma'am," he said when she answered. He had called Leona at 7:30 a.m. again. He didn't have any other time to bother her. She left home too early most every day, and hung out at the library. Story was she was writing a book about the state she came from, some sort of history thing. People said sometimes she put articles in the local paper.

"Is there anybody here but me? What is it Art? I was asleep, you know. "

"I'm remindin' you that somebody burned down your cabin over at Concrete. Well, you know where your cabin is, and how a neighbor found it when he saw the fire. You know that's where King's body was discovered." He paused to let her answer, but she didn't so he asked "Have you been up there lately?" He sure wasn't going to mention Ole Man Smith.

"What makes you ask me that, Art? You know I'm too old to be driving that many miles from town alone and nobody's cleaned it up for years. I couldn't even hike in there. My legs won't take the trauma. How did you find out about the cabin? It's not close. Who did it?"

"Whoa! One question at a time. I don't know, but since they did find King's body in there, Leonnie, and you own the cabin, I'm naturally goin' to ask you questions. The cabin didn't burn all the way, the wood must've been petrified, so old it didn't catch good. Roof leaked, didn't it? The killer didn't stick around to see the job finished, so we have King's body and maybe enough evidence to catch us a killer. Don't plead ignorant about DNA, Leonnie. What was left of his body was all swelled up from the heat, but not gone. Could've set the whole country side on fire this time of year. Too dry to be burnin' things."

"Yes, it leaked," she answered Art's question about the roof, ignoring the rest. "That's why I abandoned it. I didn't have extra money for a roof and Ted was the only one who loved it.

He's been dead for ten years now. If you think I care that King was found there, you have another think coming."

"But Leonnie, I'm rememberin' all the things you said about what you would do to anybody who touched your kin. Now ain't that a coincidence, the guy who had your granddaughter just happened to've died in your cabin— mutilated?"

"No! You're kidding, Sheriff. All I've got to say is somebody did a monumental good deed. I'd like to take credit, but like I said, I'm too old."

"Leonnie? Well, forget what I was gonna ask, you bein' in bad health and all. Besides, you ain't no murderer, just a loose cannon with that mouth."

"Art! For shame. We've been friends for years. I've voted for you in every election. How could you think such a thing? I did my part, the only thing I'm strong enough to do, I looked him up on the internet for you. My cabin was abandoned and anybody could've put a dead man in it."

"I said forget it. It's just odd, that's all. By the way I saw your friend Laurie in town the other day. Is she still ranchin'? She looks it, so stocky and all. I bet she can toss a bale of hay or a fifty pound sack of feed without thinkin' about it. Wouldn't be anything to toss around a body."

"I wouldn't know about that. We just have lunch together now and then when she's not busy running a tractor, or whatever. Any kind of a sheriff would figure that out," Leona said. She paused and then asked: "Have you been to my cabin, Art? Did you scope out the scene where King's body was found, or are you just taking your deputy's word for it?"

"Yeah, I've been there. Drove up there the day they found the body soon as I left the courthouse," he answered. "Stopped to get my bearin's at a historical marker about the old college out that way. You know, the one that reads "Concrete College 1865-1881."

"I've read the marker. In fact I can quote you a line or two from it: "One of the most respected schools in Texas in its day....In 1881 the college closed after epidemics broke out and the railroad bypassed town of Concrete...Years later rock walls of the main building were crushed and used to surface roads.

Only rubble marks site today."

"I have to say you got a memory on you woman, but then everybody knows how you love the history part of Texas." Art had to admit when she told him what he had just glanced at recently. But he had also noted on the marker that pupils were apparently severely disciplined, if that was the right word, in that they rose at five a.m. and took a brisk walk. Heck, Art had done that every day he attended school. He was a country boy who rode a school bus stopped on the main road and he had walked a half mile across a field to catch the bus every morning.

"Things sure changed, Leonnie, but back to findin' the cabin where Raleigh died," Art said. He was tired of her. "Gotta go, Leonnie, you take care of yourself. If you got insurance, best report it and have them appraise the damage. You know my term's almost up, but I sure would like to catch a killer before I leave office, and it ain't just my case. It's Brown's case too, where King's concerned. You know Bridges is runnin' next time for my place. It'd be a feather in my hat, though, to find the killer just for Brown and Bridges before November." He hung up.

Art pondered her lack of use of Texas lingo. He always grew suspicious of Leona using southern slang. She was too northern, even after these years here, but she disappointed him this time. No slang. Too bad Smith didn't recognize the people at the cabin in his "eye witness account." Smith did say they had on sheets and hoods covering their identity.

Plus, Smith wore coke-bottle glasses and even in a dream he would be wearing them. All he knew from his position outside the wall was that one was tall, the other short. One fat and the other not so fat. For now Art would keep this under his hat and not say a word unless sure. Bridges might run with his conversation with Art about Smith and it was too soon.

The tired sheriff recalled the incident of a stranger found murdered in a fancy conversion van Leona sold after one of her trips north. The sheriff's department never questioned her about it. The little girl involved—one lured into the van near the school— wasn't hurt. Somebody saw her climbing into the side door, yelled and the man shoved her out, ran around to the driver's side, jumped in and drove off. Art investigated, but the man said she asked him for a ride and they couldn't prove otherwise. The man was very much alive then.

Art had opened his PC, looked for the sex offender register and he wasn't there. The man had apparently moved into Cuero from some other state. With his body sliced up and his hands chopped off, there was no way to identify the man. His face was smashed and it would take a reconstructive expert to build a facsimile. It never occurred to Art or any of the authorities to question Leona about the body.

Too bad it wasn't January, Art thought. He would be out of office and Bridges would be taking over. A new sheriff could handle the situation with more objectivity than Art could muster at the time. If his coffee buddy was guilty, how would have to handle the ramifications of being too lax on the job and allowing the investigation to grow stale.

His heart pounded furiously as he thought of arresting the quartet at the center, Leona, Laura, and no telling who else was guilty of deciding who would clear the county of sex offenders if the law couldn't be written to incarcerate them for the rest of their lives. The dilemma of keeping children and teenagers safe in a small town like Cuero, not to mention that DeWitt County had twenty thousand plus souls depending on a few deputies, a smattering of police officers in each small town in the county stuck with the sheriff.

Brown was right to argue with the town council and all other chiefs should be on their toes when it came up budget time. Art's own salary was not enough to carry the load he was elected to bear. If his wife—God rest her soul—had not worked, they wouldn't have the money for the little scratchy patch of land they called a ranch.

She loved the ranch, especially the magnificent old Mesquite tree which had lain its enormous trunk along the ground across the front yard. The tree sported several branches along the trunk, and turning up into the air with limbs reaching so high to the sky, Art could hardly see visitors pulling up out front. Dang!

Art's mind floated back to the annual Turkey Fest with the famous turkey trot competition which preceded the election in

2005. Another stretch of limited manpower. Nora always enjoyed the celebration, even with Art tied up keeping the peace. The big race with Cuero's Ruby Begonia defending against the twin city of Worthington, Minnesota and their turkey Paycheck, every year brought out people from all over the nation seemed like.

Art had heard that a documentary of the town and its alluring events was being planned for 2007. Good! But how could small county, city and precinct peace officers oversee such crowds? Bring in the state, that's what.

Children running wild in the streets, parents chasing, hungry visitors busy buying big turkey legs to gnaw on, washing them down with beer; shopping at the booths set up at the park; all beginning with the big race as the highlight. For years the big parade was held down town, and still was on Esplanade — augmented with a Kiddie parade. The annual big carnival, dancing at the park; great entertainment and most years it was just that: fun for all. Problem this year for city, county, precinct, state and committee personnel was the stink of sex offenders dirtying up the town and county, hanging around the park.

Then there was the problem of all kinds of places along the streets and in the park available for perverts to lurk, waiting for some lone child to wander by. Maybe this year the perps would have heard what a mysterious, vengeful town Cuero could be when it came to "Pred-o-files" slinking around in the shadows. Maybe there would be no report of a child disappearing—just "temporarily misplaced."

Still, he enjoyed the exciting atmosphere of the event every year, especially when Ruby took both heats – the one in Worthington and the one in Cuero— not that he had any money down on the race. Nah!

The only thing Art was prouder of in Cuero was the champion material high school Gobblers playing football every fall. He hated to miss a game. The teams always ended up in a high bracket. Cuero had a lot to offer in spite of sex offenders.

High School baseball was fast becoming a good sport to watch if a person had time. Art wasn't so keen on golf but had heard the game was going quite well: championship playing.

Chapter 12

Predator Highs

In mid November, an excited young man waited for a ride from a young girl he met on the internet. Budgey Wayne had a change of clothes just like she instructed so he might stay more than a day since her parents would be out of town. He had on his best smelling cologne. He also considered himself good-looking with his blonde hair, blue eyes and tight pants. She had emailed the day before, wanting to meet after three weeks of communication.

A shaky hand brushed back oily hair before he reached down to tighten his belt, make sure his shirt tail was tucked in. He wasn't thinking of the young man found murdered who was being tried for molesting a teenager. He only had one thing on his mind and it wasn't death.

A pickup truck slowed, then stopped. The windows were darkened like a lot of Texas trucks and the excited Budgey couldn't see inside. The driver honked three times as was the signal the two e-mailers agreed on. He was smiling as the door opened, but attempted to run when he saw who was inside the truck. He stopped when a gun appeared.

"Get in," a voice ordered, "or get shot here and now!" He hesitated only a moment before realizing he was doomed either way. He started to run, but hadn't noticed a second person had stepped up behind him.

"We said get in," another voice ordered.

The baited man gave up and slid onto the seat of the pickup. He looked around. He hadn't noticed the four doors. It was a crew cab and two more grim faces peered at him. He hadn't learned a thing from the murder of Raleigh King, alleged sex offender. Wayne had allowed his burning burning fever for young things to overrule common sense. He was a trapped wolf.

* * *

It was late November when Art instructed Bridges to question three families as to why their kin was failing to register on birthdays as required. One by one the sex offenders were reported by their families to have taken clothes and left town. This was a repeated response to inquiries from the sheriff's department. The disappearance dates were scattered—nobody was unduly upset.

"Everyone of 'em said there was clothes missin' from the closets, so the families assumed they had left town for a few days maybe," Bridges explained.

"You asked each one, did you? How come all of 'em said the same thing?"

"Well, not exactly the way it sounds, I had to question them some," Tom admitted. He wasn't about to let Art know he led the questioning so that they admitted to clothes missing.

Deputy Bridges was reporting the information to his boss over a cup of coffee at the Doll House. That was okay with Art—his term was almost over. Until the end of December he would pretend to ride out King's killing and let somebody else solve the crime. He wished he could have found Raleigh's killer. In fact, he knew he wouldn't rest until somebody did.

The fever around town against molesters wasn't dying down like the city and county hoped. In fact, too many appeared to be suspicious of their neighbors, friends, relatives, strangers, the law. Several fights had to be interrupted. The town was in a fever pitch and no solution in sight. Art hoped the registered offenders skipped out of town before something happened to them.

He had no trouble discovering the three missing men were part of the ones listed on the registry of sex offenders in DeWitt County with photos and addresses on the website. The city had passed a law the year before demanding signs in every yard where one of the registered offenders lived, but only after the ordinance took effect. Cuero had no new ones registered, therefore no signs. Of course anybody with horse sense could look on the internet for names and addresses. Didn't Leona Broughton? Since Art's office was in the county seat, he always had privy to action on lots of things, and he didn't care where they got the news some of the perverts left town. Bridges would let him know.

Art clicked on his old '94 PC and looked up every last one

of them. He knew who they were, but wanted to learn what the the computer listing had to say as to how they became labeled as known sex offenders. There was one on the other side of town—not close to the school—twenty-two years old. He messed with an eight year old, Art noted. Dang! He knew the mother. She was reported to be half a deck shy. Stands to reason the boy would be also.

The mother, Joyce Murdock, had the boy with her when she moved into town and common-law married Rudolph Jordache to take on him and his three grown boys to take care of a two-story house up on the hill off Esplanade. Added to that, Jordache's father, George, lived there too. He owned the house.

Rudolph was a lifetime resident of DeWitt County, retired now, but the boys were still home, never having married. He had no grandchildren and didn't appear he would get any if nobody in the family ever went out with the locals. His wife died twenty years ago, left him with the boys to raise and it seemed he had done a reasonable job.However, this new "marriage" brought in the sex offender, Raymond Murdock. It was a definite embarrassment to Rudolph, but Art knew the man wasn't one to go back on a commitment. Surely, he had watched after the twenty-two year old.

Art decided to call on Rudolph and inquire as to why the young man suddenly left town.

"You know, we wondered that too," Jordache said. "His ma said he had been fiddlin' with the computer, packed up his clothes, and left. He wouldn't say where he was goin' she said."

"When was the last time you all saw Raymond?"

"Well, he was here—Joyce!" he called his woman. "When was Raymond here last? You remember—he packed his overnight and said he had to meet somebody, might be gone a few days?"

Joyce came to the door, wiping her hands on an ugly brown apron. She looked at Rudolph and he nodded like it was okay for her to talk.

"It was in the first part of November, I think,"she said. "He'd been at his computer all morning. It wasn't the first time he went off for a few days." Joyce didn't linger, turned and retreated to the kitchen.

"There, you have it, Sheriff. Me and the boys, well, and Grandpa, haven't seen him since."

Simonds chatted a few minutes and paused, feeling dissatisfied with their answers. Dang. That was a fruitless journey, he told himself. Jordache is one of the good ole boys. I won't have to worry about him, but Raymond Murdock's mother seems none too happy with her new life. She was a fine looking woman when Rudolph brought her here as his "Wife."

Art turned his thoughts to old Elsworth Jordache, the actual owner of the house. He was visible, lifting a bottle of beer to his face, but didn't acknowledge Art's presence. Senile, maybe, or just hard-core. Art had heard rumors that he was a wife and child abuser—whipping the devil out of them, it was said, not sexual abuse. So much for Elsworth Jordache. Art's interest was in where the Murdock boy went. The bunch was good ole boys, drinking and carousing; there had been no calls to this house since he was sheriff.

Art had taken his leave with a hand shake. They grew up together: Rudolph shut the door.

"Shh!" warned Rudolph when his sons started laughing and yelling at the thought of Raymond being a pervert. He'd embarrassed them all. Their step-mother came into the room to see what the hullabaloo was about. She looked around, wiped her hands on the ugly apron, turned and left. What had this quartet done now to bring out the sheriff?

* * *

In the comfort of his home, Art returned to the PC and looked for the next one to check on. The second offender on Art's computer was thirty-one: Tom Johns, reportedly messed up a twelve year old girl. Neither offender's info showed a listing as to "high, medium or low risk." Art didn't know if somebody programming missed that part or if it was some kind of privilege the labeling was missing. The programmer didn't know he was once told.

A third one, Eduardo Ruis, was twenty-eight, listed for a fourteen year old boy. They were all judged, but this one only received "deferred adjudication." That aggravated Art, these homo's —as he often referred to them—doing anything they wanted and not going to jail permanently. Somebody's twisted idea of how to get rid of them, Art reckoned, the prisons being full all the time.

The sheriff was heated up over the soft way "perverts"were treated. Hanging's too good for them, he thought, darkness spreading across his face. But, along with the rest, Art breathed a sigh of relief when the news came out about the crud leaving town. It was about time. The kids could play safer now. There were four more on the list, but he let it go until something else happened.

Leona Broughton was smiling a lot lately, possibly thinking her grand-daughter avenged and people wizened up about these predators in the area. She even accepted his offer of jelly beans one day when he was sitting in his vehicle outside the post office. Art couldn't ask for more.

* * *

The phone rang early one morning. Art woke from a fitful sleep.

"Art..." Leona said, and he noticed from caller i.d. it was her cell phone.

"Yes, Ma'am," he answered, hoping to hear a half-friendly voice, even at this hour.

"Well," she hesitated, then "I'm gonna have to renege on our coffee date. Sorry, but I'll be busy the rest of the year. I won't be able to have coffee with you all at the usual time, or even to have lunch with Laura for awhile. I told her not to find a new partner for lunch," she said and laughed, "but I wouldn't mind if it was you. Say hello to the bunch at the center." She almost hung up. She just couldn't tell him what was on her mind, exactly why she called.

And that's important for what reason? Enough for her to call me? Art pondered for a spell on what she might be talking about. Was there something she wanted to tell him other than she was going to be busy? What?

"Well," Art said, "are you gonna be so busy that I cain't drop by once in awhile to fill you in on things from the sheriff's office? Bridges will let me know."

"Oh, I'm sorry, Art. I can't. Maybe Laura can. I'm busy writing a new mystery about our sex offenders and them sneaking out of town. I got the idea from our sheriff, Art," she said and laughed.

"Wouldn't be a murder mystery, would it? Why don't you just stick to history of the state you migrated from? You're good at that," Art told her. "Let me read the new story, Okay?"

"I'm running out of time, friend, and ya know I am. It won't be long now until I'm in the last stages of this cancer. I have to hurry. I'll let ya know when I'm not busy and we'll do lunch. I've a great list of names and photos, and things to do."

"Okay," Art said, noticing Leona's use of the "yas" not you and he grew more suspicious. "Is there somethin' you want to tell me, ma'am? It sounds like you're hintin' around that way." No answer.

Leona wanted to tell him something, but the sound of his official voice stilled her voice. She couldn't.

Art hung up and called Laura. Just when he thought she wasn't home, she picked up and answered. She seemed out of breath, but he had to ask:

"What's going on with Leonnie? She's got no time for you, her best friend, and to talk with me. We've been havin' coffee regular for years now. To top it off, she called from her cell phone, not home, tellin' me she was short on time. Where you two been?"

Laura Rogers sighed and all she would say was, "I'm really tired of this lunch thing. We just got back. I wish Leona would let up on the dining and we'd get back to where we used to be. Where'd that y'all thing she's using lately come from, Art? She never talks like that unless we're in among locals."

This was getting nowhere."Talk to you all later," Art said, without asking her to lunch.

* * *

Across from John C. French school, a K&N customer pulling away from the drive-up window, lunch on the seat beside him, stopped short of entering the street when he noticed a parked car on the lot facing the elementary school yard. The windows were closed in the heat, the motor running, but most noticeable was the occupant—a middle-aged man—holding the back of his head and leaning forward.

The by-passer stopped, parked his vehicle, got out, pecked on the window and asked "Anything wrong?"

No answer. Again the concerned man pecked on the window. The driver sat with his hands locked together on the back of his head and wouldn't answer. He clearly was in a state of panic. The K&N customer tried the door but it was locked. He stopped short of breaking in to open it from the inside. He asked again if anything was wrong.

"Call 911!" was the only response. Asked again, the man responded with "Call 911. I've been shot in the back of the head and I'm holding my brains in!"

"Oh my gosh! Hang on, I'll get help."

An ambulance arrived followed by three squad cars: city, county, and Precinct One. Emergency personnel didn't hesitate to break in the rear window, reach in and unlock the front driver side door when the man refused to cooperate by unlocking the door. They were successful in snapping a brace around his neck before leaning the man forward to look at the back of his head. He held tightly to the back of his head through the whole thing yelling "I'm holdin' in my brains!"

"Where did this happen, Sir?" he was asked, failing to unlock the grip of the panicked man.

"Sittin' right here! I was just sittin' right here, mindin' my own business."

"Do you always park across from a school on the K&N lot? Where'd you been before you arrived here?"

"At H.E.B. buying groceries, " the man whined, "and somebody drove by here and shot me. It must have been the same one who killed Raleigh King."

"And why would anybody be wantin' you dead, Sir? I ask again, why are you parked here across from the school?"

"You know why my life's in danger. Never mind that. Get me out of here to the hospital!"

The first emergency medical technician took a long look. He turned and walked away, motioning the second one to take a look. They looked at each other, fled to the back of the car, hid their faces and almost fell on the ground laughing.

"What the heck?" asked City Officer John Thomas.

"Do you know this man? Would somebody shoot him?" one EMT asked trying to control himself.

"Yeah, he's a registered sex offender name of Tony Jones, and not supposed to be anywhere near this school. He moved in here last year from another state to be with the only person who would have him—his sister."

The newest DeWitt County deputy, Walt Perkins, walked up to the man now sitting in the back of the ambulance still gripping his head. "Where's the blood? Why ain't he unconscious, men? Where's any hole in the window if he was shot from behind? The windows are rolled up."

"Why ain't somebody doin' somethin'?" Jones screeched. "I been shot and my brains are spilling out of my head. Look at me!" He jerked one hand around filled with grey and brown slimy material.

The deputy took off his Stetson, bent down and looked at the back of the man's head where a hand squeezed tightly to keep something brownish-grey from falling off. Jones was a weak-chinned, parrot-faced man, with wild hair gelled and sticking up like a porcupine. Grabbing his mouth, the deputy walked away without comment to hide behind the ambulance and split a gut laughing. His lean abs showed against a tight uniform shirt as he sucked in air.

"Yeah, I know this man too," he said, laughing. "He's short on brains. He's one of them Pred-o-files Art told us about. Where'd he say he'd been before he was shot?"

"Shoppin'. He'd been shoppin' and guess what he bought before he decided to sit in the heat watchin' kids on the playground: canned breakfast rolls. One of 'em blew up in the heat and hit the fool in the back of the head. He's been sittin' there—oh my gawd, I cain't say it for bustin' inside—he's been sittin' there holdin' raw cinnamon rolls to the back of his head afraid to move for fear his brains would fall out. Serves the dirty pervert right."

"Oh G-God help m-me, I c-cain't s-straighten up," stuttered Thomas, rotund body shaking and his brown eyes invisible. Not one officer, not one rescuer regained control as they looked at each other. The constable joined in the fun.

A photographer from the Cuero Record slid his car onto the parking lot and jumped out. He heard of the shooting incident over a scanner and rolled up just in time to photograph the wounded man's head as he whined that he was dying and nobody cared because he was one of the "registered."

Jones fainted when the flash went off.

The reporter looked, held in his burst of amusement and had to flee the scene. He had his pix and one heck of a story. He might win a Pulitzer if he handled this right. Cuero Record reporter Jesse Rogers, new on the job, asked just enough questions to go with his back-of- the-head view, and turned to leave. He wasn't getting any serious cooperation from the cracked-up bunch.

"Too bad this wasn't a woman," he remarked as he slammed his car door, grinning.

"Why?" Thomas asked, laughing.

"Heck, he's got blonde hair."

That did it. "Oh heck. Take him away," the EMTs were told. "We cain't let the hospital miss out on this one. Have him checked for possible heat stroke. Let his sister know where he is for gosh sakes. I won't forget to tell Art Simonds one of his computer list Pred-o-files got shot," Deputy Perkins said as he slammed the door on the man inside the ambulance.

He stumbled along, bent over from laughing as he headed toward the "victim"s car to scope it out before it was towed to the nearest impound lot since the registered pedofile would be arrested and not returned home. Was he ever glad Bridges told them about Art coining a new word for perpetrator-pedofile types: "Pred-o-file."

What mileage that would be in the coming days.

Chapter 13

More Bodies

Christmas, New Year's Day, the year 2005 already on Art, it was time to step aside and allow Bridges to assume command. Other things filled his long awaited retirement days: fishing or hanging out at the ranch. Fishing would require movement to Hogue's Bait shop on Hunt Street. It was tempting, thinking about the cheese bait Hogue developed.. Art had left the office in Tom Bridges' hands, newly elected sheriff.

The ranch was lonely, Art had lost his wife, Nora, married thirty-four years, right after Christmas a year ago. He was bored. He never knew she was sick until the end. Always too busy with duties, he never knew how much he depended on her until now. He asked himself what's left for me now? We were gonna travel some, never had time before. Then to spend the end of his career planning only to be left by himself with no children, kin—just nothing.

Thoughts of fishing flashed thorough his mind. He'd have to look into that sport tomorrow.

* * *

Relaxing in a wicker chair and sipping hot coffee on the porch came to a halt in February.

Bridges drove up in a cloud of dust, leaped over the mesquite tree trunk, limped up the steps, flopped down in Nora's chair—still sitting by the side of Art's whicker—and without so much as a hello, shouted:

"Art! The dispatcher informed me four more listed offenders apparently left town in the weeks following the holidays. They hadn't reported in. It was quiet until after Christmas when families began reporting their men gone, one by one," he said after drawing a breath.

"How did you deduce they left town?" Art asked. "These were old cases with no signs in their yards. They were from the prior days."

"The news came from families we questioned about their kin failin' to register as ordered. They said their kin just up and left town," he said, "took some of their belongings with them. I sense somethin' wrong about this picture. There ain't been any mandate to run them out of town, so why are they leavin'? They were all registerin' every year like they're supposed to. We've even had one on High Risk who registered every quarter. He raped and strangled a woman. She lived and wouldn't testify. The state complaint did him in, but he was turned out to live on the streets with our kids." Bridges had no children Art knew of— he wasn't married, but should be.

"Is this another one of them jokes you fellas are so fond of dumpin' on me lately?"

"Heck no, Art. This is real. This ain't no raw can of rolls thing."

"Well, I wouldn't know what's goin' on, but maybe since Raleigh died like he did, them other perverts thought it best not to stay, " Art evaded, "and I don't really care, Tom. You take care of it." At least they could account for the exact whereabouts of the blonde-raw-rolls-shooting victim—in jail.

He hurried back to his PC soon as Bridges left, not amused by the cinnamon roll incident. He clicked to the space where he could look up the offenders he thought the new sheriff was referring to. A twenty year-old, Budgey Wayne, labeled high risk because his victim was a four-year-old, Art thought probably was one who disappeared, but it wouldn't hurt to check with his mother if he had one.

Then there was a black eighteen- year- old, Bruce Leeds, listed for molesting three kids, a four, a five, and a seven year old. He received a five year sentence for that and then was let out to live among the innocents. Sick, sick, sick! He wasn't labeled low, medium or high risk on the internet program Art clicked into, and no reason as to why he was loose.

Art didn't want to omit another "deferred adjudication" perp, Roger Moss, a forty-four year old who messed with a twelve year old. He had greasy brown hair. The photo showed a dumb-looking man who would think his brains were in perfect condition. That would be another one Leona would want castrated, Art thought, but there again, no info about the risk level on anyone but the young man named Leeds.

The last one Art looked up was a Tex-Mex , Jose Juarez, old enough to be a fourteen year old's grandpa. No risk level mentioned. "Now I sure would like to find them perps," he said aloud. "Like to know why they're leaving our town all of a sudden. Could it be Leonnie visited 'em? That would be interestin'." Art learned it was okay to talk to yourself when noone else lived in the house.

* * *

In March, in the middle of a good nap, somebody hammered on Art's door. He opened it to a frustrated sheriff. With more than enough experience under his belt, Bridges still was not too sure he was performing the way he ought to Art guessed. *Here he stands, knocking on my door.*

Bridges didn't wait for an invite, just busted in, pushing Art aside. He didn't keep house that well now, and felt embarrassed. He hadn't picked up since Nora died.

"Art, you ain't gonna believe what happened!" Bridges burst out. "A hunter lookin' for a place to build a deer blind in the woods near Leonnie's scorched cabin stumbled over a skeleton hand, probably dug out by wolves or a pack of dogs!" Bridges flopped down on the nearest chair, yelled out, not waiting for Art to ask him to have a seat. "He called me," Tom said, all out of breath. "I was smart enough to call Justice of the Peace Kate Sorensen, like you told me. She drove hard to the scene. You know how she drives."

Bridges was as red-faced as a black man can get and about to bust a blood vein on his forehead. Art guessed he didn't know it wasn't hunting season, so the ex-sheriff kept silent. This was no joking matter he could tell, but Bridges was always getting tips. Art never was allowed to know from whom, like Bridges had a great secret. Of course he had friends Art never knew existed in the county. Probably it was a precinct constable who might've been "hunting" and Bridges wanted his source to himself.

"Sorensen came barreling into the brush scratching up her new four-wheel drive pickup," the sheriff shouted, pulling Art back to the subject at hand. "She came off the blacktop from Hwy 183, just short of Concrete, right into the mess of law vehicles leading the way to the grizzly scene. Dust chokin' all of us, she leaped out and stumbled through the weeds and burrs. She looked at the first body and turned white. At the same time she was knocking them burrs off her pants as she talked."

Art remembered Bridges talking the same way when Sorensen appeared at the cabin when King's body was discovered. He had called on and talked to her when King was found. Being the first female Justice of the Peace, she had faced good ole boy criticism and joking without flinching in any way. Art had wondered what she thought facing his deputy and the others.

His memory of Sorensen's face was that it was blank when he had talked to her about King's death, but he almost knew what was running through her mind. Dang shame such an attractive woman wanted to be in politics when she could be gracing some lucky man's house having babies.

Sorensen had stared at the older man and leaned back in her chair. It was good that older peace officers had the option to retire. This one appeared beat down with overwork. Simonds didn't know what was on her mind or he wouldn't be enjoying Bridges so much now, Kate was thinking as Art talked. These macho men should be used to women in law enforcement by now. She knew her job and ignored the expressions of those who resented her. After all, this was 2004, not the seventies.

One three-year-old cold abduction-murder case left undone by the sheriff and police chief had plagued her daily. This county didn't need any cold cases on the books. It caused everyone to look bad. Production and closure ingrained in her mind told her they were not diligent. Townspeople were calling with venom in their voices about the sheriff and the chief not doing their job—not trying attempting to solve anything, just going to coffee with everybody in town they called friends.

Time to discover the problem involved in this and rectify it to the best of her ability and duty. She reached for a Rolodex and her desk phone. Now where was the ranger's number over in Victoria? She had watched as Simonds, silver-toed boots sticking out of faded jeans, shirttail hanging out, clomped across the floor.

* * *

Pulling his mind from Sorensen and the visit to her office in 2004, Art listened to Bridges, laughed and talked but he didn't remember the Jay-pee acting in any particular way with her new job.

"Ain't that just like a city woman?" Bridges was saying. He didn't see the humor and ranted on, drawing Art word pictures. "Well, Sorensen yelled when she saw that body. Great horned toads, she said. She was lookin' over at two other bodies already exposed. Chief Brown's men were pokin' around through the limbs and leaves, right along with mine and Constable Dag Braneski. Art, we ain't ever had a killin' scene like this in DeWitt!"

And who else yelled when he saw the bodies? And who else is city born and bred?

"Who called in Brown and Braneski, Tom? It ain't basically their territory. Is everybody listenin' in on our radios?"

"Well, the city has been lookin' into the disappearances reported by the perps' families," Bridges said, "along with fendin' off questions on the unsolved King case."

As with the rest of the area's law enforcement, noone remembered out loud the van murder case. He dropped the question. No use pointing out that Brown had more experience and could be useful to the new sheriff. Constable Braneski was no tenderfoot when it came to experience. Bridges had some learning to be done.

Sweating with excitement Bridges ranted on about Sorensen. "She guessed there could be more bodies than the two we already found. 'Ain't this the site where Broughton's cabin burned last year' she asked me, Art. Then she ordered me to get men out there on the double, and tell them to find plenty of shovels, maybe even a ditch digger! Heck, that's county business where the cabin is. It's not in the city so it ain't their business. How we gonna explain all this to the state boys when Sorensen calls them in – without involvin' Leonnie and her talk?"

Art asked him what he was doing, letting in other peace officers since they had no "business" there. He stood, ignoring his old boss again. Art tried to read into the stance whether a hunter, maybe not—out of season—called, thinking he was obligated to let Chief Brown know.

"It didn't take long for me to call it in to the justice of the peace," Tom said, letting the excitement rise again. "The state boys came out too after she called 'em. Can you believe we uncovered seven bodies in shallow graves? It took us five hours, even with dogs lookin'. But whoever buried 'em didn't dig deep. What stunned us was the way all of them men was naked from the waist down. Some of 'em were preserved enough we could tell they was missing organs, you know, castrated like horses. The private parts, Sorensen called 'em. Fire ants took care of the any holes in the face. But, I don't think animals did that to their gonads."

"My chief deputy Walt Perkins puked when he dug up the freshest body," Tom continued. "Just like the rest, it was cut between the legs and his tools missing. Blood was dried on his face and up into his nose, shirt stained from the trail leadin' down to his face from the sliced out area. The body was so fresh the ants didn't have time to do their work. Rope burns were on his ankles and his hands were tied behind his back just like the rest of 'em. The deputy called me over and turned away to puke upchuck again. I didn't feel so good myself," Tom said, but wasn't finished.

"Sorensen, well, she says there's a serial killer in our community, y'all," Bridges aped Sorensen's woman-voice. Bridges then allowed as "How long did it take the judge to figure that out with all those bodies lying there?" He laughed.

Art found nothing funny, but Bridges added:

"Art, our former precinct justice wouldn't have said that where anybody could hear, but this new Precinct One justice ain't that experienced."

Both men laughed: Bridges at his clever wit and Art at Bridges' far-out thinking on women. The topic was not funny enough to cover up a sharp noise. They stopped and stared soberly at each other. Art rose and took a quick look out the window for his next door neighbor who was always somehow outside his door. It was to make sure Art was all right, she always said. Nora would've wanted her to. Yeah!

He failed to see a tall, tight-jeans, booted young man with a star on his shirt scurry around the corner.

"Sorensen cautioned me to get the state in on this," Tom said, drawing Art back to the subject at hand. "I already told you that, didn't I? 'We'll need a forensics expert to i.d. the bodies,' Sorensen said, 'and we'll need this ground gone over with a fine-tooth comb. Maybe the killer or killers left somethin' behind.' Well, Art, the killer did: them bodies. Do you think the coroner from San Antone could become involved? I hope not."

He wasn't laughing any more, but inside Art was. Those two out there together in the woods —both of them totally unaware of long past entitlement programs which gave them an opportunity that was not available when Art was younger—unconsciously trying to one-up each other in their legally gained roles in society. Bridges had no experience except what Art taught him, and naturally resented that he had to work with a lesser minority, a woman. Well now, that wasn't funny. He liked Sorensen.

By now it's obvious that Bridges didn't cotton to a woman justice of the peace having authority, but she was the one with the power over the sheriff.

"She might want to take advantage of her position without offending anybody," Art reminded Tom. "Chief Brown won't interfere," he said, "especially after the publicity of the trial. He has a cemented job. I only hope you were friendly to him in case you ever need to correlate crimes."

Bridges nodded, and ran on with the story, uninterested in Art's advice.

"By the way, Sorensen, I said to her, there's something odd here. There was seven men disappeared from town who were known sex offenders. Guess how many bodies we got here. Now that makes a connection to city and county, don't it Ma'am? Sorensen, she didn't answer, but I could see her mind grinding. This wasn't her problem. She was there to get things in order and that's what she did." He paused.

"Art, you got to hear this from me," Bridges drawled. "I believe we found all them missin' perverts from DeWitt. How the hunter found them bodies and knew to call me, well he was one of my deputies. That's why I was called out there, the scene bein' in the county and all."

Well heck, just what I feared, Art thought. The town's gone mad. I'm not hearing this, he told himself, but asked, "Why do you have to have a connection to DeWitt County, the town and the precinct, Tom? "

"Ain't nothin' like this come our way since you been sheriff, Art, and I want to lead in the solvin' of it. Them victims was all from DeWitt County, if it's who we think. Don't that give me the lead connection? Might want to run again, you know, like you did."

Bridges, bless his young bones, was serious, face crimson with excitement as he pushed on.

"Now let me finish tellin' the story, Art. Everyone of 'em was mutilated, I'm thinkin', from the look of things since some jeans pants were still on but sliced or ripped, it could be they all bled to death. Didn't see bullet wounds to the heads. The last one was still recognizable. A kid named Leeds. The animals didn't get to him yet. Did I mention they were buried up there by Broughton's burnt cabin?"

"Yes sir, more than enough times. Don't even say it. Don't keep repeatin' that stuff. I'm beginnin' to feel it myself. It's your territory. Leonnie's cabin's in this county. I've talked to her and she's not capable of hurtin' anybody. She's not strong enough and not young enough to lure any of 'em out of their houses, is she? Would you go meet somebody like her if you could see her? Good gravy, Tom, she's seventy if she's a day."

"Prob'bly is seventy, Art, and she don't look too good lately, but she's crafty. But like you said, it wouldn't be fun for 'em to meet up with the old woman. Do you think she's too sick?"

"She's capable of plannin' it, but not strong enough to do it alone," Art said in answer to Bridges' question. "She told me too much of her past about her own rape and her so-called prison sentence. I hope you ain't spreadin' this info to the state boys. Let 'em find out on their own. When she told me what ought to be done to molesters, I ignored her ranting. You know she's dying of cancer and wouldn't care if they were all killed by her. Hindsight, well, we should've pulled her in when Karly Young's molester was found in the burned cabin. But if you want that family after your hide, go to it. My money's on that bunch of seniors down at the center I heard talkin' about King not showing up for work."

"Why them, Art? Nobody would think them or Leonnie done it. I don't, and I've known her as long as you."

"No... no you haven't. I knew her before I ran the first time. She was a dang nosy retired reporter from up north, married a local, and moved here in the Nineties. She always found out too much, even stuff she couldn't print. She did some work for the local news, but not anything important. She was fair about not publishin' things when it was for the good of the office, but this? I don't think so."

"Should I pick her up, or what?" Bridges asked Art as he looked at the floor. He didn't relish facing Leona or her kin alone. He liked her and hoped she liked him. She had been almost a mother to him since he'd known her, but that bit of news was none of Art's business.

"No, no you shouldn't." *Good gravy, let her rest in peace. She's been through enough lately.* "You don't have any evidence she's involved." Art said aloud. "Let forensics and the state handle that part. You know the ranger from Victoria will be on the scene as soon as Sorensen calls him. She'll be ordering the bodies to forensics and identified by the Austin pathologist, just like when they found Raleigh. If it's your sex offenders, remember they all had to give up DNA when they were judged and labeled. There won't be any problem in identifying 'em, Tom, just takes time that way. If the bodies are decomposed, it'll take several days, won't it?"

Bridges didn't grab an opening. Art continued.

"Meantime, keep Brown informed if you want, since he was a witness to the bodies. You might need him someday and if you get too close-mouthed he won't be available. He'd do the same. I don't think you need the Texas Rangers involved—Sorensen has the call on that—unless it comes to those bodies being carried out there from another county. You and Brown could be unable to handle it from this end without the state involved, but that's the way it is. It's better if you do what you can yourself, but don't get in the way. My last word on this is if you don't give the city an invite, they won't give you one when you need it."

"Gettin' back to Leonnie, Art," Bridges persisted, like everything Art said flew over his head. Reaching into Art's jelly bean jar on the table, he popped a few into his mouth, and mumbled "Would she do something like out and out murder?"

"I don't believe I'd chase that maverick if it was me. Somebody like her, you have to have a cut and dried case." Tom was causing Art to drawl in his need to get a point across. "She knows the ropes and she'd get the best lawyer in the state to put you in your place. Remember her lawsuit against the town? Remember how everybody said you cain't fight city hall?"

"No. What law suit? Why?"

"When they tried to get her for that body on her porch? This is Texas, Tom, and there was a time when we could shoot an intruder for being on our property without an invite. She won."

"My gawd, is she that cold-blooded?"

"Be careful how you use God's name when you talk, Bridges. You don't have to do that. Only men who have no vocabulary resort to usin' descriptions like that. If you want to look professional clean up your language. Anyway, don't pick up Leonnie unless you want to mess with her kin. She gets mighty riled up and afraid of nothin'. Maybe we should've warned the judge about her mind wonderin' about his easy way of lookin' at teenage molesters."

Art paused to give Bridges time to react, but he didn't so the retired law man continued.

"This question would never come up about Leonnie if Judge Toby hadn't been so eager to let King out on bail for allegedly keepin' Karly Young over to his place. I hate it that Leonnie was disgusted, rememberin' years ago. In fact she was more than disgusted, she was fire-spittin' mad. You don't know — you're too young— we didn't punish them so much durin' her day as the law says to do now. I wager she's probably hardened to all us men, especially judges, when it comes to that."

Bridges wasn't registering that he heard Art. The ex-sheriff pushed on, hoping something would penetrate Bridges thick head.

"Thing I cain't figure out is where the strength would come from to kill, if she did. How would she get them out to that place? She'd have to have a helper, maybe two. She'd have to have a truck. Maybe that strong farm woman. I almost feel sorry for Leonnie. She'd probably die before the case was tried if it was her. I for one ain't gonna believe it was her. She's too visible and too old. Best swing your rope on another cow, Tom, or more likely another bull. In fact, how come you ain't lookin' at Tom and Sue? It was their kid. They'd have more stake in not wantin' King or the others around. We don't know but what vigilantes are operatin' in our little town."

"Probably Leonnie's innocent," Bridges suggested, ignoring Art's pondering, bored with all the talk which produced no solid answers. White woman like Leona helping a black deputy become sheriff was enough for him to believe her innocence.

Art realized everything he said went over Tom's head, but he could sense hope in the new sheriff's voice. Bridges liked Leonnie. She promoted his election all she was able.

"Of course, she's innocent," Bridges said again, and Art had to agree.

"She ain't no killer, just loud," Art said. "That many bodies, why it would take several good men to kill that many that fast. And you know how that lane is grown over to the cabin. It don't take long here for the mesquite and weeds to move in. She couldn't drag them in. They'd have to walk in on their own. Was there any sign of them being dragged to their death? No, well, they were killed at the scene."

"Not to my knowledge. Let the state boys handle that one. I'll just stay on the sidelines to take credit when it's over. You know, when the news shows up." He laughed and walked off.

With Bridges out of the way, his house once more his own, Art could replay all the scenes of numerous bodies in his mind besides Raleigh King. He mulled over Bridges' description of the piles of grave-filled bodies. Here the county had seven more bodies, maybe all registered sex offenders from DeWitt County, and as of that sighting over at Leona Broughton's cabin.

From what Bridges said, they appeared to have been hung up by the feet, castrated and the blood allowed to run down into their noses, mouths taped shut. That would surely choke them, he thought. Why hadn't there been a more serious investigation at the reported lack of registration from listed offenders?

Sheriff Bridges was excited to have this much going on with him elected in November and taking the position of sheriff in January when Art retired at Sixty. Bridges said one thing as to Leona's innocense, but was ready to suspect everybody from the senior citizens and Leona Broughton to Tom and Sue Young, Karly's parents. Art knew Bridges could be trouble, and felt sick, believing now that Leona wanted the men dead.

Chapter 14

Questions Rise

On Sunday, Art Simonds did something he would never have done. The action revealed to him the concerned citizens weren't the only ones gone wild. Art went to see for himself what kind of church Leona attended. He had dropped by the funeral for Raleigh King held there last year. The church people, all nationalities and types, apparently did not condemn the man-boy for what he allegedly did to Karly Young.

Maybe the church was weird like everybody who did n't go there said, he mused. Maybe that's what she thinks like. Maybe she's guilty. I could see her killing the one who had her granddaughter, but not the others. I've been in law long enough to know revenge from execution: I ain't insulting anybody, just wondering.

The church door was open and a lot of friendly folks shook hands with Art, but always the question: "When will something be done to keep our kids safe?" Some Art knew and some he didn't.

Although Leona apparently wasn't present, he sat through a whole service of two and a half hours. It started out with singing and some heavy young fellow walking up on the stage, raising a twisted trumpet, maybe an antelope horn, Art didn't know, but the sound blasted Art's ears, not once but three times. It raised the hairs on his arms. Everybody rose as one and began yelling and clapping. It was fascinating how they threw their arms in the air, shouted and all. Some even danced around the room while music was playing the same song over and over. The more they sung it, the more emotional they became.

Dang! Art almost said. He didn't think it weird, just different. He hadn't been in a church since his parents dragged him to the Baptist one downtown except for King's funeral. He didn't recall how that went, the forced attendance at a Baptist church. Rudolph Jordache and his family sat two pews behind Art and he had to admit he never pictured the old man, George, Rudolph and the three boys being at church. Rudolph's wife being there Art could believe. She seemed like a church-going type even though her son, Raymond by her first husband, was a registered sex offender. Art nodded but the Jordaches hurried from the church before he could strike up a conversation.

On his way out, the pastor of the curious church invited Art to visit his office sometime, asking at the same time if Art had a Bible." Was he asking because he wondered how people saw his church, or wondering what Art was going to say next?

Art remembered thinking that particular Sunday he should've said yes, he had a Bible, because the pastor said "Wait a minute" and went down the hall to get one. Art already had a Bible, it was Nora's. She churched all the time, but down with the Baptists. Art wondered does the President attend church? He had heard he did. He kept the thoughts to himself. The reverend waited for Art to continue, but he needed time and walked out of the church after shaking hands.

Rev. Jack Lester rubbed his young hands together in satisfaction as he watched the sheriff leave, believing that he was the one finally able to reach this particular peace officer in this town. His church could be the leader in converting the unbelievers and lifting the good citizens up to God for favorable judgement. Not that he wanted to be guilty of proselytizing from other churches. That would never do. Solidarity and the annual community holiday get-together would be jeopardized.

* * *

Aching to learn all he could about the slaughters led Art to ride with Bridges on a visit to Leona's the next day. The two inquisitors stepped up and knocked on an ebony door. Funny how she trimmed everything in black on the bright yellow house. She was smiling a warm welcome, and Bridges wanted her to be innocent. How many times did he tell Art that on the way there? He just wanted some idea, he said, if she knew who could be mutilating bodies like these men and boys and burying them on her place. Had she given some fool the idea maybe with her ranting? He kept asking: Art had ignored him.

"Y'all come on in," she said, drifting into a drawl and smiling that new smile developed over the last few months.

"Hey, Bridges. Hey, *Mister* Simonds." They were greeted

not by Leona so much as her son, Tim Young, stepping out behind his mother and standing where the Sheriff and Simonds couldn't go in if they were a mind to. "What can we do Ya for?" he asked and laughed at his own joke.

Art realized by the attitude it was true he was glad when Art wasn't Sheriff any longer. Was he worried Art was after his mother? Ten years older?

"Why aren't you out looking for whoever buried all those bodies over Concrete way?" His northern voice irritated Art today. Young hadn't been eager over a black sheriff, letting his prejudice show when he talked to Art a few times.

"Always the joker, Young," answered Bridges. "We just want to talk to your mother some, about the business over in her cabin a while back. Shame it burned. Ted always was proud of that little place. Must've been a hundred years old. King became our problem where his death's concerned, the body found out in the county all."

"Well, I wouldn't know how he felt since I didn't grow up here, but Mom didn't use the cabin anyway. She's too old to drive that far out of town, don't you think, and Sue and I have no use for it. Karly always hated to go there, so bushy and all. "

"Miss Leonnie," Bridges said, touching her by the elbow. "Could just me and you walk a ways and talk?" He never failed to let Art know he didn't like Tim Young since he married the Clements girl. Art knew from his and Leona's conversations that young Karly could make anybody mad. Probably never had a whip to her bottom, he thought, like it used to be for lack of respect. Art had heard reports of her behavior at high school and around town. There was even report of a bomb threat attached to her name.

* * *

"It took several days for the bodies to be identified, doing the DNA thing along with dental records," Bridges told Art when he saw him again. "Forensic DNA evidence was willingly supplied – all registered offenders have to supply DNA when found guilty of a sex offense. All they had to do was ask for the lab." He wasn't informing Art anything new.

Otherwise they wouldn't have identified them so fast: this

Art knew from his past days and before the famous Simpson trial. Forensics also determined the way they died. The state police had brought in three experts from maybe Austin or Houston at Sorensen's bidding. The seven sex offenders Art brought up on his computer had been slain, apparently by castration and neglected until they bled to death. Dang! What a way to die! He wondered briefly if any had been buried alive with their hands roped together and tape covering their mouths. He knew any good roper could tie those knots Bridges described and thought about one senior citizen in particular.

* * *

National headlines spotlighted Cuero and DeWitt County pricking Art's pride in his home town:

SMALL TEXAS TOWN RIDDING BLIGHT FROM NEIGHBORHOODS

Below that was a sub head "County Becomes Hotbed for Sex Offenders."Dang! What followed was not anything Art would call a complimentary article.

He wondered if President Bush heard about it. Why would that be important? It wasn't in the county where Bush had a ranch, but it was in his state. It was here in mid-state, out in DeWitt County where the bodies were discovered. If the president hadn't heard, Art would be surprised. What time Bush wasn't living in Washington, he was in Texas on his ranch. His assistants would keep him apprised on whatever happened in the president's home state. Art had wanted to contact the President for some time relating to sex offenders all over the country, not just Texas.

Funny how things go through my mind and distract me, Art thought, when he heard through Bridges' deputy a comment Bridges made concerning the missing sex offenders: "Funny no kin reported them gone until we questioned. Guess they were just relieved they were out of sight." Of course it was reported to Art. He was sheriff too long for the deputies to forget.

"Less work for us," Deputy Jose Gomez said, and laughed when he told Art, like the retired sheriff needed to keep up on Bridges' business. "It was plain to Tom," he added "that nobody really cared these men were dead. But Bridges, he told us it's his job to find out who, no matter if they're slime. He wants the publicity. I sure hate to think it could be them old geezers down at the center like Bridges thinks. They might think different than us younger folks, he said."

"It still ain't my business," Art said for the umpteenth time, and resented being part of the old geezers referred to by the Hispanic deputy's words, being sixty himself.

* * *

"Nobody much turned out for the funerals," Art mentioned to Bridges one day shortly after hearing the news from Bridges' chief deputy—Art's second-in-command behind Tom before he became Bridges' right hand—but Art left out the part about the deputy telling him what went on in Bridges' office.

"I know. They got what they deserved, prob'ly, but I have to look into this, no matter who it hurts," Bridges replied. "Murder is against the law, even with perverts. Makes a county unsafe when things like this happen. We got us a bunch of vigilantes, or just one, do you think?"

"Well, now, I don't have a clue. You take care of this mess alone. I'm sittin' this one out 'cause I don't want nobody on my back for interference. Just stay away from the Center unless you all got plenty evidence. Them old folks got you elected."

"I'm gonna question some of the registered offenders' kin," Tom said. "Maybe they saw or heard somethin' when their men disappeared."

"You do that. Let me know if they cooperate."

Even though Art couldn't legally interfere in any way, or get involved in the city's murder investigations, he could use past connections with the state department and the local P.D. to influence investigation into any suspects he or Bridges might have.

The ex-sheriff replayed King's funeral of last year in his mind, remembering he was the only law in town who cared enough to attend. He thought he saw Leona and Laura several yards away, but his mind could've been playing tricks. Suzie King was so torn up nobody could console her. Her neighbors were kind enough to show up, but looked around to see who else was there. It was a sad day. Art noticed an older woman he hadn't met standing to one side, wiping tears and blowing her nose. Who could she be? He wouldn't ask. That was last year, this was now.

* * *

"Ms. King, ma'am," Sheriff Bridges addressed Raleigh's mother when she opened the door to insistent knocking as his first contact concerning the eight murders. Art was along again, just for the ride, but this investigation was becoming more interesting every day and Art wished, a little, that he was still sheriff. He would have done the same—invited Chief Brown along—when he was sheriff located in Brown's city. Ms. King sure was short, and no longer a looker. She'd let her hair go. Art had noticed that when she was on the witness stand last year.

"Yes Sir, whatcha want? My boy's dead, I'm alone and I don't want no truck with y'all anymore." She wiped a strand of dirty blonde hair from her jaw and pulled a ragged housecoat close with one hand as she placed the other hand on the door ready to slam it in Bridge's face. Art was glad Raleigh didn't inherit the pock-marked face of his grandpa. At least there was that good memory.

"Did your boy say anything about where he was headed?" Bridges asked Ms. King. "We were informed he moved back with you the afternoon he left the courthouse. I know you slept a night or two since he died, but if there's anything— You know he was the first victim, and there's all them bodies buried out in the woods. In fact, he was in the scorched cabin, not in the woods."

"Yeah, I know about that. You don't need to remind me. It hurts too much. I don't miss his troubles, Sheriff, but he was my baby." Tears flowed easily down Suzie's cheeks and Art dropped his gaze. "There was only one thing he said, and I worried some about that," Ms. King answered, and reached up to brush a tear from her cheek. "He said there was a new girl in town he wanted to meet and he had an invite from off the internet, I think."

Suzie King paused to remember, then "Yeah, he said he had to meet her out to Concrete at the old Stage Coach Inn in the middle of the day. But I wouldn't loan him my car. Too old and

I need it. He said he'd have the girl pick him up, and I just made sure she wasn't a teen. Come to think of it, it was the next day after the law loosed him. Yeah, through the internet, that's what he called it, the thing he left behind, is how he met her. He was smart, my boy, he could work that thing."

"Would y'awl mind if we take it down to headquarters and have an expert look at it? Could be we might find out who he chatted with." Bridges could really come down on that drawl of his when he was trying to pump somebody for information.

"Do whatever y'all like. I never touch it, don't know how," she said and opened the door for him and a deputy to find the computer in a back room. They carried it out, dusty and unused, to where Art was talking to Ms. King.

It was none of his business, but Art had to ask: "Ms. King, did you have enough funds to bury your boy?"

"Why yes, I did. You might've not known, but my son's Pa, he gave me money to pay for insurance on my son. He did that much, although he would never admit to being Raleigh's daddy. Did you see his grandma at the cemetery?" Changing the subject, she pointed at the computer. "How come the city ain't asked for that thing? What about that feller who came by here with a round badge on that said RANGER?"

Tom looked to Art for that answer, and all he could offer was "Ma'am, that's Chief Brown's territory, and I know nothin' about a Ranger. Bridges here cain't get into that. If ya want him to find out who killed your boy just keep this quiet and we'll let you know as soon as we can."

Raleigh's mother offered another piece of information they probably didn't care about.

" I handed my boy a bag of his favorite jelly beans—liquorice—on his way out the door."

Suzie King had only one person to blame for her son's death. She had heard all the talk Leona Broughton spouted at the senior center. These so-called lawmen had no answers and didn't even care that her precious boy—who did no harm to anybody—was gone and she, Suzie King, had nobody. Yes, she knew who to blame.

Raleigh's grieving mother closed the door in their faces.

* * * *

Art met Bridges at the Doll House the next day.

"What's happenin', Tom? Why'd you ask me for coffee?"

"Got me a room full of computers from kin of those victims. Set 'em up in that old storage area we quit usin' Art. Got me an expert from Houston comin' in to read the hard drives," Bridges bragged. Simonds could see him mentally rubbing' his hands together and waitin' for a pat on the back. "Only one who wouldn't cooperate was the Jordache family out on Deacon Hill. Their son didn't live with them no more anyway, the mother said. Told me "he just up and packed his clothes and left. Rudolph, he didn't know either where my boy went," she said.

"They weren't friendly, Art, just stood with the door half open. I could see two or three overgrown boys lounging in front of a TV. There was an old man in there, could've been your friend Rudolph. Couldn't do much about it, so I left. The one PC I'm most interested in was King's I'd like to know if he made contact with anybody — I'm not sayin' Leonnie—before he was killed. Since he was the first, maybe somethin' was on that PC that would tie in the rest. All of the missin' men was from DeWitt County, and if the city ain't interested, I'm goin' ahead with my own search. What do you think?"

Art's answer was automatic.

"I plan on doin' what I'm doin' and that's keep out of yours and Brown's business." This was not the time to offer any solutions to Sheriff Bridges. Let him get in hot water and Art would do what he was doing. "If you got any sense, turn King's computer, or at least the findins', over to Brown so's he can figure this out," Art advised, then asked, "How'd you get Houston involved?"

"I lied a little, Art. Told 'em the city and me had a task force goin' and Brown allowed me to help out from here since King's body was found out in the county. Well, actually, I kinda asked Brown in a roundabout way did he want me to look into the families of the men who died. He didn't say no, so I rounded up the computers from the families and it was all left up to me. Just a little lie, Art," he pleaded for his former boss to understand.

"Brown ain't gonna fade away if that's what you think.

Why should he waste good manpower when he has a county dummy doin' it for him? They're prob'bly just glad you did it," Art said, sipping coffee and pondering on the moves made by Bridges. "Wish I could help you," he said, "but I'm retired. I say again I don't want involved." *Brown wouldn't just let Bridges get away with using his name. He'd let the eager beaver do all his work. Why not?*

Thinking back to what he last said to Bridges about being retired and not wanting the involvement, like heck he didn't. Art was in this up to his eyeballs just like King's killer. He finished his coffee and rose to drive his favorite vehicle home to a little ranch outside town. He said "let me know if any chattin' on them computers is Leonnie," and changed the subject.

"My new SUV beats heck out of the ole Texas standard Suburban truck all to pieces. With Norrie dead, it ain't no fun to go home. Wonder what that friend of Leonnie's is like? Could be she'd like some company some time. Of course, not me, I'm newly widowed." Art turned toward Tom and waited for encouragement.

Bridges felt uncertain. He sure wasn't interested in Art's love life. He wanted Art to be proud of him and his investigation. Art trained him, didn't he? Only thing, Art wouldn't be so open to what he was doing about collecting computers that are evidence.

The ex-sheriff watched as Tom rose slowly, pulled himself off the chair, paid for two coffees and limped out the door heading back to his office. He'd once told Art his leg hurt all the time now since he stumbled over a log by Broughton's cabin last year. Must've pulled something, he said. Couldn't worry about that now. Tom better worry about the city's interest in this investigation. He better make his mark high as the first black sheriff of DeWitt. He could be cutting his political career short.

* * *

Another interference was nosy insurance investigators coming around asking questions about the murders. Art learned that each and every one of the murder victims had been insured for enough to bury them and then some. He asked himself did the families have something to do with the killings? They could use the hubbub surrounding the King killing as inspiration.

Art Simonds couldn't tell his former deputy-elected-sheriff that Chief Brown had contacted him about Leona's cabin when it burned, and he couldn't, or wouldn't help Bridges investigate his coffee-drinking buddy, Ted's widow. He had spent all the time he was going to searching for clues in that tangled brush and in the smelly, half-burned cabin.

One thing Art couldn't face was Leona's hurting for the wrong done her in the past, Art told himself repeatedly. That smile she was wearing lately didn't fool him for a minute, and he wasn't going to let anybody persecute her, not even Bridges.

Chapter 15

Copy Cat

Art wasn't surprised when Leona called him the next day, saying she thought she heard something last night outside her front door.

"I looked through the peephole, saw nothing, but thought I heard a man walking across the yard. It was dark, but there was a street light," she said. "I moved over to the window and peeked from behind the drape. I could see he was limping. Doesn't Bridges limp now? But then the man appeared to be heavier than Tom. What would he be doing over here nosing around, anyway?"

She stopped and then, sounding sheepish, said, "You know I keep a gun, so I reached behind me and slipped it out of the holster hanging on the wall where Ted always kept it. You know, the one he carried years ago when he was in law enforcement – the antique.38 colt with the hair trigger. I waited for awhile, then decided it must be that old man down the street who peeks in people's windows. He's been doing it for years, but never harmed anybody. I dropped the drapery and turned out the lights. Might be well to keep the blinds closed at night from now on. I went to bed to think about it tomorrow."

But then she said just as Art was gonna hang up, "Hey, I could've used that gun on King if I'd thought of it."

"Have you ever used that gun on anybody, Leonnie or threatened to?" Art pried. No answer. She hung up.

Leona was thinking how Art would not believe she could identify the intruder staring into her window. Hah! If she shot him, however, the law wouldn't believe Art was a peeping Tom.

Dang! The man limping across the yard saw her looking and decided he had better be quiet from now on. That man was Art. He hurt his ankle picking up some stuff at the ranch, but for now, let her wonder. Good thing it was dark enough she couldn't see my belly, he thought. That would be a dead giveaway. She was crazy enough right now to shoot Art, and nobody would do a thing to her. It was her property. Art just wanted to see if she was using a computer this time of night. She was. He was curious as to how all the alluring little girls got on chat rooms this time of night like Tom said. Art didn't find out a thing. Leona was reading a book the whole time he spied on her, glancing at the computer now and then.

He didn't notice a slim young man following him that night at Leona's.

* * *

"Leona phoned me the next day," Laurie said, when Art used an excuse to call. He was getting too involved, but couldn't help himself. Of course he didn't need a reason, and said:

"Leonnie told me about the man in the yard and I wanted to find out if y'all knew anything I could use."

"Somebody's been snooping around her yard at night," Laurie said, "and Leona said she's thinking about opening the door and taking a shot to scare whoever it is. It wasn't just one night, it was three times. She's not herself anymore. Hasn't been since the trial. Won't go out for lunch or talk much on the phone, Art. What do you think?"

"I wouldn't draw attention to myself that way, if I was her," Art said and thought, boy, I could get shot at that, and I ain't been saved like them church people talked about the other day. Thing that bothered Art was that he had been there one time. Who else was snooping? To Laura he said:

"Advise her to have the city post a man outside first. That way, her butt's covered if, or when, she does shoot. Who would snoop around her yard?"

"I haven't the slightest idea," Laurie answered. "It's not like she's a killer or anything."

Art ignored Laura's loyalty and asked, "Are you goin' to lunch tomorrow with Leonnie, Laurie? I'd like to go too, if you don't mind. I'll call her and ask."

* * *

"Well, I'm busy working on this new manuscript, you know," Leona evaded when Art called. He had asked, but she countered with, "I think I can finish it before I die if I keep at it. Why don't you pick up something and bring it over? We'll just have a snack out on the patio and talk awhile. I can spare that much time. By the way, there's no sign in the Henton's yard. They moved a sex offender into their place. I heard it was their grandson, Bobby Knight from Oklahoma. All out-of-State offenders have to register too, you know. He's already on the internet. He had to have been tried here and convicted, wouldn't he, to have a sign in the yard? You'd think they'd be careful to not let that out after all that's happened here this year. Nobody would be wiser if they kept shut."

"Yeah, you'd think that," Art agreed and laughed. Lunch was gonna be fun.

* * *

Lunch was fun until Bridges interrupted. He couldn't wait a few minutes to tell Art that Bobby Knight's body had been found southeast of town, down by the Guadalupe River.

"Dang Art, he was cut up just like the others! Difference is, he was shot later like a mercy killin'if I don't miss my guess. What've we got goin' on here?"

"Bridges, I'm eatin' lunch with the women folk. Cain't you leave killin' to another day?"

"No! You advised me to leave King's death to the city, but things have changed. We're involved. All these others were out in the county. We're in this up to our eyeballs!"

"Don't say up to our eyeballs. I've heard that somewhere else this year." Art looked over at Leona and Laura and they were staring at each other. He couldn't read their faces, and didn't want to either. He folded his napkin after wiping his plate with it like his Ma taught him and stood to leave the ladies to their lunch.

Sheriff Bridges pulled Art aside and handed him a piece of paper.

"Open it, Art," he said.

Art opened the paper into a foot square size, then looked at the women. He walked away without another word. He was too angry. He wished he hadn't brought Leona the package she hadn't even opened yet. It was a jar of black liquorice jelly beans, her favorite.

Neither woman said a word, just wiped their mouths with a

napkin and took a drink.

"Come on, Bridges, now that you've ruined my day." Art was perturbed to have to leave Laura. She was some woman with that flaming red hair, and he was lonesome.

"Aren't you going to let us see the paper, Art?" asked Laura Rogers.

"I think y'all know dang well what's on the paper, Laurie, and you too, Leona," he growled.

"No, no, we don't," one of them said and for the life of him he couldn't tell which one it was. He could feel them smiling without asking twice for the note contents. He slammed the door.

* * *

Bridges led the way to his squad car and Art hesitated before climbing in like Tom suggested. Art really didn't want any part of this newest killing because it was too close to him. The Hentons were nice folk and it was going to be hard on them even with Knight labeled a high risk. How did this town manage to raise this bunch of nobodies? Art hated to admit Clinton's wife was right, but maybe it did take a village to bring them up. At least Art and his wife had no children, so Art had nothing to worry about on that score. He did miss out on the little league and little girl dances, teaching them to ride and shoot, but was just as glad now that he did.

"Where're we goin'?" he asked Tom.

"Down to the river where the body is. The coroner and the state boys are there. I told 'em not to move that body til you got there. I didn't let them see the note on the body, Art. I wanted you to see it first."

Art took the note from the car seat and read it again. The note was obviously printed on a computer.

LET THIS BE A LAST WARNING TO ANY MAN WHO LOOKS AT CHILDREN AS SEX OBJECTS. OUR TOWN WON'T TOLERATE THIS ANY LONGER.

REVISED HOME PROTECTION CLUB OF CUERO.

Art stared at it, attempted to recognize the style of the author, thinking he knew darn well who wrote it, but he could be wrong. In answer to Bridges' last statement, he said:

"Why? I'm not involved any more. My advice would be to keep this out of the press. How long's the body been there?"

"You're gonna be involved as long as I'm sheriff, and to answer your second question, the blood was dried, but the fire ants hadn't taken over yet. Not long, probably done this mornin' early. This is a little more than I expected as sheriff. We never had to face serial killin's, Art."

"Okay," Art said, faking a sigh. He was flattered to be involved. He was glad the county had a reason in DeWitt to investigate serial killings. That way he would know everything going on in the county.

The pair drove out Hwy 87 towards Thomaston and took the first blacktop to the Guadalupe River where cars were beginning to block the way.

"First thing, Tom, clear this area. Use the state and city boys if you have to. Them sight seers are muddyin' up the scene and how come y'all didn't face this with King's killin'?"

"Well, maybe we kept it quieter, Art, I don't know," he evaded and Art knew he was afraid "Chief Brown didn't want the county in on it since he was losing the notoriety of the King killing with so many other bodies discovered. He believed his involvement was ongoing and I couldn't stop Brown on my own. That's why I brought you, Art, to the scene."

In answer to the question Art forgot he asked, Bridges said: "The hunter who found the skeletons wasn't the gossipy sort, maybe. Anyway, I'll take care of it. You go find out what you can from Judge Sorensen."

"And what makes you think she'll tell a former sheriff anything?"

"You go way back and she'll work with you if I say so." He was confident Art had an in with the JP.

Wow! This was what Art wanted all along, but did he actually want to catch the real killer or killers now? Heck no. Not if his coffee buddy was involved.

Bridges would have all he could handle when the killings hit the national news. Art didn't want to be any part of a national investigation, but he knew Bridges did.

* * *

Later in the day, Art received a call from Brown.

"You boys need my help?" he asked, laughing. "I got me a clue over here on our favorite serial killer. Come over and have coffee, Art. I think you're gonna be interested in what I found."

Not needing any further encouragement, Art climbed in his SUV and headed to Cuero. If Brown wanted to tell Art anything Bridges could use on this new case, he'd be more than obliged. Funny thing, he thought. everybody's forgetting Tom is the sheriff now, not me.

Art was driving the hot miles to town—too short a time for the air in his SUV to kick in—sitting there trying to figure out why this victim was shot. This was really a copy cat killing. Leona couldn't have done it because she didn't believe in mercy killings, just torture. Who would stand to gain from this one? He could think of one and he didn't want to go there. Surely not, he reassured himself. No, he wouldn't. Art kept telling himself over and over as he pondered the events leading up to this last murder.

No matter, it was in DeWitt county hands unless it could be proven the last victim was killed in the city limits. Bridges would get his excitement without involving Brown. He might have some idea of connecting this murder to the DeWitt County offenders who died, and just where they died which would become Bridge's problem if it was proven they were killed in the city. If they died in Cuero, Art didn't know what to expect from Bridges. Maybe I'm too old to be involved, he thought. Best find out what Brown has that I could be interested in.

Brown was busy when Art arrived. Not with reporters: they left with the sheriff on the Bobby Knight case because of similarity to the Concrete killings, and the fact the body was discovered out in the county. When Brown saw Art in the hall, he came out in person to lead him to his office, away from two state boys looking at files in the outer room.

"Art, you're not gonna believe what we found over at the Broughton land. By Grib it sure surprised me. It was a notebook with your friend Leona Broughton's name on it. All about history in the first part, but the second part intrigued me. She was writin' about killin' sex offenders. Looked like she was takin' down stuff you talked about at some time or other, or she knows somethin'. Know anything about that? And I ask you, know anything about the bunch she hangs out with at the center, Art? I know you visit there often enough, allowing how you like to eat. I visited with them one at a time, but got nothin' out of a one of 'em."

"Don't go messin' with them old people, Brown. They're my friends, at least I like to call 'em friends, and I don't want my avenues of rumors blocked due to you foolin' around askin' questions."

"Handle 'em your way, then. I'll leave it alone and stick to my own investigation. Okay?"

"Yeah, Brown, it's okay if you stay the heck away from them. As to knowin' anything about the bunch Leonnie hangs around with, wish I didn't, Brown," Art said. "And I'm wonderin' what you were doin' at Concrete recently since that ain't in the city limits."

Evading the notion he had no business in Concrete, Brown just looked at Art and smiled since Art was no longer in office. He left secret that he was looking for evidence of just where all the men were killed, but hadn't found any thing to tie Leona Broughton to the scene except maybe an empty jelly bean bag lying along the weed-filled path from the blacktop. Of course, Art could've dropped it when he visited the scene. Everybody in town knew Art and Leona ate jelly beans. It was no gosh-darn secret.

Realizing Brown wouldn't reveal his moves, Art said, "I hate to think Leona was even out there. Been tellin' Bridges she wasn't able. She has cancer, you know."

"No, didn't know that, but if she's involved, cancer won't make a heck of lot of difference when it comes to killin' of this magnitude."

"Brown, let's go over some facts about these sex offenders. I just happen to keep a list in my computer of each and everyone. In fact, I know parents of a couple of 'em. It's beyond my imagination as to why they're all out runnin' loose, when the crimes call for incarceration. If you take a look, they didn't even enter risk category on some of 'em. You know what I'm talkin' about. Whether they was high, medium or low risk. I only found one high risk, but he raped an older woman and almost killed her. Brown, you can print out your own copies, if you're interested."

"I don't like it anymore than you do, Art. There's a female listed over in Lavaca County for messin' with a fifteen year old boy. Can you beat that? I asked Sheriff Ernie Falco about her just out of curiosity. A woman. I already thought of printin' out the info." He laughed. "There's plenty of us older men she could have – why a boy?"

"Well, when I was young, I dated some older girls. I'm not so proud of it, but we didn't have the laws we have now, and nobody told, and nobody got hurt."

"Okay, I'll drop over to your ranch in a day or two and we'll hash this thing out. Do you think your friend Leona could have done this?"

"Well Rich, I didn't, but now I'm wonderin' just how much she is capable of. In fact, I'm wonderin' if she even has cancer. She runs a lot for a sick and dyin' woman. Brown, don't you wonder why the body was left out in the open? It don't fit the M.O. of the other murders."

Brown didn't answer and Art left. He couldn't take anymore because if Leona was involved, that could only mean Laura was too, and he knew he was taking a shine to that redhead. He wished wholeheartedly that Nora was alive.

* * *

Art had one fine deputy in Bridges when he stepped up to his new office of Sheriff, rising from Chief Deputy for years. Now, Tom grew more and more the armadillo in spite of all the teaching Art gave him. When he "found" the body down by the river south of town, it brought the attention he wanted to take heavier charge of the investigation avoiding the city chief. The news media invaded DeWitt county again. Bridges couldn't resist talking about the note pinned to the body. Odd thing, he wasn't asking about interrogating Leona any longer.

The death was a copy cat killing – not like the rest he pointed out. The news hounds made big stuff out of the note, he remembered. The details of the river killing reminded Art of the dead man in Leona's van she sold, and he told Bridges what he thought. The killer had mercy and shot the alleged pervert before he bled to death slowly from castration. Art's old deputy-turned-sheriff was blood-red with excitement over this latest mess.

Art wondered if the family had insurance on the Knight boy like all the other families. They would have been considered high risk with their records. It would've been high premiums, but a bonanza if the dead men were murdered.

The next day he remembered a mental health counselor he used when he was sheriff, the same one who testified at King's trial. Art needed some information on how a woman like Leona could, or would do something like this. She hadn't retaliated in all the years since she was branded by her perpetrator, so why would she risk herself and her family now? She didn't look or sound demented.

Art reached for his address book, looked up a number and dialed. "Come in tomorrow," Floyd Birchman said.

Chapter 16

Grandma Arrested

"Howdy, Floyd," Art said as the health counselor motioned him inside his office. Art had met with Birchman on more than one case over the last few years. They were not close friends, but had no trouble.

"What can I do You for?" Floyd asked.

Darn! It ain't enough Tom Young has to joke with that phrase, Art thought. Here's Birchman doing the same. Cain't just one man say what can I do for you?

"Floyd, I need some answers, and since I been invited by Brown and Bridges to work with them on these serial killins' I find myself short on mental health questions as to why, or if, a normal person would suddenly up and kill."

"I'll have to know at least what gender this person is," he said as he leaned forward, put his elbows on the desk, then folded freckled arms and hands over each other. Art knew that move. He'd pulled it himself. He wasn't here to reveal anything to Birchman, just pump information out of him. Art looked into dark blue eyes, up to dark red hair, and tied it all in with Floyd's sun burned face. Can he be trusted for sure Art asked himself as Floyd sized up the ex-sheriff.

"Well, this one's female," Art said. "I've known her for some time, she's not young, and she's normal as far as I can make out. She had trauma over a pervert some fifty years or more ago, and I'm wonderin' if she flipped out over these perps bein' allowed to live like normal folks. They're all over town and no way for anybody to know just where and who without goin' on the internet. Now, how many parents do you know who control their kids on the computer or even take time to sit at a computer drawin' names and addresses off the internet?"

"I think I see where you're going, Art, and I've wondered myself. You know I hear the gossip too, what with being in here week after week listening to troubled minds. Now if this is who I think it is, and mind you, we're not using names, just theory, she could have cracked when a certain perpetrator was turned loose. It could've triggered her mind into what we call a victim of 'catathymic behavior' in some form or other. Unlike a psychotic killer, this person would— to put it plain—just have had it up to the chin, triggered for instance by court findings. I did testify then you know."

He looked at Art like he could assure him it was court findings which set off this hypothetical person. Not from these lips, Art vowed silently.

"It takes something traumatic to trigger that kind of behavior, something not normal for the person," Floyd continued. "They would suddenly react without thinking of the consequences, and feel more guilt overtaking care of an impossible situation. In technical terms, Art, catathymic behavior is described in this book I rely on somewhat since I delved into writing—*THE CRIMINAL MIND* by Katherine Ramsland, Phd.—as a 'sudden explosive act from a buildup of tension.' It's an urge to carry an idea through to a violent act, according to one psychologist's notion," Floyd explained.

He sat there waiting for Art to digest his words, then continued explaining.

"The person equates violence with symbolic meaning, and..." Art interrupted with a wave of his hand. What in the heck did "violence with symbolic meaning" mean? Floyd stopped.

"Good gravy, Floyd, do you all think she would?" Art had to interrupt, finally getting to the answer in his head. "I've been wonderin' how it could happen. I have thoughts myself of why some people don't deserve to live, but no thoughts of takin' the law into my own hands. I ain't no vigilante. I was laughin' the other day about the old Home Protection Club that was organized back in the 1800s and wonderin' if somebody revived it into savin' boys and girls from predators since the law seems to need outside help. By Grib, I've got to think on this. Thanks for your help. Now, give me the name of the book where you read that stuff and I'll chew on it for awhile."

Art rose, information in hand and hurried out. His over-taxed mind couldn't take in this new stuff just then; he needed to do some reading at the library on this catathymic behavior thing Floyd read about.

Floyd leaned back in his chair and reflected on what he told Art and realized the words he used were from a psychologist view-point and might have gone over the law man's head.

Art checked out the book on criminal behavior at the library with help from the head librarian and researched what Floyd was talking about. There it was, in chapter three, just like Floyd said. Art read: "Violence is imbued with symbolic meaning." What? "Thinking becomes delusional and becomes rigid and incoherent," Art read on out loud until the librarian shushed him. He always had read out loud. It helped him think. He read on, lips moving in silence.

"The action culminates in a violent crisis from a situation the thinker encounters. When it's all over, the person returns to normal and the tension leaves." The writer apparently knew something.

Dang, those mental health words ain't in my vocabulary, and I cain't hire a Philadelphia lawyer to explain it to me. He wouldn't ask Floyd again either. But if this explanation was correct and Art's understanding was correct, and if that didn't describe what Art thought of Leona's behavior if she was guilty, he'd salt his Stetson and eat it. Anyway all of this information would be kept from Bridges.

The next lines he read heartened him some when it was explained that "Any repeated action would depend on circumstances surrounding the situation." Art had no thought Leona would need to keep on killing. She just blew her mouth about anybody who hurt her kin "would never get to court." King got to court, but he was turned loose on bail. Could that trigger what Floyd said: that catathymic thing?

Art had never heard there were so many kinds of behavior, but then he wasn't a health counselor, just a weary ex-sheriff. The other thing he wanted to know was how much would it take to get somebody he didn't want to consider to do a copy cat thing like the Bobby Knight killing. That burr was under his saddle all day every day, he thought. He couldn't stop thinking he knew who killed Knight and certainly did not want it to be who he thought. Dang!

Needless to say the books at the library were more than Art could handle. He decided it'd be best to leave the criminal books to mental health counselors—somebody who understood the lingo. Throughout his career, Art thought psychopaths were the only ones who up and killed without rhyme or reason. He would just take Birchman's word on it and if it came to court, put a bug in Trent's ear and, he'd recommend the prosecutor buy the book if he wanted the skinny on the human criminal mind.

* * *

That afternoon Brown decided to make his move and called Art, not Bridges. The eager ex-sheriff rode along, trying to explain what Floyd told him about people who suddenly became dangerous, hoping he himself could see something to prove Leona's innocence, or at least excuse her guilt. It went over Brown's head just like Art's.

Two car loads of law enforcement pulled up in front of Tim Young's house and Art took it upon himself to get out and knock on the door. Good gravy, this two-car thing was overkill for one old lady. Leona answered. Why didn't she just go back north and hide? Brown found out easy enough she was staying at her son's lately and that's why police were here instead of her place. Art knew she wasn't hiding, just getting sicker.

"Fooled you for a long time, Art," Leona said, not even letting Brown ask questions when she saw the two of them together. "I was going to be executed anyway, so I took care of the lot of them, didn't I? You can't get me on that last one, Art, that was a copy-cat except for the shot to the head. I wouldn't have had mercy for a child molester. He would've died a slow death."

She appeared eager to get this thing over with. "I was tired of luring men into my clutches through the internet."

Where in the cotton-picking cornbread heck did Leona come up with this nonsense?

Art wasn't eager for the officers who followed them out to Young's home to drag Leona away without him saying at least something, but he stepped aside. Brown had agreed to let Art go along, but only after the ex-sheriff reminded him Leona's and his friendship went back to when she first arrived in Cuero and married Ted Broughton.

Her son Tim Young expressed his outrage that the chief could even think such a thing of his mother. "What the heck do you think you're doing, picking my mother up for questioning in the killings? Let her alone, Brown, or I'll have you fired."

Brown ignored the outburst and motioned an officer to handcuff the old lady.

Karly, who shouldn't have been around, smiled. Satisfaction gleamed in her eyes at the thought. She must be fourteen by now and Art heard no word that she was ever pregnant with King's child. Her last words as the officers escorted Leona out the door and into the sunlight were: "She's a mean old woman who thinks she knows it all. She probably loved killin' people."

"I love you, too, Karly," Leona shouted as the door closed on the squad car.

Art could've sworn he heard that brat say "and all for nothin' 'cause Raleigh King never laid a hand on me, you silly old woman. It was somebody else."

"What did you say?" Art asked as he turned and looked at Karly.

"She didn't say a thing, Art," Tim Young shouted back at Simonds, "she was just coughing and clearing her throat."

My God, Art thought, I'm not hearing this. I don't wanna hear this. He loaded into the car and left with the city boys.

* * *

"Brown," Art began, "how do you think this is your move when the body was found at Concrete? I think this is a county case and the only reason for the city to be involved is because King disappeared while on a city charge."

Brown didn't answer. Was Art exhibiting jealousy out of office?

Art didn't expect the new sheriff to be alarmed, but he would put a bug in Bridges' ear to get him moving on his own case. He kept his mouth shut the rest of the way downtown.

"I promise to not let Leona get executed for somethin' she didn't really do," Art told the chief when he dropped him off.

He had suspicions as to who really killed King, and as to who slaughtered the sex offenders, but if this is the way Leona wanted it, then by Grib, that's the way it was gonna be for right now.

Art's money was on the real father and grandfather of Raleigh King, with the young man embarrassing them like that. Everybody in town wondered who the father of the pervert was. Suzie King wouldn't talk.

After one vigilante act, why not the rest? But then, Art had to consider Leona's son and his smart-mouthed wife. They had a good reason. Then, Art had to think the unthinkable: the Home Protection Club of the 1800s was alive and well. Might even say it had a branch membership down at the senior center for Women and Kids Protection Club, he thought. He might've become one of its strongest members himself if he wasn't steeped in law, but Art was no vigilante.

Instead, he was thinking the best way to get the law off Leona's back lay in the latest convicted sex offender, the one who should've had a sign in his yard in this town. Somebody figured to get rid of him and bring this investigation almost solely to the county, leaving no room for the city to say it was their case. Art had suspicions as to who really killed Raleigh King, and pretty danged sure he knew who killed Bobby Knight. Leona was right, it was a botched-up copy cat. Art was sorry Brown allowed him to accompany his boys to arrest Leona. It looked like he was on their side in this. She was innocent and he determined to prove it. Where was the Texas Ranger Bridges thought Sorensen brought to town?

Art didn't believe Leona killed the seven men found in the woods. He thought she confessed too quick. That wasn't her M.O. Suspense and plots were her operations, like book writers. Somebody took that on to help her out, since she's an old woman now, and more sympathetic than anything. Well, not too old, heck. He was pushing sixty himself. Art banked, no, he hoped the killer could be somebody else so he could court Laura. She couldn't be guilty, he vehemently declared.

He had read where an eastern city racked up a few deaths when somebody started killing sex offenders with signs in their yard. He had no reason at that time to substantiated a TV report. It gave him ugly thoughts as to how repeat offenders ought to be treated. He wondered it Leona had heard that and decided to do something herself. Nah!

Art drove to the county jail. Brown allowed his old friend leeway to visit Leona as a city prisoner. "I'm thinkin' you're coverin' up for somebody to confess without a squabble," he said. "Now tell me who really killed those eight men. You ain't strong enough. I'm gonna prove it."

"Stay out of my business, Art Simonds! You aren't sheriff anymore. Tell Bridges to keep out of my way. I'm doing what's right for everybody."

That remark slapped Art into reality. He didn't have as much pull with Leona as he thought. Her sharpness decided him right then and there. It gave him the unspoken right to consider her fair game in the King killing.

Brown was with Art on the belief the elderly woman wasn't guilty. He didn't believe Leona did such horrible butchering to the men. He asked Art if he came up with anything to clear her, to let him know —he was open.

Art knew he needed to talk to the state boys about his suspicions. He couldn't deal with who he thought committed the first killing, and for sure couldn't deal with who he just about knew did the last one. *God help me, I'm in over my head.*

Art's life swam before his eyes: from the time he first wore a badge—everything he fought for as a law officer in his younger days—to everything he believed in; every principal learned over the years. These ingrained beliefs were fading with his aging outlook on life; why and what his present responsibilities were concerning friends, protegees, himself, but most of all the people who entrusted him to perform to the fullest extent of his abilities as sheriff.

Chapter 17

Too Much Info

In Bay City, Michigan, a forty-something year old man picked up the newspaper, walked into the two-story house shared with wife and kids. He opened the paper, glanced at it, laid it down, then grabbed it up in disbelief: There was his mother-in-law's photo staring at him from the front page!

TEXAS GRANDMOTHER QUESTIONED IN SERIAL KILLINGS screamed the headline.

"Oh, Dear God!" He scanned the first paragraph, flung the paper down on the kitchen table. His daughter and son couldn't see this! What would his wife say? How would she handle seeing her mother as front page news? Should he get rid of it and lie? It wouldn't be the first time the paper wasn't delivered. She would never know and the kids? Well, would anyone at school know? He snatched up the paper and read in smaller type: "Grandmother Connected to Bay City Area Through Daughter."

"Leona Broughton of Texas, mother of Sally McKeefer of Bay City, has been questioned in the serial killings of eight registered sex offenders in DeWitt County, Texas in the small town of Cuero." He stopped reading.

No way to hide this. Reporters would be calling if they hadn't already. He checked the phone messages. Sure enough. They would be bombarded. The doorbell rang. He tip-toed to the front of the house after dropping the paper on the table, peeked through the narrow aperture of a window, and saw a stranger on the porch. News reporter, no doubt. Charlie McKeefer refused to respond to the insistent ringing. It wasn't in his nature to be bothered by anyone he wasn't interested in. This could ruin his standing at church. Looking in the mirror, he checked out his Clint Eastwood look-alike face and grimaced.

He called Sally."Don't come home just yet after you pick up the kids," he instructed, " and don't read the paper until you get home. We can't let the kids see the paper."

"Why?" she asked, suddenly alarmed. What could be in the

news so terrible he would warn her? Of course she would stop and buy a paper, then take the kids for a burger. “Okay,” she assured Charlie, knowing it would be impossible to not look at the paper.

Charlie hung up and Sally immediately determined to find the nearest convenience store for a paper. She had to find out what was so awful the kids couldn’t know. Did he think they wouldn’t?

Customers turned to look when the pleasant looking woman shouted: “Oh my gosh!” Sally almost fainted. Good thing the kids wanted to laze around in the car while she went into the store. Folding the paper, she straightened her face, hurried out to do what Charlie suggested: “Take the kids out to eat.” After ordering, she motioned the kids over to a table and her son went into the playroom. She knew the oldest would watch out for her little brother.

Sally excused herself to the restroom, paper clutched, secreted herself in a cubicle and opened the news to stare at her mother’s photo. “Oh God help me, help me with this!” She looked in the mirror, shut her eyes, then stepped out to face the kids.

* * *

In Reno, Nevada a mid-age truck driver bought a paper to read while he and his wife were held up for a fortnight to catch another load. They hauled all over the U.S. and Canada, leaving out Mexico for the braver drivers.

When he tossed the paper inside the cab, his slender wife picked it up, started to glance over it, then screamed! The driver jumped, almost spilling hot coffee he carried over to his wife.

She read part of the headline *TEXAS GRANDMOTHER QUESTIONED*....and screamed again.

“John, look at this!”

“What?”

“Look who’s picture is on the front page under a headline about a grandmother being questioned in Texas about serial killings!”

“Not your Mama?”

“Yes! Mama! Oh dang! Oh dang. What has she done now?”

"Liz, calm down and let me look."

"Here, take it, I can't read another word."

John stared at the white-haired smiling woman on the front page, UPI photo caption blaring the words Leona Broughton.

"There's nothing in here to connect us," he said, nonchalantly, "but it does mention her connection to Michigan. Ain't you glad we don't live there?"

"John, how can you be so nonchalant about this? That's my kid's grandmother."

"Well, there's nothing we can do. Wanna go to Texas?" He asked with a grin on his slender face. He knew the answer.

"No!"

* * *

In Cuero, Texas, former sheriff Art Simonds picked up the phone.

"Tom," Art said to his protégée, Sheriff Bridges. He called to give his former deputy a chance to explain some things to him. "Come out to the ranch and have coffee tomorrow or even today if you get free. I need to get some facts straight."

"Yes Sir, maybe today, later in the evening."

Bridges appeared at four and Art opened the door before he could knock. Art didn't want this, but somebody had to.

"Tom, it's great havin' those murders directly here in DeWitt, ain't it? Looks like you're really involved now, so what have y'all found out about Knight's death? How'd you like them reporters hangin' around? Have you hooked up with the ranger yet?"

Again, Bridges ignored Art's questions. Tom...Tom, Art begged silently. Tell me it ain't so.

"Art, I'm havin' a heck of a time gatherin' clues. Them state boys walked all over everythin' down at the river. Took stuff with 'em and I'm left hangin' to investigate cold."

"Talk with her about the killin'? Find anything at all?"

"Nothin' that would put Leonnie at the scene. No tire tracks, nothin'. I still don't think she's guilty, Art. I'm leanin' toward families collecting insurance and riddin' themselves of their embarrassin' kin."

I don't think she's guilty either, Tom, at least not of that last one. Somebody pulled that off to look like the others, but didn't have the guts to let Knight suffer as he bled to death. They shoot horses don't they, when they're sufferin'? I know you got a report from forensics on the bullet, but it could be anybody's gun in this state."

"Yes Sir, they do shoot horses, but they're animals. Art, where's this line of questionin' comin' from? You don't think any of us know anythin' about it, do you?"

"Bridges, I'm just askin' 'cause you all ain't been around lately to fill me in on what's goin' on at the office. I don't like to hear from your deputies. You're the one invited me to get in on this killin' thing. By the way, did you get a warrant and take Leonnie's computer? You know, like you did the others."

"Yeah, well, Art, you bein' retired and all, thought I'd leave you alone and take care of this with the deputies," he said, not answering Art's question and looking everywhere but at his old boss. The computer would sit where it was and it wasn't Art's business any more.

Art sat still, wondering if he should let Bridges know what he thought. No, he decided, best leave it to the state boys. Age was getting the best of Art; he didn't want to hurt one of his own.

"Have a cup, Tom, and let's drop the subject. I just wanted company, I reckon. Gets mighty lonesome out here. I should start lookin' for a woman."

"Yeah, Art, you do that. Me, I've got to get goin' on another case right now. It's out this way, so wasn't out of the way to drop by. Take care."

Bridges rose, stood with his well-pressed uniformed back to Art for about five seconds and Art thought he was going to talk, but he opened the screen and left. Art watched him walk down the little path Nora lined with bushes, and a tear slid down his cheek. He swiped it off and flopped on the recliner. Dang!

Art jumped up and drove the miles to the DQ. There he consumed six tacos, something he well knew better than to do. They always gave him a stomach ache and nightmares. Since nobody he was well-acquainted with remained in the frequented restaurant, he sighed, rose and left the building, depressed and returned to his ranch for a good nap before bed time. He fell sound asleep in three minutes.

* * *

The phone rang.

"Art Simonds?" a strange voice asked.

"Yeah, I'm Simonds," Art said.

"You all don't know me, Mr. Simonds, but I'm thinkin' we might oughta get acquainted. Name's Roscoe Wilson. I'm the granddaddy of that bastard King boy. I've got some mighty interestin' news for ya, if you're interested."

"By Grib, Mr. Wilson, I'm interested. I wondered who King's unnamed folks might be. You bet you're boots I'll meet with you. Just tell me where."

"You know where Ted Broughton's land is located. Meet me there in the mornin', but come alone and don't tell Brown. This ain't none of his business."

"Mr. Wilson, count on it."

Art walked over to the stove, poured himself a cup of coffee, thought better of it, set it down, moved to the front room, plopped down on the couch, popped a jelly bean in his mouth after making sure it was lemon, leaned back on the cushions; gone to dreamland, jelly bean glued to his teeth.

* * *

Morning found Art so excited he woke with an urge and had to hit the bathroom. He could've peed his pants like in younger days. *This has to be good, but for sure I'm taking Peewee along.* The .22 pistol always was somewhere on Art. It hid real well down in a pocket and palmed well. It might not kill anybody, he reasoned, but it could give him a head start just in case.

The drive was the longest mental trip Art had taken in a while. He missed the overgrown lane that led to the cabin, and wondered how he could have with all the yellow stringers that must have been left in place with the investigation pending. Art's mind wasn't slipping, he was over extended and refused to recognize a weakness.

He pulled onto the cattle guard leading up to the Old Stagecoach Inn, paused to admire the marvelous build of it, backed out and drove slowly to the spot where entry could be made from the road way to Leona's cabin. How could anybody find their way in there? It was beyond him. If it wasn't for all the tramping around when the bodies were discovered, it would be hit and miss on how to find the cabin. There was nobody in sight and he thought to put one foot out at a time, get out slow and look for a vehicle. Never know when it's a trap.

The man who called had to drive up here, surely. Art remembered Ole Man Smith's nightmare tale saying he didn't see a car when he witnessed the killing last year. *Dang! I don't want to remember stories no more, especially Smith's.* Where would a car be hidden unless there's a road back in the woods? The trees in Texas aren't that tall, the winter weather had stripped a lot of green off but were dense. What with the heat and all, and were beginning to re-leaf after the winter rainy season. but Art didn't see any shine from the sun on anything. The only reason trees live in south Texas heat, he thought, was the long roots reaching down to under-ground water.

"Hey! Art turned around to recognize the long drink of water he saw at the courthouse last year during King's trial. He was older than Art thought, but then he hadn't paid much attention to the stranger at the time.

"Mr. Wilson?"

"Yes Sir, that's me, but you can call me Roscoe. If ya want, let's walk up to the cabin."

"Well, Roscoe," Art said, "I didn't see a vehicle anywhere, so I guessed you wasn't here yet. How'd you get here?"

"Ain't hard, Simonds. I live back of here away from the Mott of live oaks over there. Got me a nice ranch, well outside Cuero city limits, passed on to me by my Daddy, and I don't cotton to things goin' on around here that bring attention. I'm sure you heard of my spread, ain't you?"

"Well, yeah, Roscoe, and you can call me Art, since we're bein' so friendly."

"Saw you at the courthouse last year," Wilson said, and Art nodded. "You ain't hard to find with your big Stetson. It's kind of a trademark, that and the six-gun you pack on your hip. Notice you've abandoned the gun since retirement. Good. I've got news for ya, and bein's there's no witness, I'll lie if what I say is taken anywhere. You ain't in law enforcement any more, so I can tell ya what I think really happened here. Are we clear?"

He had a rifle and he used "ya" for you like a lot of German descendants in the other county. His name wasn't German, however, so Art swallowed and nodded. He knew enough about generational ranchers to recognize the drawling language used by Wilson and to realize it wouldn't be anything for the direct man to shoot a hole plumb through him if the situation was right. Well now, he told himself, I've got myself in a knot here.

Art led the way along a path now visible from all the tramping in and out. He sidestepped through the burrs, ticks, maybe a copper head or rattler in the rocks looking for sun, and whatever else could be there, including fire ant hills. Art didn't need any of them varmints up his pant legs today.

He hadn't been here since King's death and discovery, except nosing around the scene when Bridges told him everything that happened with the last victims buried here. The place was burned some, but it stood as a silent reminder of murder. Off to the left he could see where the bodies had been dug up—nobody bothered to fill in the holes—and Art felt a chill race up his spine.

"Art, I'm gonna tell ya straight out. I hired that high dollar lawyer, Merriwether on a recommend from my own lawyer. You don't have to wonder who was that crazy any more, to hire a lawyer for an accused sex pervert. My boy, Jared, is Raleigh's real Pa, and he was so ashamed we decided that our blood needed to pay if he did what he was accused of. We wanted to have it fair. My boy is responsible in an off-handed way for Raleigh's death, gettin' a slow-minded girl pregnant. Raleigh's come-uppance got out of hand, and I know because I was there watchin' every bit of the accident from behind the trees. I watched the cuttin' to the patchin' up of my grandson's tools. Got that?"

He peered intently into Art's dark eyes. Not finding any condemnation there, Wilson continued.

"It's a family honor thing, shame for all of us. It was an accident, like I said, him dyin'. We didn't mind him fixed so he wouldn't bother any more girls. In fact the person doin' the work knew exactly what to do, like bein' experienced in castration. We didn't want no more Wilsons runnin' around the county with our blood. Got it?"

Art nodded, but no, he didn't understand what this was really all about. Why would a well-heeled rancher come forward and tell this story? Was he admitting to killing Raleigh King?

"That Karly Young girl was innocent and not like Raleigh's Ma," Wilson was saying. "My boy got Miss King pregnant when they were teens. He didn't know any better and he wasn't old enough to have a family. We provided for her good and she kept her mouth shut. That's the way it was handled back then. When the judge turned Raleigh out on bail, I looked at the situation and her Grandma Broughton and I judged Raleigh guilty. We wasn't gonna have no more fatherless babies runnin' around the area, embarrassin' my wife. She's a good woman and she never got over not knowin' her grandson. It was my idea to keep that fool boy of ours from marryin' at sixteen. Now to my way of thinkin', the bad blood—incest—came from Suzie King, not us. Ain't the same with Leona Brougton's granddaughter, her bein' only thirteen."

"I don't know what to say, Roscoe," Art said, the unfamiliar name sticking in his craw. "My first question would be how did anybody get King to come the ten miles to Concrete? Since he don't own a car, how did he get here? My instinct is arrest, but like you said I ain't the sheriff any longer. I think I'm obligated to tell Chief Brown and the new sheriff however, and you know that. He might not understand this family honor thing. I do but I'm not your average law man. In fact I've been thinkin' on how good it would be to revive the old Home Protection Club, and wipe out all the pred-o-files."

Art laughed.

Wilson didn't. Where did the ex-sheriff come up with a wrong word like Pred-o-files?

"First off," he said instead, "did you hear me admit to lurin' Raleigh out here? We didn't and we wasn't into punishin' all of them perverts, and we don't know who did. We was just interested in this bastard of ours. It wasn't meant for him to die, just be rendered harmless for little girls. Careful castration by them sheeted vigilantes was a good plan. He accidently bled to death, or suffocated or somethin', but Art, you cain't prove anything."

He stopped, waiting for reaction from Art, but none forthcoming said:

"I hate it that Brown has tagged Miss Leona with Raleigh's murder. We don't want her to take the blame for her ignorance about Raleigh, and a castration-gone-bad. I think she lost a notebook Brown found diggin' around out here one day later on when she came out here to look at her husband's cabin and all the diggin' the state did. You know the notebook, the one she carries everywhere she goes takin' notes. Brown has it. You don't have witnesses as to who the sheet-clad persons were. Make myself clear?"

Art could only stand there, head down. How did Wilson know Leona carried that infernal notebook everywhere? And when did he become such good friends with Brown to learn so much? The perplexed ex-sheriff wheeled around, turned his back for a second to get his thoughts together. How could he get Leona off without knowing who Roscoe and Ole Man Smith saw decked out in sheets? How could he believe this wild tale when Smith had told him another wild story. Dang!

What's wrong with this picture? Did Ted Broughton's friendship with this neighbor of the cabin property have anything to do with this? Something was wrong — mighty wrong. He shook his head.

When Art dared look around, Wilson's shadow wasn't stretching out on the ground. He had slipped away as silently as he came. Well, that takes care of Ole Man Smith's tall killer, Art decided, so is Roscoe's boy short and stout?

The other thing, his voice don't sound like a woman. Where did Smith get that? And he didn't talk like a northerner the way Smith inferred. Maybe Smith knew something else and wasn't telling the truth. Maybe this Wilson wasn't even here and this conversation didn't happen and maybe Smith never was here, or in my office, but the sheet thing sounds like both of them saw something. Maybe an old fool was just hunting something to pin on somebody, something to vindicate Leona. Dang!

Art glanced quickly at the remains of the cabin, shuddered, leaped and jumped his way back over brush to his SUV for a slow drive home, thinking how he had this serial killing all wrong. He had been sure Tom and Sue Young did the killing because they had good reason. He wondered if he was wrong about Leona confessing because she thought her son and daughter-in-law killed King. Maybe he was just too dang old and was also wrong about who killed Bobby Knight. Dang!

* * *

An alarm woke the sleeping ex-sheriff. Rubbing his eyes to rid himself of all the questions dashing through his dream-drenched mind like wolves after a new-born calf, Art put the pot on the stove for coffee. He never had attempted to use Nora's new-fangled speedy coffee maker. It boiled over and down the sides the first time. Coffee boiled in a pot on the stove was the best tasting and it wasn't that hard to settle the grounds. His Ma had taught him the art of dropping ice cubes in to settle the grounds and a little salt to bring out the flavor. He never forgot and revived the practice after Nora died.

Mulling over his findings and hear-saying, he decided if his life was going to hinge on wild tales and suggestions—or worse, clairvoyance—from now on this could be the right time for the state to bring in a profiler. Art didn't feel a need for one himself to see how this scenario played out, but Bridges might. Dang!

The new factor entering Art's off-the-record investigation in the form of a well-off rancher almost confessing to knowing who the perps were in the killing of his bastard grandson stopped Art in his tracks. He couldn't function the rest of the morning. Dang! Wilson, at the cabin implicated, but did not accuse; hinted that his son was the actual killer, but did he imply his wife knew about it and approved? No answer on that thought.

Wilson had denied any killing of seven other sex offenders. Wasn't interested in them, just his bastard grandson. Didn't sound right, and who was Art to question his meeting with Wilson at that time? *Maybe God's trying to show me something.* But then, Art had never had much use for hymn-singing people talking about God and seeing visions. Smith and Wilson were real, not characters in nightmares.

As for the other killings, Art was thinking by this time he should question Smith—his other killing-scene informant—and three other senior citizens at that. They would be into the "Home Protection Club" idea from listening to their granddaddies. Ole Man Smith told Art a wild tale of two killers dressed in sheets, but did he really see Wilson and his son up close and got the idea to fix the town perverts once and for all, as well as send out a message for sex offenders to leave town or die? No, that wasn't it. Wilson also mentioned sheets. Somebody was crazy, maybe it's this ex-sheriff. There would have to be an elaborate plan to confuse the issues. Art didn't consider himself a stupid man, just not college educated like the present-day lawmen.

He was also wondering how Smith could know so much about the cabin and why he would be out there, but just now Art had no clue. Why did he listen to that wild, hard-to-believe tale about Smith stumbling in on the killers in Concrete? Art heard enough times how Leona's answer to the problem of sex offenders was stringing them up and mutilating them. The old man would know too since he used to do heavy ranching a few years back, but castrating animals ain't the same. This vigilante plan was growing, he decided, and invading his sleeping time.

* * *

Art drove to town and visited the Senior Center. Lunch was over but the wizened sheriff knew the ones who hung around all afternoon playing cards and other games. To that end he ambled over to Smith's table, feeling somewhat goofy about doing so after the tale he heard in his office last year, and then the one yesterday. He asked in a whisper: "Where did you get a list of the sex offenders, Smith?"

The old man looked up and motioned Art to sit.

"What list?" he shot back, not whispering.

"The one you used to find out who to kill, Smith. I think you saw somebody kill that King boy and whoever it was shut your mouth with money, didn't he?"

"Don't know what you're talkin' about, Simonds. Y'awl

ain't sheriff no more, so why the questions?"

"I ain't gonna let you send Leonnie to jail for somethin' she didn't do, that's what."

"The town's better off, ain't it? She don't care," Smith countered. "She's dyin' she said. If we did it, and I ain't sayin' we did, she'd be proud of us now wouldn't she?"

"Be that as it may, you ain't gonna let her go to her grave with a legacy like that for her family. I won't let it happen."

About then Art was riled and compassion deserted him. He was glad Laura probably wasn't in on the killings though he suspected she was, and he had to say he was glad somebody had the guts to rid the town of crud. Experience taught him that if people got away with vigilante action, there would always be another need spring up. Art hated to stop the old man from wise-acre talk but wanted to keep his mouth shut until he could figure out who was in on the vigilante raids with Smith if it was him and the women.

"Smith, you get smart with me and I'll hang you and those smart-aleck friends of yours out to dry. I'm ain't into forgettin' the time you four cornered a cat on the floor of Ranch House Inn on Cheapside Hwy where you hung out a lot forty years ago. Yeah, I was young," he said, "but it wasn't funny to see you older men splittin' a gut when your knife escapade missed the mark and pinned the cat's tail to the floor. Not only blood flyin' everywhere when the cat split its tail wide open right down the spine gettin' away from a bunch of fools, but the bartender had a lot of cat crap to clean up all the way out the front door. You boys have a suspicious mean streak. I'm gonna be watchin' every dang one of you, so don't go anywhere."

Smith laughed. Art wasn't done with him.

"Those boys out there remodeling that old building for a church ministry witnessed the knife marks in the walls and on the floor where everybody did target practice. You ain't even ashamed of such a cruel act, are you? You could easily kill somebody like a pervert, couldn't you?"

"Hey, Simonds, you ain't in a position to throw stones from what we hear."

"So long, Smith."

Carlton smiled and waved as Art left. In fact, Art heard clapping sounds coming out of the center after the door swung shut. He smiled, but knew he had to get to the bottom of this question and clear Leona. The law could put all of them in jail. And how could they lure seven men to their deaths except over the internet? Art needed to see Bridges. He must have discovered something from the PC experts by now.

Smith sat smiling at a thought that it would have been easy to do what Simonds suspected. He had castrated bulls and stallions for years. Somebody needed to do something. He recalled the Home Protection Club—a neighborhood watch of the 1800s, if you will—only more serious. The sex offenders could have been taken care of one by one. Maybe they wouldn't all die like the King boy, but if they did, "just burn 'em." Each killing thought made him sicker, but apparently there had been no stopping point for the do-gooders who took care of the perverts.

Where did Simonds come off accusing him or his "cohorts" as Smith had called them in front of the dumb sheriff. His buddies: the cattle roper, the PC expert, and the strong hay bale lifter could have been characters in a book written by Leona and titled *LOST TOOLS.* What a name for one of Leona's books! He laughed.

Chapter 18

Getting Nowhere

"Chat rooms," Bridges answered when Art arrived at the sheriff's office and asked about information off computers he remembered the new sheriff confiscating. "Our expert found chat rooms where teen impersonators told the victims to meet them at spots around town. Then they were apparently taken to Broughton's burned down cabin. Each one was lured out on different days, and the PCs at the library were used to contact them is how I figure it."

He stared at Art, but nothing came out from his old boss.

"Now, there's no way to find out who used the computers," Bridges continued. "I asked at the library, but they didn't remember just who. They showed me a long list of everybody who signed up to use computers each day, but I couldn't tell who it was by that. Art, your pred-o-files didn't all die at once, accordin' to forensics. The state boys told me it wasn't unusual for chat rooms to lure young girls out of safe homes, so why would our perverts be any different?"

"Well that's nice to know, but my question is, why didn't anybody see unusual activity out that way, or did you even check on that?" Art waited, then stood up to leave. "Had any word on Knight's killer?" He had to ask. Bridges ignored him and picked up the phone. Dang!

* * *

Art rung up Brown when he got home and Brown told him he had a visit.

"Cain't say who," he said when Art asked. Then Brown told Art he was letting Leona go.

"Why?"

"She confessed she dropped the notebook when she couldn't stay away from Ted's cabin any longer. A witness came forward telling about her dropping the notebook. Said she was with her. Do you know somebody named Laura Rogers, said she was Leona Broughton's best friend?"

Brown could out silence most people and Art was easy. He

smiled to himself.

"Yeah," was all Art could get out of his mouth. Well okay, that's good, he thought. I won't have to worry now if I want to court Laura. But, I'm wondering just how far this Wilson will go to free Leona if he was the one to talk to Brown. Why would he get involved? Would he get in touch with Laura and have her provide an alibi for a woman he only knew as his late neighbor's widow? Yeah—he would.

If Art was looking for clues to prove the old people killed seven men, he would be looking for clues to who killed Knight. He was almost positive he knew who, but he was now convinced he was wrong about King's killer. It would all come out in the wash, as his Ma used to say but he couldn't let the thoughts alone.

* * *

"Leonnie?" Here Art was, calling her again at 7:30 a.m. and she probably needed sleep.

"Dang it Art! Why must you call me at this hour every time? I got no sleep in that mangy jail and now you call. Haven't you done enough damage to my family? I confessed and they said it's no good. Art, if it wasn't my son and his wife who killed the King boy, who was it? I was only protecting my own by confessing." Anger at her old friend grew as she held the phone.

"Leonnie, I knew that. Brown and I both knew that, but your notebook was at the scene where you said you hadn't been. Did you drop it there on purpose?"

"Yes, but that's none of your business, Art. If you know who killed King, why don't you say so and get my son off the hook. If my son did it, like Brown thinks, I'm proud that he would stand up for his daughter. I'd gladly go to prison for that. My own father did nothing for me when I was hurt. Why do you care now, you stinking old gluteal maximus perforation?"

Not knowing that her words meant the hole in his backside, Art ignored her outburst and didn't tell her anything about his meeting with Wilson. He sure didn't want to offer an opinion on whether her son had the guts to avenge Karly, so best keep shut. Art hadn't decided what to do about tacos and dreams. He did understand shame and family honor, which would be a reason for Wilson and his son to put Raleigh out of misery, but Art didn't know what to do—d idn't want to do anything. He hung up the phone. Then thought better, lifted it and dialed a familiar number.

Art called Laura anytime under any excuse which was better than none; he liked the sound of her voice. She didn't answer. Well, that was okay, she might be out in the barn. He would just run up there and see. Better take something along.... how about some of Norrie's flowers. She wouldn't be needing to see them anymore and he didn't want to take care of them.

Leona had held onto the phone for a moment after Art hung up, wishing for a replay button that could be used to look back on the last two years. Maybe Raleigh would still be alive and maybe her granddaughter—wait! Who's knocking on the door? Leona wasn't opening the door to anybody today. The cancer pain was really taking a toll on her. She thought she heard something: maybe not.

* * *

Driving up the tree-lined lane to Laura Rogers ranch-style house, Art was angry. Dang! There sat Ole Man Smith's car in the drive, right next to a picket fence. It ruined the image of the immaculate yard Laura kept. She had preserved all the live oaks surrounding the ranch and their presence lent an air of Texas taste to the place.

Art asked himself what the cornbread heck is Smith doing out here? He ain't got anything to offer Laurie. He's older than dirt. That's why she didn't answer the phone. She was out here with him. What could they have in—

"Hi, Art," Laura said. "We were just talking about you, weren't we Smith?"

"Yes Ma'am, that's what we're doin', talkin' about the law."

"Which one? Me—Bridges—Brown, or the Rangers?"

He didn't answer. Art shoved the flower pots at Laura and asked "Do you want these? I don't like tendin' flowers. Norrie would like that, don'tcha think?"

"Why thanks, Art. Be glad to plant these up the path there," she said, indicating the stones laid end to end to the patio. "Seen Leona yet?" she asked as she set the plants down.

"Yes ma'am, we've talked. She's not too happy with me. Thinks it's my fault she's out of jail when she confessed," Art said. "Know anything about her gettin' out of jail?"

He was boldly staring at her with her hair all wild and not braided like she usually wore it. The red hair shone in the sun like a new penny and he had to jerk his mind back to the business at hand.

"No. I was surprised when she called me," Laura lied. Art had no business asking questions about her best friend.

Dang! Art didn't want her to lie, not to him. What else was she hiding?

"Laurie, I've got to get back to town," Smith was saying and Art was glad. He wanted to talk in private.

"Bye," she said as Smith walked over to his old car. He didn't answer and Art knew he had broken up something, but what he couldn't figure. Smith still had a good body on him. Maybe he had designs on Laurie and Art didn't stand a chance. Why did she lie to him?

Invited in for tea, Art leaped at the chance. How often did an old bird like him get to talk one on one with a good-looking red head? Who knew? They might get better acquainted and Art might get over this stirring inside him every time he looked at her red hair shining in the sun. He followed the shapely older woman inside, thinking how nice it would be if she would warm up to him. She had a strong build, probably from ranching like she did. Even old jeans and a wrinkled flannel shirt looked good on her. He couldn't see her being involved in serial killings.

It was cool in the house, and Art liked the way Laura took care of it. His own house was filthy since Nora died and he wouldn't let Laura in if she showed up. Too ashamed.

"Laurie," he started to say and she put a finger to her lips. Now what? She tiptoed to the door and peeked out. Then she tiptoed back and sat down quietly, still with a finger on her lips.

"He didn't leave," she whispered.

"What and why was Smith out here anyway?" he whispered back.

"He was askin' questions about you, for one thing. The other was he wanted to know if I had any idea who killed all the sex offenders. Of course I don't," she whispered for the truth.

"Well, he might be thinkin' since I asked him about his part in the killin's," Art said, not bothering to whisper. He realized Smith would know more than he did, so why whisper. "I more than suspect him and his buddies. Of course, I ain't the law anymore."

Laura didn't dignify his remarks with an answer. He continued.

"Laurie, well, I was thinkin' that Smith and a self-appointed bunch down at the center killed off them men and thought they did it for Leonnie. I would like to have done it myself if it would make her feel better. I'm a lawman, badged or not and I cain't get that out of my blood. If you could help me prove Leonnie's innocence, it would sure be appreciated."

"Art, I wouldn't help you if I knew. I think you know that. What made you think I would?"

"Yeah, I know, like when I called you about the beach thing last year. You didn't care enough to go with me to pick her up. Why would I think you would help me now? Just hopin' I'm wrong about the lot of ya," Art growled, and let her see the disgust on his face knowing she lied through her teeth. He couldn't like this woman now – she'd betrayed his trust by lying about knowing why Brown let Leona loose. Dang!

He stood abruptly, slammed down his cup and rushed out of her house letting the door slam behind him before he felt any sicker, not at her but at himself for wanting her company more than the truth. That settled that.

"So long, Smith," Art called out to the bushes under the window as he left.

* * *

Although not his duty any longer, Art investigated the senior citizens, tried to trip up the new sheriff, found out Leona's friend Laura had become a liar, and mourned his fate. At home, he pondered his findings. Then he pondered Sheriff Bridges' fate; Leona's and Laura's and Smith's fate. Heck, he pondered the whole county's fate with a sheriff like Bridges, his pride and joy at the helm. Where did Art go wrong in bringing up an inept sheriff candidate? Art thought how Tom, as the first black man in DeWitt County to become sheriff, was ready for great things in law until he got crazy to get involved in solving serial killings. Wonder what they would do to him if they found out for certain what Art already believed in his heart?

Wonder what would happen to Wilson, his wife and son? Wonder if Wilson would feel guilty about Leona's granddaughter and would give a confession thinking to help her. Could be it all hinged on Wilson being a neighbor of Ted Broughton when the late husband of Leona lived that far out. Maybe he would confess if he wouldn't face jail. If he's lived there all this time he had to be acquainted with Broughton, and that's likely a good reason to feed me bull.

Heck, Art decided, and wondered if he could walk amongst them any more. He sure wasn't gonna be the one to solve the serial case. He'd leave that up to the rest of the good ole boys. He was no longer sheriff—well not as far as the law was concerned.

* * *

Art considered visiting Little John at his new church out on North Terrell Street, maybe discussing Leona with the little evangelist. Would he say anything or would he send Art to Leona's church for answers? Art gave into his instincts, lowered his pride, made an appointment to talk to the preacher he met at Leona's church. He thought maybe Rev. Jack Lester could help him get a handle on what his obligation to the law and his obligation to God amounted to. Somebody had told him once, maybe his mother, that the Bible said "an eye for an eye."

He looked it up in Nora's Bible with the index in the back, but couldn't see how it applied to the here-and-now and was that what Leona would be capable of? He read : "Thou shalt not kill," and all he could figure out was killing that wasn't self-defense was wrong. So Leona couldn't even hold onto her Bible and feel right if she was guilty for King's murder.

Leona had once told him when she started attending the church with Ted it shocked her religious sensitivities, but after awhile and experiencing some unusual happenings herself, she fell into line. But, did that include an eye for an eye?

* * *

Newspaper reporters, television crews, local and national were hanging onto the cases. Nobody was safe from their prying eyes. Art was no exception. They remembered his part in the affair prior to January. The law couldn't keep serial killings out of the limelight. It was like Bridges said, it was too big. Art went against everything he ever learned and kept his mouth shut. Let the new sheriff and Brown figure it out. There wasn't any reason for the FBI, but Art wouldn't have been surprised if they were on hand. There were rumors of sightings of a Ranger from Victoria, but—

Let Leona's God handle her. This collateral damage thing was real, anyway for Art's little county. Perverts hurt everybody around and the fall-out tore the county apart as far as Art was concerned. Friends couldn't be trusted and it was all the result of sex offenders not being jailed for good. Art mentioned to Bridges "Maybe children weren't killed, but looking at the number of killings that tore up the county, it had the same effect on our homes."

What could Art do at that time? Leona's own children seemed to care less if she was in or out of jail. None showed up that he saw, not even after he contacted them himself from Tom Young's address book. For that matter, he wondered if Tom and Sue cared. If he butted in and proved who killed the first perp, then proved who killed the rest of the pred-o-files, and finally proved who killed the last one, the county would never be the same for Art and nobody could trust anybody. They shoot horses with broken legs, don't they? Why not men with broken minds? Dang!

The senior citizens haunted Art's mind day and night. He didn't pretend to be psychic or a fancy profiler, but his mind was working from years of experience. He replayed what he knew, not what he pried out of the old geezers. There was Ole Man Smith who was expert at castrating horses and bulls. There was Toady Wiseman who could tie a mean knot and hoist a bale of hay in the air with pure strength of a rope over a limb. Then the county had Rodeo Bob who could throw a mean lariat. Art couldn't remember the actual name of the other one they called

Amigo, but he was alert for his age they said. He knew a lot about computers, somebody said.

Art also never stopped suspecting Tim and Sue Young. He called. "Young, I'd like to talk to y'all," he said after Karly's father stopped razzing him about not being sheriff any more.

"We're home for the day. Come over and let's get this out in the open."

Art didn't know what Tom Young meant by out in the open, but he jumped at the chance and arrived full of hope.

"We need to set the record straight," Tom said when Art was seated with a full cup, double sugar and no cream. "We didn't tell you everything at the hospital and the way things turned out, it was a sad mistake. Karly was at King's house all right, but she wasn't touched by him. She admitted to us but didn't want her grandma to know that it wasn't King she had sex with."

Art's shock registered. Young leaned forward in his chair to explain before the ex-sheriff could get in a word. Sue Young sat still as a mouse eyes unblinking.

"She was seeing a fifteen year old behind our backs and that's our fault for being so lenient with her," Young said, "letting her run loose over the neighborhood as long as she came home at a reasonable time. It wasn't until after the trial that we discovered she had been downloading porno cartoons from the internet and some were very graphic. Sorry, Art. She's all we've got and we didn't want her reputation shattered any further."

"Hell fire, Tim!" Art yelled. "Don't y'all realize what this means where your mother is concerned? Cain't y'all see what this kind of thinkin' did to Leonnie? Do y'all see what tore this investigation up and it's your fault?" Art couldn't hide his disgust. Tim ducked his head; Sue still didn't blink. It was eerie to Art. He had to get out of their house and think.

He entered his SUV with shocked mind, but asking himself questions. Did Raleigh King die for nothing? Did all the other registered sex offenders die for nothing? Not that Art thought they deserved to be free to ply their sick trade, but murder? He couldn't look in his own eyes in the rear view mirror. He had failed everybody, including his deputy-turned-sheriff. If there was a God up there analyzing all this, he must be disgusted with this biased investigation. Time to get busy, but rectifying what? Saving his faithful former deputy from prison? Saving Leona, Laura and the vigilantes from prison? Dang!

* * *

Art couldn't function the rest of the day, doing nothing but sitting in his favorite chair and rock. He rationalized better in the rocker. Nora knew that, and left him alone when she was alive. He was alone now and missed her. He greatly desired to go back a couple years and start over. Of course that wasn't going to happen. Raleigh's ma suffered for nothing and all them parents and wives, girl friends, whatever, suffered for nothing when their boys or men died for no reason except that they registered as sex offenders.

Dang! Who could Art go to with this information and how much should he tell? His world in DeWitt County was now upside down and he had nothing to show for it. Panic shook him, but it was important for somebody to remain sane. He called the City Chief.

"We have to talk, Brown. I've news that you should've ferreted out, but be that as it may, we need to get together—now!"

"Okay, Art, on my way out. You sound almost hysterical. Calm down and I'll be there. Put on the coffee. Sounds like we need it."

By the time Brown arrived Art was walking the floor, leaving the coffee pot on so they could spend a full night getting their act together. Should they get the state in on this, or let it stand with an unsolved serial killing suffocating their county? Dang.

"Now Art," Brown began as soon as he walked through the door. "I can see you're stirred up about somethin' and I think I know what. I got a call from Tom Young just after you left there today. We're gonna be here all night, figurin' out what to do and when."

"Brown, you don't know the half of it. I have to fill you in on what I suspect, what I know and what you can do with any of it, or do about any of it."

"You might be surprised what I know, Art. You ain't the

only one who's been around the law long enough to figure things out. I know about the seniors and their talk at the center. I know about Leona's breakdown after King was loosed on bail. That much I do know. You ain't the only one acquainted with our non-resident mental health counselor. Now what else can you add? Let's do it by the book or don't even go there. You're partial to the bunch from the center to the point you're negligent in your duty. Gonna do anything about it?"

Art ignored the question.

Brown persisted. "Art, I'm not a church-goin' man by any stretch of the imagination, but let me tell you somethin' my Daddy taught me, made me memorize, and it comes in handy. Listen: 'These things belong to the wise. It's not good to show partiality in judgement.' That comes from Proverbs, chapter twenty-four if you want to look it up. Do you good to remember."

Art failed to respond.

"Are you partial in judgement, Art?"

"No! Let the Rangers handle it—it'll make Sorensen happy. She brought 'em in here."

"I don't give a hoot how happy she is—I just want to save my job. I have a family to to feed and educate. You don't have—oh, I'm sorry, Art, I forgot about Nora."

"Yeah, my wife's dead. I have no kids, so no, I don't have any financial problems. Do you know how much my pension check is?"

"No, but it's better than the city offers. Besides, I'm younger than you by a long ways. I don't have a new SUV—my wife drives a '92 Dodge. She has a job or we wouldn't be able to keep our heads above water, let alone send the kids to college."

Art relented. He filled in Chief Brown in on everything he learned, everybody he had talked with, the meetings and conversations with Smith and Wilson, most of all what he suspected about the county's new sheriff. Brown didn't blink. Somewhere in the telling Art realized none of it but Art's doubt of reality in his findings was news to Brown. "I talked to Wilson, him being a neighboring rancher to Broughton. He brought in a notebook Leona dropped out at the cabin. You didn't get all of the story," Brown injected into Art's rambling and raving. "Didn't you tell me the whole thing was a taco dream? I suspected Tom Bridges of things, but I'm not talkin' at this point. Are you goin' to talk? It's your move, Art. I'm done with this rotten investigation except for puttin' on a front. The government did little or nothin' about the collateral damage in Oklahoma that amounted to anything. Should we do anything here? The state has effectively taken over. It's out of our hands for all intents and purposes."

He grew thoughtful as his coffee grew cold.

To occupy his screaming mind Art rose, walked over to the counter top and heated up his coffee; didn't offer Brown a warm-up, then plodded back to his chair. The coffee was tasteless, so Art set the cup on the table and drummed his fingers until Brown grabbed his hand and stopped the aggravation.

Art looked down at the hand on his arm and absent mindedly thought he needed to keep himself presentable. He was slack about changing shirts lately.

"Art, what good will it do to attempt exposing all these good people?" Brown was pointing out. "We cain't bring back the dead. This was a terrible mishap and mistakes were made on all our parts. Will we let a feedin' frenzy of the press into this mess, or just leave everybody guessin'? You know how nosy news hounds won't leave anything alone until somethin' else more horrendous comes along to fill in the white space. Let it be for now, Art. We'll clean it up later."

Danged if Art knew what to do. He couldn't talk just now. Brown leaned back and stared at the aging ex-sheriff, but that diligent soul couldn't get a word out of his throat. Rationalizing the situation was not the answer. Finally Art spoke:

"I'm a lawman in or out of office. It's my duty."

"Art, what are you thinkin'? I cain't tell by lookin' at your face. The town's quieted down. The runaway girl came home right after all them—to use your new word everybody's talkin' about—pred-o-files went missin' and we don't need to go into that any more. We ain't had many phone-ins lately from fights or scared parents. Are you gonna ruin a lot of good people who just felt the law wasn't doin' its duty, or will you let the state handle this mess? The press has temporarily left town. We can stay mostly out of it, Art, if we keep our mouths shut."

"That's just it, Brown. Can we keep shut about serial killings if we know this stuff? Can we ignore vigilante actions in this day and time? This ain't the 1800s, you know. There's law now that will get us for hidin' evidence. It's called neglectin' our duty or malfeasance in office or something worse: guilt. Do ya want the country to think we're ignorant enough to put the law aside to favor a few citizens who don't want to wait on the law to act? Do we want the Rangers to stay here? What about all the stuff, Brown? What about all the stuff we know?"

"Know what stuff, Simonds? I know nothin' and I didn't have this conversation," Brown said and stood up to leave, turned and left a comment hanging: "The state has control over the investigations now and we have no realistic part.I'm not ready and I'm not gonna retire. Chew on that."

His piece said, Brown walked out the door. He left it up to Art to rectify the lack of a sufficient investigation to arrest half the town.

Outside, Brown considered the predicament he and his old friend were in. He liked Art—in fact admired him for years—but this thing of withholding information from Leona's confession and the interviews of others, especially if he as city chief failed to question Roscoe Wilson, was a bit much. The combined years of law enforcement wouldn't permit leniency for friends in murder cases. It didn't take a profiler for old heads like him and Simonds—it only took reasoning and uncovered knowledge. How long before everybody blamed them—maybe even arrested them—for not acting?

Inside, Art was sorry he talked to Brown. He decided he could do this thing by himself, chief or no chief. He never bothered to tell Brown the suspicions he had about Leona Broughton that if she was guilty, she might kill herself or have help to end everything even now. So much for years of friendship.

Chapter 19

A Time To Die

Art decided the next day to take a ride into Cuero and visit Raleigh's Ma.

Suzie King had a smile on her face until Art told her the truth about Raleigh being innocent. He couldn't reason why it was important for her to know, but he knew she should be told and her son cleared.

"I knew all along my boy was innocent and I knew who to blame," was all she had said to the once-around-again sheriff and slammed the door in his face.

In another part of town, Laura Rogers was having coffee with Leona at her house when the cancer-plagued woman suddenly asked:

"Laura, have you ever thought about dying? I mean like killing yourself?"

"No! Well, at times I did, wanted to since I was a kid, even tried several times, but it always backfired. Have you, Leona?"

"Lately I thought about how nice it would be to have no more fear of this cancer, but then who would take care of Art's pred-o-files?"

Laura laughed. "Nobody I guess, unless Smith and the boys want to. They're gettin' old however and don't have much oomph left in 'em. We did our job and it's over. Right?"

"Yes, it's over for Raleigh. Too bad. Ted and Sue told me the truth as you know, that Karly lied. They hid that during the trial and especially after the poor young man was murdered. I never faulted him for the label hung on him as a teenager. We never did that when we were young, so why has it become the thing to do now? I'm surprised all the little boys who hug their teachers don't get arrested for sexual harassment."

Leona paused to let the truth sink in. Laura said nothing.

"Can't blame the teen boys when girls want to experience life, except the reason Raleigh was labeled a sex offender was one of those teen things. But, the job will never be over, with these other perverts on the loose. Unsuspecting children, even grown women are ever in danger. Somebody has to take a new stand. Couldn't it be us?"

"Not anymore," Laura answered. "You made it plain what you would do to one of them and when they found Raleigh, you were the first suspect. Just by association, that friendship dragged me into the mess. Leona, don't go there again. Enough!"

"Well, if anybody finds me dead, I assure you it won't be suicide, Laura, getting back to the question I asked you. I did consider it a time or two years ago and might have said a thing or two about that, and," she paused, "I did receive a threatening phone call from Raleigh's mother. She figured it's my fault her son is dead. I know what I would do if it was my son murdered for no reason. Maybe that's the way out of this mess."

"Keep Ted's old .38 Colt police revolver by your bed, or if you're at the computer, keep it on the desk. If you hear a noise, shoot first and then ask questions." Laura wouldn't say the thought on her mind that if Leona went down, she would take her with her.

"You sound like a play write, Laura. Shoot first? Did I tell you I had to buy Winchester and Remington cartridges for that old relic. They don't make Colt ammo for them anymore. It could blow up if I used it, don't you know. I have an antique sawed-off shotgun from the gangster days in the county I came from up north. Should I use that? Ted's son-in-law gave me ammo for that one. If I hear a noise, you bet your shiny boots I'll shoot and then check it out. Remember when I first moved here?"

"Yeah, I remember. Everybody in the county does. Do you have anything to do with Ted's family since he's gone? I thought they stopped speaking to you when he left you all he had in his will. Did his son give you ammo before Ted died? Well, I've got to get back and feed. You take care and let Art know about the threat. Okay?"

"We'll see," Leona said. "Hey, isn't he seeing Naoma over at the church now? You lost out."

Laura didn't answer. What did she need with a has-been sheriff and city bred rancher?

Leona knew she wouldn't talk to Art again unless necessary.

* * *

It would be easy for a night visitor to enter Leona's home. It wasn't hard to find, stuck up on Esplanade like all them other muckity-mucks, as Suzie King's son had said in the past. It was no longer true. The more well-to-do lived all over town and out in the country.

The back door was unlocked on the screened-in porch since Leona let the stray cat in for milk and forgot to put him out. She dared anybody to enter her home unbidden. She had a gun and hadn't she already shot one intruder with it? Got away with it, too. Maybe this was a good time for a visit from the Reverend Pastor Lester. She called. They talked.

Leona forgot to close up after Rev. Lester took his leave from consoling his church member for the pain in her heart from killing an innocent young man. Lester read to her from the Bible, prayed for her forgiveness from God, gave her a list of scriptures to search out and called it a night. She picked up the book, opened it to the prescribed place the preacher said.

Tears over her misguided acts since coming to Texas flowed down pale cheeks. Who did she think she was? Surely God could forgive an old woman for the insanity which plagued every waking moment from the time the known-only-to-her sex offender bought her beautiful van to the killing of the Knight boy. She had nothing to do with the other seven. Only God knew. Art Simonds didn't believe her. *Forgive me, Lord. I'll not sin any more. You said never let your left hand know what your right hand is doing lest they deliver you to the judge. Well, I'm keeping my mouth shut for the sake of my children and grandchildren. Is that wrong?.*

Suzie King didn't know the story about the shooting at Leona's house and how the old lady got away with it through the law. She didn't care. She slipped in the back door, crossed the kitchen, saw an old shiny pistol lying on the counter top by the coffee pot. She laughed silently thinking. God must've been in on this. Here lies the means to get revenge on Leona Broughton. Hah! I'll just creep up the stairs of this old mansion and look around—get my son's killer by surprise.

Leona heard a noise but dismissed it as the cat she had forgotten to put out. She turned back to the computer. She had to get the book done, the doctor gave her only weeks and it would be enough. Laura promised to see it through to publication if Leona didn't make it. It was a play-by-play how-to-kill-a-sex-offender rendition.

Satisfaction swept through Suzie's body as she thought about the look of fear Leona would surely have on her face as the vengeful mother held the old woman's own pistol to her vicious, crazy head—her husband's pistol—and this act of revenge would be reward enough. Yeah, she might be slow, but she'd heard about Ted Broughton and his treasured .38 Colt. They don't even make bullets for these anymore, she thought she remembered the boys down at Ruby Begonia's talking, but some gracious soul loaded it just for Raleigh's Ma so she could avenge her son.

Suzie had considered mutilation for the old fool, but with cancer smell lingering all over the room, what for? The fool woman had the gun lying out in the open inviting somebody to put her out of her misery. Suzie was the one to do it. She had grabbed it after she sneaked into the unlocked door. There was nothing upstairs but a bed room, just an empty second bath. She slipped back downstairs.

"Hey, old woman," she said and Leona jumped. "You should've stayed out of my boy's life. And you should suffer slow like you done to him. Now sit back down at that desk and write what I tell you, you old fool."

Leona gasped but saw this was not the time to argue and obeyed the manic woman. She typed the letter on her computer as Suzie talked. Raleigh's mother couldn't read well, so she talked.

Surely this old fool would type what she told her to. She could read well enough to know whether Leona told what Suzie was doing there. "I want everybody to know my son was an innocent victim," she said aloud. "He should've never been labeled to begin with. He wasn't no sex offender, just a young boy with limits who fell for the wrong girl. He never laid a hand on that brat granddaughter of yours and you know it."

Leona was wise enough to keep her mouth shut and type Suzie's dictation.

It was turning out delicious for Suzie the way Leona kept typing and added other stuff in the letter about some man in a van and signed it after Suzie made her repeat word-for-word what it said. She ordered Leona to bed in the guest room—it was apparent she had started using the downstairs room when it was painful to climb stairs.

Suzie forced the gun into Leona's hand—a hand too weak to resist or the woman no longer cared. Suzie forced Leona's finger to pull the trigger. The chief and that old has-been sheriff the letter was addressed to would never know. She carefully placed the gun so as to look like suicide like she and Raleigh saw one time on TV.

Suzie's life had been hard until she met Jared Wilson, Raleigh's real Pa. They were in love, her fourteen and him sixteen. Jared's father, Roscoe, wouldn't let them marry, but he made sure she and Raleigh never went without. They had a house to live in, but Raleigh got in trouble with a fourteen year old. In Suzie's day, nobody yelled rape for teenagers, they just put everything aside and ignored the victim—especially if pregnant like Suzie had been.

Leona Broughton should've been left alive, maybe, to suffer. Anyhow she really did the old woman a favor, the cancer and all considered. But now, too late, she regretted not letting Leona live it out and suffer the way Raleigh did–slow-like. Actually, Suzie didn't know what all Leona wrote, she had never learned reading all that well what with her eye trouble. If Raleigh's grandpa hadn't taken care of her and the boy, they would have starved. She couldn't get any good jobs with a handicap like poor reading and bad eyes. Her looks had brought only pregnancy with her boy and nobody to help raise him. Money wasn't everything.

* * *

"Art!" Brown addressed the former sheriff in a phone call early next morning. "I need you to drive like the devil was after you over here to Leona's house. She's dead!"

"What?" Art couldn't believe his ears. "What did you say?

Say it again!"

"Just get over here, Art. Don't delay. Sorensen's here and you know how fast she works. She already has the M.E. on his way. I don't like the looks of this death."

"I'm there, Brown, I'm there! Keep the examiner away from her body as much as possible."

Art jerked on a clean shirt, pulled his hat down, left his gun behind and ran to his SUV with fire in his heart. Not Leona...not yet. Wonder if Laura knows.

At the house of his long time friend, Art leaped from the vehicle, forgetting his bad ankle, loped into the house and almost fainted at the sight of Leona Broughton lying on her downstairs bed with mouth gaped open and blood spilled over the pillow. She wouldn't stain a perfectly good pillow in her right mind. Not that neat lady. Her attitude was not depression the last time he saw her. She was calm, collected, and having lunch with Laura. He didn't know what they were talking about—he wasn't invited to sit—but they were smiling. No sign of depression.

Brown pulled him aside and slipped an envelope into his hands. Art turned his back, read his name on it and stuffed it into his pocket. Sorensen was looking the other way talking on a phone.

"Did she leave a note saying it was suicide?" He asked where nosy ears could hear.

"Art, I saw none," Brown answered, then whispered, "but I don't think from looking at the position of the gun and knowing Leona, that it was self-administered. I got here before Sorensen and took the envelope from the table beside the bed. It had your name on it and that's all it took for me to decide."

"Thanks, Brown. I owe you. I'll read it later. How did you find this out?"

"Phone tip, Art. I'll talk to you later about who we think called. I want to tell Laura Rogers before somebody else does. Let's go outside and read it now."

"No!" Art wouldn't read it now. He wanted to talk to Tim Young and find out if he had informed Leona's daughters of their mother's untimely death. They never appeared when she was diagnosed with cancer or after the headlines hit the paper, so maybe they could care less. Well, this time was different.

* * *

The funeral was the saddest one Art ever attended. It had been held up for days with Leona's body on hold at Freund's on Gonzalez across from the courthouse. Seemed like all the noise and work going on at the landmark courthouse since early last year would distract from the seriousness of Leona's funeral. It was the only funeral home in town for years now. When family arrived—the two daughters Art had never met and Tim and Sue Young—the services could be held and life could go on.

Forensics hadn't taken much time deciding it was a true suicide. Art didn't agree, but for the sake of his old friend, let it lay. The letter Leona left him was not right. He read it three times.

"Sally," he addressed the one daughter who he watched shedding shed tears beside her mother's grave, "Your Momma was my coffee-drinking buddy for a long time. I didn't see her doin' this. What do you think? I sure thought one of you would take her body back north for burial, with your father maybe, but she'll be okay here beside Ted's grave. I'll tend to flowers when I come out to decorate my wife's grave. "

"She's gone, she'll be with God. What does it matter?" Her two children weren't at the funeral. Charlie decided they shouldn't see this, Sally explained, and church friends in Michigan kept them from the mess.

Art walked over to the other tearful daughter, Liz, and asked the same question.

She shrugged, looked at her husband, he looked away.

"We have to go over Mom's things at the house. She left us all those books not sold. Then we have to get back on the road," she said.

Yeah, Art thought, that's what matters, the things; the books. She loved her kids—

That left Tim Young and Sue. They walked away before Art could open his mouth.

"Hell!" Art yelled and hoped his sainted mother wasn't looking down on him. "I at least expected some sort of deep sorrow, but this? They ain't seen their mother for years I heard."

"Who you talkin' to, Simonds?" Laura Rogers asked.

"Nobody, just nobody." It infuriated him that the two daughters and son of Leona didn't even talk to each other. Now what in the cornbread, cotton-picking heck could have happened in that family that they were apparently estranged? He didn't want to be near the house when they rambled around looking for things of value, especially Leona's books. Was that all they wanted from the woman who raised them? He had wondered for years why the daughters and grandchildren never came to Texas. Leona had always traveled north to visit them at her age.

* * *

It was shortly after the funeral Bridges decided his life and career were down the tubes when he allowed Leona to convince him no one would ever suspect him of hiding the murder of the Knight boy when he went to her for answers. All he had to do was keep his mouth shut, she said. He believed Leona guilty of the killing, but she couldn't say it out loud. She kept insisting on silence.

Wrong! She didn't know Art Simonds as well as she thought. Bridges knew. Art wouldn't leave a stone unturned until he discovered the truth behind Tom's silence. Art was too smart, too cagey, and he knew how bad Bridges wanted publicity in the serial killings; he knew about Tom's ambitions to grow old as a black sheriff, maybe more. Too bad. Leona may have helped him get elected—but at the same time the Knight killing would destroy him because he couldn't, just couldn't, arrest her.

For Art's sake, and to keep his own reputation intact, he took a position in Harris County offered during the height of the murder investigations, turned in his badge suddenly to a surprised county board and left town. He left instructions as to where his benefits should be sent. Better get on with life while his reputation was intact without revealing anything and without letting Leona down. For a white woman she had been a grand supporter and a great help during the election. He thought he loved her like the mother he never had.

* * *

In the end Art decided he couldn't do a dang thing when he accepted the sheriff's badge temporarily from the county, and knew he couldn't keep it. The county would have to hold a special election—something which would cost an arm and a leg—especially since the state took over from Bridges and it was out of Art's hands. He never had the opportunity to talk to Bridges about him leaving suddenly and couldn't read anything into the note the young sheriff left:

"Goodbye Art. It's been a hoot. Regards to Leona and the vigilantes."

Art decided right then and there to give Bridges a recommendation if he needed it, but not in law enforcement. Bridges hadn't told him where he was going and if it was in law. Now appointed to fill out Bridges' term, Art stood around with his hands dangling while the Ranger and the state boys did the work. He wouldn't give them the case on a platter. He just sat back and watched things happen like it was none of his business anymore who, what, why, where and how.

Art hoped people wouldn't judge him until they heard the story of the vigilante's revenge on sex offenders. He hoped, even prayed, that the law would do something about controlling sex offenders, not allowing them to run the streets freely, knowing they would never change. Leona would like that. Maybe he ought to start a drive in that direction.

He had a solution, one he would sit down and write about for the President, or for the Texas Governor, neither of which was going to like it, because it would take an act of Congress and the Texas State Assembly to get anything done, plus a lot of money. Everybody studies history, Art thought, and everybody knew what England did when they settled Australia back in the 1700s. They shipped their overload of prisoners to an unsettled land to survive the best way they could. They called it a penal colony–should this one be a penile colony? He laughed at the thought of what to write on the gate of such a colony.

He asked himself where in the United States does the government have control of enough land to house hundreds of thousands of sex offender and throw away the keys? Then it hit him! Alcatraz, the abandoned prison! It would hold a lot of men and could be refurbished by the prisoners. They didn't deserve any better.

Art didn't keep up on geography stuff, but he was sure the President could find out and get a bill passed to settle any problem of collateral damage from sex offenders by keeping the perverts caged, or fenced, or something; put them in the wilderness behind electric fences, somethin'. They shouldn't be allowed to run loose to rape, maim, and ruin people's lives.

Private citizens should never have to form groups to avenge wrongs the law couldn't seem to get a handle on; just a thought, not a demand. It could be something however for the President to think on, him feeling so good about signing the Walsh bill.

Art sat down to write a story—off record—and not reveal all his investigative findings to the state concerning who killed who. Some day, maybe he could report just what happened to all of them: Leona, Laura, Ole Man Smith and his vigilantes. Maybe some day somebody would read his version.

He paused long enough in the writing to pick up Nora's Bible. It fell open to Proverbs 24, just like God wanted him to see something. He read: "These things.......belong to the wise: It is not good to show partiality in judgement." He remembered Brown's admonition. Well, nobody made Art God, so he didn't have to judge. He read on in verse 25: "But those who rebuke the wicked will have delight and a good blessing will come up on them."

Art knew he was guilty of failing to rebuke the wicked—he'd let his friends and their "evil ways" slip by the law. Dang! He closed Nora's Bible, not knowing whether he would ever open it again.

Chapter 20

Truth Will Out

Art replayed the day Leona's son had to view his mother's body in bed with Ted's pistol beside her right hand. When Art heard the news, went to the scene and saw the body, he too believed she had become worse, beat down by cancer and when finally told by her son that Raleigh King didn't do what her family let everybody think, Leona's strong resolve to live life to the fullest just broke. She died before anybody could gather enough evidence to indict her, which was a good thing, considering.

Art went to a drawer and dug out the note addressed to him, the one Chief Brown hid from the J.P. Sorensen's sight and handed over to Art. He wanted to read it again–to understand why she would really take her life. Art had ripped it open when Brown led him outside that fateful day to look at the message, but Art couldn't concentrate on the contents; it could be studied later for truth.

Art, old friend, if you have this letter, then I guess you know by now that I killed a man for nothing. I let my emotions overrule rationality and avenged myself for all those years of self-hatred involving a sex offender of another decade. Karly is just a fool kid who was full of fear her father would find out about the teenager she was lying with. I should have made sure of the facts as I would have in my reporter days."

Art put the letter down to wipe tears from his cheeks. A grown man crying. That beat all. He picked up the letter again when his eyes cleared. He hadn't let Brown see him in tears when it was handed over to him. Why cry now?

This tragedy could have been avoided and all the things my misguided friends at the senior center maybe did. It just ruined too many lives. Please forgive Smith and the others, and especially Laura. They mistakenly wanted to give me the revenge I never had and I let them. I was sick, Art , sick with years of not being understood and accepted.

Poor Suzie King. I took away her son, and she had no one. Please forgive me and don't be too hard on Tom Bridges. He only wanted human dignity and worth and would be innocent of letting blood. He covered for me. I shot the young man found by the river. I was sick of watching him suffer, so I put him out of his misery. Not that I cared about the sex offenders being taken out. It didn't matter anymore since I was dying anyway, did it? And Art, you don't need to blame yourself that Bridges handed in his resignation. He just couldn't handle you questioning him. He believed he had failed you and he knew about me killing the Knight boy. He just couldn't face putting me in jail. I tried to be the mother he never had, but I was misguiding him in the actions of his office. He cried when he told me that before he left town. Too bad, I liked that handsome black sheriff. Have a good life."

Your friend, Leona Broughton.

P.S. I know you think about the unsolved murder of the man who bought my oversized conversion van: the one I brought down here when I went north last time. We talked about that, Art. Remember? Guess what. I didn't recognize him at first and sold him my vehicle. I found out later from my son that he was a "pred-o-file" I vaguely knew from newspaper days in the north—one who raped a little girl and nobody did anything about it. I don't know what he was doing in Texas and it doesn't matter much now. It just became too much for my mind to realize I sold him that perfect "love wagon" with its queen-size bed, TV, video player and all. Perfect set up for a pervert to lure children in and do his thing. It was a straight shot to the head. First time I used Ted's pistol. I castrated the pervert first, just like King, but nobody heard the screams: I taped up his mouth. He deserved it: King didn't. It was my fault for not checking out the first man's background, so I righted that wrong. Oh, yeah, I chopped off his hands so you wouldn't find out he was from the same area I came from. You can find them buried out at the cabin if you need to use them for cold case identification. Of course, the flesh would be rotted off.

There wouldn't really be any use in digging them up. I knew he wouldn't be stopped by you or anyone else. Laura doesn't even know. Hope this helps you to close that cold case. You couldn't know about him being a pervert, he wasn't registered in Texas. Tell everybody I killed him if you want. Thanks for being my friend. I'll take some of those jelly beans now. If you don't mind, just sprinkle them on my grave. Bye.

Dang! Art cussed the scalding tears running down his cheeks, but not where his angelic mama would hear. He had never even suspected Leona of that van murder and would now tell nobody about this confession. Did this mean he was wrong about her mental condition at the last-minute killing of Raleigh King? If she and Laurie had been indicted for killing the King boy, Trent could've introduced Art's mental health expert, Floyd, at the trial and let him explain the catathymic behavior syndrome he thought his theoretic friend was operating under after King was turned loose. Of course if this letter came out, Art would be the fool.

Art believed it was like Leona was raped all over again and nobody doing anything about it when King made bail back when Karly was gone three days. Leona ended up in Port Lavaca out of her head, which fit Floyd's explanation of the theory. Of course neither of the two men suspected a van-killing incident. Art would be labeled a fool sure enough if this got out. Friends with a murderer, indeed. And he wasn't convinced she really killed the man in the van. Maybe she was covering for somebody; he wasn't going to find out who. It was too late: she wanted it that way.

Art would keep in mind until he died that the van killing was Tim Young's doing. Trying in any way he could to alleviate the hurt in his mother's eyes when he realized it was stupid to tell a mentally troubled woman who she sold her van to. It could have been left alone.

As for Tom Bridges, Art believed the young sheriff actually took part in the Knight man's death even though Leona confessed. Once again she took the blame, knowing she was on her way out. She suffered mightily her last days with the bone cancer. Maybe that was her punishment. He didn't blame her for ending it all. He didn't know just how this God thing worked, if suicide was a sin, since it was almost like murder— no chance for repentance—but Art was the only one knowing about the secrets, the only one left to punish the guilty parties without the law taking matters to hand. Art had no excuse for Laura except she was Leona's best friend and would do anything for her.

It occurred to Art that Leona being the kind of person she was—knowing she was dying—did a Jesus-on-the-cross thing, taking the sins of others on her head that they might go on with life. Nah! Well, maybe—

The circuit court clerk couldn't set a trial date for anybody without an indictment. Art never did get around to showing his letter to Brown. Told him it disappeared. There was one thing he remembered: if he had been in charge of giving out Oscars in Hollywood, he'd have to nominate his two friends, Leona and Laura. Talk about sincerity! Perfect acting! And that included Smith and the gang.

As far as Tim Young and his wife, they never admitted to anybody but Art, Brown, and Leona what really happened with Karly. They sent her off to school in another state where she couldn't think about her part in the whole affair. Maybe that was best, Art mused. At least she didn't have an illegitimate kid to mess up her parents' life and fourteen is a tender age to carry all that weight. It didn't serve any purpose for Raleigh's Ma to hear the truth now, except she could go to her God with Raleigh cleared.

Brown called as Art compiled his story in his head.

"Well, what did the suicide letter say, Art? You never did tell me exact. It's been weeks now. Tell me or I'm comin' over there."

"You'll be better off not knowin' what the letter said, Brown. Leave it at that."

He decided to rid himself of this bit of evidence in case his house was searched. He wadded the letter and stuffed it into his pocket. It would be burned later. He failed to notice the letter falling out of his jean pocket, and a lean young man bending over to retrieve it. Right now, he had people to tend to.

Leona's family deserted the town and went home. They left when it was discovered Leona did the right thing and left half of her estate to Ted's family, not that they ever showed her any appreciation either.

The sheriff in Art had to make two phone calls: one to Neal Sturm and one to Terrence Trent. They had a right to know about Raleigh King's innocence regardless of the outcome. Neither would want to rehash the bitterness of a man dying for no reason. There was no obligation to let either know, Art just wanted the record straight. He knew bitterness himself towards Tom and Sue Young, Leona Broughton, and most of all against Laura, the woman he had designs on for his next wife. The only way he knew to put this behind him was to forgive them. How? When? Could he? Would he dream again?

Neal Sturm was grateful for the call. He always enjoyed when an innocent man was proven not guilty, but King never had a chance. He grieved for the young, slow-minded citizens of the town, and he grieved once again for his guilt from childhood that he didn't save his father in time for his mother to have the love of her life back in her arms. He failed King too. The next case a judge dropped on him concerning sex offenses, he would diligently press for hard and fast evidence of actual criminal wrong-doing, or by dang, he would give up the career he loved dearly.

Trent, always the prosecutor, wished Art had kept the information to himself. He felt bad enough that Raleigh King died the way he did, alone and scared in a cabin full of nothing, a cabin full of hate, choking to death without his asthma inhaler handy. Suzie King told him about the asthma. Now he would look at every young man askance, wondering: are they really guilty? That question would not prevent him from doing his duty as a preserver of the law: it would prevent him from pushing aside nagging doubts concerning future alleged perpetrators. He needed an able private investigator on hand for such doubts. He needed to know for certain that a defendant was guilty. Would Art make a good investigator? Nah!

* * *

Art Simonds sat in his favorite rocker on the porch of the cottage he and Nora had called home, mulling over the conversation he had with rancher Wilson confessing to him with compassion for Leona's hurt, because Roscoe Wilson thought his illegitimate grandson was better off. Maybe he just didn't want Leona to pay for it. The talk was so crazy, and Art had eaten too many tacos—it could be part of a spiritual, no, maybe not spiritual, plot to sidetrack the good sheriff.

Art made a decision, looked in the phone book and called Wilson, He asked for information on what Wilson might know since his ranch was located close to the Broughton cabin where somebody witnessed fire and smoke rising from the midst of overgrown land. He asked and he got it. Wilson agreed to talk, but strictly off the record he said. Art agreed.

"I had no business bein' on Broughton land, Sheriff, but I'll tell you what I saw. You're right that I'm the one reported the fire. I hid in the trees and witnessed my own grandson's murder. It didn't start out to be murder, but the boy accidently died. I saw three people covered in sheets, like vigilantes, with holes cut out for lookin' and breathin', one tall and one short, take Raleigh into the cabin with a pistol to his head. I assumed it to be Miss Laura and Miss Leona after the trial when the news got out finally about Raleigh's death."

Was Art listening? He was rewarded with silence as he held the phone.

"I'm plumb sorry if I led y'all to believe anything else. I hired the lawyer from Houston: Raleigh deserved a fair shake. You probably know that by now. I've heard of you and your bulldog ways. Maybe me and my boy killed Raleigh indirectly, you think? Me or my boy did nothin' wrong is the truth. We neglected Raleigh's upbringing due to the shame of having a bastard in the family. Nowadays, it ain't no shame for kids to be born out of marriage, but it was in my day and yours."

Oh God, help me! Ted Broughton's antique pistol must have been the weapon if it was Leona and Laura. Wilson didn't know about that I hope.

"Anyway," Wilson said, "they had gagged Raleigh; nobody heard him scream when he was sliced. They took everything, not just the sac. It was too late to stop. I know, I watched. He wasn't dead when I sneaked off and two vigilantes were wrapping Raleigh up. I assumed he would live. Horses and bulls do. When he didn't, thinkin' my own blood, my grandson, had done this thing to Leona's granddaughter, I wanted to save your friend. I thought my standing in the county would give me a better chance of gettin' away with an accident, but, well, I didn't step forward. You know some things are better never told."

He paused, but Art held his tongue. Wilson continued:

"There was an old man standing guard for them, and two others helpin' out, but I didn't recognize any of 'em. I beat it back to my ranch, and when I told my family, they agreed it was for the best. Raleigh wasn't dead then. We're sorry he died later. My son grieved for the years we deprived Raleigh of his birthright. My wife grieved over the photos Suzie King sent to us over the years. I have to agree, he was a good-lookin' boy. I'm sorry more than I can say, Sheriff. I'm plumb sorry about your deputy who became sheriff. He just wasn't cut out for it, and you maybe are, but this thing has to stop. You're the one can do that."

Dang it, Art thought, the whole county is in on this thing. Maybe he was exaggerating, but the taco indigestion sessions caused him to believe his visits with Carlton Smith and Wilson in the past were a portent of things to come—things that happened. Nah! God wouldn't tell a man in advance about something like this. What had the world come to? The entire county would be lucky if half didn't end up in prison or an institution. Art wasn't claiming to be a fortune teller or have a vision. He was confused.

Art weakened while Wilson waited for a response, and told Wilson about Leona's letter. Roscoe needed to know his grandson was an innocent young man, just foolish and a slow learner. No need to stir up memories now, but Art wanted to clear the board, let Wilson live with his conscience where Raleigh's neglected life was concerned.. They were all settled in—Roscoe, his wife and son. Art couldn't leave the boy's plight alone.

"We're all guilty of hiding things," was all the consolation Art gave at the moment. A*nd seems like we're all destined to be liars. Wilson, what's your stake in this?*

"If I was of a mind to turn this information over to a Ranger and reveal the chat I'm havin' with you Wilson, y'all would probably be guilty of withholding evidence, which would certainly affect Mrs. Wilson. Ever heard of collateral damage? Well, your wife would be a victim. Maybe, Roscoe, in some twisted way you thought Leona did your job for you and you wanted to exonerate her. I don't know."

Art was right about northern lingo in Smith's story and the difference in Wilson's Texas slang. Why didn't Wilson reveal who the old man was at the scene? Such an ugly, mixed-up, cotton-picking conspiratorial mess. Especially when the young man was innocent. Dang! The rest of the late predators weren't innocent, but did they deserve to die that way?

"Let me think on what you told me, Wilson," he said, remembering the confession letter from Leona. "We've done enough talkin' for now."Art sat wondering. He would never know why Raleigh King confessed to a rape he didn't do. Maybe he didn't really confess. This case was too complicated: too bizarre.

Wilson stared at the phone briefly, turned red from the shoulders up, started to raise a fist, but stopped just short of breaking the hall mirror and slamming his wife's furniture into the wall. That was the last time he would speak to the man, sheriff or not. He slammed the phone in Art's ear, stomped out of the house before he weakened and grabbed his rifle to drive to town and put a bullet in the stupid law officer who withheld information for his own personal gain.

With the slamming of the telephone in his ear, Art knew it was time to get something out in the open. "How can I tell everybody Raleigh was innocent?" Art asked out loud. "Before Tim Young lets that little fact slip someday? Raleigh would be avenged, but my word would be dirt."

Breaking the silence of an empty household with his own voice was becoming quite the habit. As to why Raleigh confessed, lack of intelligence, he guessed, or maybe he was proud to have the attention. The law never proved the young man admitted to anything.

Art argued again with himself on whether to allow Roscoe Wilson any more particulars. Should his wife have something better to remember than her neglected grandson dying like he did? Maybe someday he would get the courage to tell her in person her grandson was not the child rapist the papers alleged. Heck, the Wilsons might even take it upon themselves to prosecute Art, the city, the county and sue Leona's kids for her estate. More fall out. Maybe he would just let it lay. Politics are all about doing what has to be done with the least possible harm to the majority. He now knew exactly what that flimsy excuse meant.

Chapter 21

Wrap Up

Carlton "Ole Man" Smith and his suspected vigilante gang of newly-formed, "secret" Home Protection Club members from the Senior Center stayed away from the nutrition site after Leona's death. The autopsy ordered by Sorensen had delayed the writer's funeral; her death ruled a suicide. The more Art had questioned the four avengers—well, maybe that was too nice a description—the more they avoided him and everybody else.

Instinct and Wilson's information told Art they were all in on the first killing and helped Leona and Laura at the cabin with King's castration-turned-manslaughter, but they didn't talk. How could he prove them guilty?

Smith needed to confess something Art guessed, but more likely he would rather brag; make up stories about King's death to any body who would listen. Those rumors sparked the nightmares Art had. Everybody was a little crazy back then. The year 2005 could've been better. It could've been that Smith decided to help out further by joining in, gathering up his little posse to rid the county of all the sex offenders.

Art guessed if the old man and his friends were guilty, it had to be some misguided idea Smith carried out to fulfill the desires of his two "girl friends." Just by knowing what that gang was doing, Leona and Laura would've been aiding and abetting the seven other killings, whether taking part or not, because they knew if caught, they couldn't do the death penalty but once. Texas didn't recognize killers as "delicate" females, just killers.

* * *

"Leona wouldn't have promised, or planned, to kill all of the registered sex offenders, just the one who she believed hurt her kin," Art told Chief Brown later when they talked. He didn't produce the letter Leona left. He couldn't find it to burn. The sheriff was surprised about the cold case death of ninety-nine she admitted to, but not sorry. With her dead and the case gone cold, who would ever know? Any Pred-o-file—Art used the new descriptive word as often as he could even in his own mind—was better off dead. He didn't need to be loose preying on young girls.

"Leona was incensed at the last, like Floyd said the theoretical —his word, not mine—person would be, since it was such a trauma for her when King was set free," Art needed to explain to Brown, "but the first killing was pure unadulterated justice in her mind, righting a wrong she caused by not investigating the man who bought her van. To her thinking, she saved a lot of children, maybe her own."

"Why tell me all this, Art? I'm not gonna give you up."

"Rich," Art answered using the chief's given name just this once, "Leona confessed she was the only killer to save her best friend Laura the time we picked her up and charged her as a suspect," he said, pulling himself back to the conversation with Brown. "Reason that wouldn't work was because Leona wasn't strong enough to lift bodies for the castrations and torture by herself."

That was enough for Brown to know. He left.

* * *

Art had to hand it to Laura: kept her mouth shut and didn't confess to anything. He drove to her ranch to interrogate her. She cried, but she had an explanation for everything.

"Raleigh wasn't supposed to die, Art. I wouldn't have helped Leona with the process if he was supposed to die."

He looked away as Laura sobbed. It wasn't his place to judge a friendship such as the one Leona and Laura had. He'd never had a friend like Laura was to Leona. In fact, he couldn't have, not as a lawman. He'd always had to remain aloof even over coffee with his best acquaintances.

"Why in the heck did you decide—you and Leona—you could castrate the boy? You didn't know how."

"That was where Carlton came in, Art. He had the expertise and we lured him into it. He seemed willing to do anything to please us, because he was afraid we would muff the whole thing. We did, but through no fault of Carlton. I think he had feelings for me but I didn't encourage him, I swear. He went along with us to the cabin after we lured Raleigh to my pickup through the internet."

"Yeah, but how did you lure Raleigh?"

"The boy was lonely, scared, eager to please," Laura explained, "and we used the excuse we wanted to find out what Karly did exactly to make him pick on her, convince him into taking her in his house. Of course we didn't let on who we were. It was easy. He thought we were his new friend Chief Brown. We met King by the park. He hung out there sometimes I guess because he was familiar with it."

"Cow chips, Laurie! Did you disguise your chat screen with little girl things or just how did you get him interested straight out of the courtroom?"

"Oh, it took some doing. We had to go on the net looking for a chat room. Couldn't locate one—we're not computer experts, you know. Carlton got on Leona's cell phone and called his buddies. They were leery of the project, but came running just because he asked. One of them, Amigo, had strong knowledge of computers. He hacked into Raleigh's chat room and away we went. We did it from Leona's house. I never cottoned to computers myself, especially the internet. Tried it once at the library, but the librarian had to keep helping me so I got embarrassed and quit. Leona, she was a whiz at it, just like writing. Practice, I guess. Anyway, to get back to how we accidently killed Raleigh— "

"Wait a minute! Which one of your strung King up on a limb for Ole Man Smith to use his skills? Leona wasn't strong enough and Smith was old."

"It was sort of gratifying that we had enough strength among us to do that, until the end. That was when we all got sick and scared. Especially when we thought we saw somebody lurking behind the trees to the north of the cabin. Nobody was there we could see, but it took out all the fun ."

"Wait another minute," Art stopped her. "You messed up here. You said you were at Leona's house when you stumbled onto Raleigh's chat room. Where was this so-called expert PC operator when you were at her house?"

"I told you that story, Art. We couldn't really find one, so Leona called Carlton, he called Toady Wiseman, who called the who called the expert. We became The Child Protection Club. Good name, sort of like the Home Protection Club Smith told us about. He learned it from his great-grandfather. It was formed in the late 1800s, I think, but we revived the idea for the early 2000s. Too bad we got sick and stopped right then."

"Go on, Laurie. Tell me the rest. I'm gettin' sick myself."

"The next day when we found Raleigh had died guess what I found in his pants pocket? One of those asthma inhaler things—you know, for when they get to wheezing—and we thought he was just scared, but actually he couldn't breathe. What a way to die, choking to death. Heck! We tried to burn the evidence, Art, but the cabin must've been too wet, dry-rotted or something or maybe God had a hand in it. We could've caught the whole county on fire. But that's when we heard a car coming, or a pickup or something, with somebody in it who probably saw the flames or smoke or something."

Art could hardly breathe until she was done. He had questions, however, ones she couldn't answer. "Who killed the other seven men and how?"

"I don't know," she answered, "unless Carlton and the boys grew serious about their new club and decided since they would get the death penalty if caught, might as well get rid of the lot of them. I know Leona and I had nothing to do with that part. By the way, Art, you know she confessed when Brown picked her up because she believed you suspected Karly's parents of the whole thing. She was so close to dying and didn't want me implicated, she underestimated how much Brown could believe, especially with her being older, weaker, dying and all."

"I have to tell you, neither one of us believed it entirely, but we had nothin' else to go on, Laurie. Let me tell you about a couple of events comin' up on me after I had a couple of my talked-about nap times."

"Art, I didn't hear about your nap times. You'll have to fill me in some time." He ignored her remark and explained last year's story when Smith pushed into his office and told him a tall tale about sheeted figures taking King to the cabin. Art told of the meeting he had with Roscoe Wilson, Raleigh's blood grandfather, and the telling of his tale. Both of them had such a proximity to the truth, it was scary now to think about how Laura confirmed the tales.

Laura forced a laugh like she didn't believe his tale of taco imaginations, but not being in a position to negate his thinking, it was crazy to rile up a lawman. That little laugh reminded her of something Leona did at the cabin: read King his "Miranda" rights, but not the legal one the law had—it was one Leona picked up in the north when she was a reporter and a police chief had presented her with his version.

"Art, read this," Laura said and pulled a small plastic card from her purse. A twisted, sad smile flickered across her face.

He read: "Revised Miranda – 1976" What followed was not something he would have told anybody from a church background, but maybe for a laugh with fellow officers—

"You have the right to swing first. However, if you choose to swing first, any move you make can and will be used as an excuse to beat the crap out of you. You have the right to have a doctor and a clergyman present. If you cannot afford a doctor or are not presently attending a place of worship of your choice, one will be appointed for you. Do you understand what I just told you, north end of a southbound mule?"

"Good gravy, Laura. Leonnie's sense of humor never ceased to amaze me. Did she actually read this to Raleigh while the poor soul was tied up and bleeding?"

"No, she did it when we arrested him for kidnaping. Smith got a kick out of it."

In the end Art couldn't bring himself to arrest Laura in spite of the confession. He had dreams of her in the back of his mind that hadn't been realized, just remembered. It was Leona's influence led her astray and both of them would pay for the *accident* in Hell, he decided. He couldn't forgive her leading him on at her house the day Smith was there. She lied then and she might be lying now. To heck with it all.

Laura would have received the death penalty, not fifteen years for involuntary manslaughter if it came to trial. At her age–Art's age–she would probably die waiting for the end, what with a good defense attorney pleading insanity or some such. Sturm would be good at that. Appeals could lead into fifteen years more for Laura. Everybody knew Texas didn't let women escape the death penalty any more than the men. He had to expose her.

* * *

Laura jumped bail shortly after the arrest. She deserted her ranch and fled north before the authorities could have her indicted. A sense of loyalty to Leona caused the lawman to do something out of character and against the law: He helped her leave. It wasn't his desire to arrest and charge her: he left it up to Brown. Art's only desire was to just not care deeply for her anymore. He knew she would eventually be returned to Texas. He was sorry.

* * *

Tired and disgusted, Art Simonds visited the families of the four "vigilantes" from the suspected, recently organized senior citizen protection club. Out of a conscience he didn't realize he had, he helped the relatives find quarters for the misguided old men in a rehabilitation facility over near Lulling. They would die there unless Laura ratted.

He hoped any such group was disbanded when he did that. Surely there weren't anymore at the center who would be in on this Protection Club thing and carry on to the point of "tradition." They were elderly, but something had kept bearing on the trio of minds they wouldn't, or couldn't talk about. Just clammed up and withdrew into a private world. Smith and his buddies got so nobody could handle them at home. That was when Art, knowing what he did, pulled strings so that they qualified for special treatment in a state institution, not having any money. Art hated that for his once-upon -a-time, church-going friends.

They had to face God, not Art. Anyhow nobody confessed to anything and Art was busy getting the department shaped up after he had to take over again. As far as the county knew, Tom Bridges just up and quit, left town and told no one where he was going. He had no reason—nobody accused him of anything. Rumor had it that he couldn't face not solving the killings. Art heard he was working in Harris County and that was good.

Vigilante action must have cleared the board as far as Pred-o-files were concerned. No more registered sex offenders made Cuero. They probably didn't want to live in a murderous town or county where the law couldn't or wouldn't protect them. Hah! Well that much good came of the whole affair, Art thought. Now, it's time to get on with life.

All the mess ruined Art's plans for a red-headed wife. Heck, he thought, I might've been next to be hung on a tree and cut if Leona and Laura got mad at me. Actually, the Rangers might never reveal I wasn't in on this whole thing myself, not being able to gather evidence to the contrary and hating what happened to friends in their little county. If only Sorensen hadn't called on the Ranger service—

Meantime, Art was avoided like fire ants because of his new cause: openly pushing for everybody to petition their state and nation to pass a law keeping sex offenders in prison for life without parole. He was even asked if he thought that would solve the grizzly murders in the county. Of course not, but it could vindicate his lack of investigation.

The whole county, in fact the nation, knew Art became sheriff again when Bridges quit after all the ugly publicity surrounding a town where no killers were found. The news media took care of that little sensation. The best deputy Art ever had, elected sheriff in 2004, had long ago quit talking to Art, and here it was going on 2007.

The Knight killing Bridges hoped would propel him into instant spotlight and love the serial killings thoroughly away from the city and and solely into DeWitt County's jurisdiction to gain him some fame, actually ruined Art's finest deputy. He never confessed to anything either, no matter how much Art pressed. The state, so far, hadn't found any evidence as to who killed the Knight boy. Now Art knew Bridges wanted to help Leona like she did him in a successful run for election to the sheriff's office. It was Art's secret to the grave.

Ranger John Irwin eventually made himself known, but wasn't talking to Art. Time flies when nothing is being solved. The cases should have been over last year. Would the next headlines concerning DeWitt County become *Cold Case Capital*?

Danged if I know what to do, Art thought. Had Leona actually reverted to using Ted's pistol again on Knight like the first killing in 2002 with the van situation? According to her death-bed confession, she was guilty of that. Awful thing was, the rest of the dead men were already judged guilty of molestation or rape to get labeled like they did; murdered like they were. Their families didn't deserve the shame, Art realized, so if there had been a pre-selected place to incarcerate them forever, there wouldn't have been any trouble or displeasure over being parents.

It was all the fault of government heads sitting in Austin and Washington, D.C. If they would do something about the sex offender population in this country, there wouldn't be a need for any vigilantes or idealists or self-righteous senior citizens or whoever in small towns protected by limited law enforcement personnel. Trouble is they would end up policing themselves if what the sheriff read in the papers and watched on TV was correct.

How many of them, including Clinton, would see their actions as fodder for jail time? Art was sorry Raleigh King was labeled for his young affair with a teenager. Raleigh's mother had to live with that for the rest of her life. From what transpired, Art knew girls like Karly could get a boy in trouble when his hormones started raging. Art's own blood had raged a time or two, but he had parents who never let him get close enough to a teenage girl to get in trouble. He sure wanted to. In fact, his Ma said more than once:

"I would rather see you dead, Arthur Simonds, than a bad citizen." Added to that she said "If you get a young girl in trouble, her parents won't have to shoot you, I will." Art believed her and did the right thing. *God bless my Momma.* One big thing Art hated was he never got a chance to tell Judge Black how much he liked—in fact respected— him in spite of the times Black didn't always side with Art and his department. The judge died of a heart attack at the young age of fifty-four after the trial for King.

Black was right about Karly not telling the truth at the trial or at the hospital. Her parents knew and that was why they fought against her being put on the stand to testify. They bore no guilt in their hearts for letting King die, Art guessed. Why would they? Everybody in town judged the slow-minded man guilty and useless for anything except keeping his momma happy.

After all these years, Art finally understood why public defenders were so adamant in proving their clients innocent. In fact, some of them actually were. It was too bad about King.

* * *

Suzie King left five messages for the sheriff to call her. She had something important to tell him, the notes said. Deep rooted guilt kept him from returning her call. He knew her son died for nothing. He let it slide, but did ask his deputy:

"Did she give you any idea why she called?"

"No, just said we'd all be sorry if you didn't."

Later that week, Chief Brown called Art Simonds with news: Suzie King's body was found by a neighbor who hadn't seen her all week. It was unusual for her not to be out and about, they said. She was hanging on a clothes line rope with an overturned chair beneath her, just inside the kitchen, flies and maggots all over the place. The stench was too much.

"She left a note for you, Art," Brown said, when Art walked through the door holding his nose. "Why you and not me, I don't know. I'm the city chief, ain't I?"

Art ripped open the note Brown handed him. He could see it was brief and printed in scraggly handwriting from an uneducated person.

"Mist. Sherf, too good to call me, Lena Brotten din't kill herself. She begged for life. She thot I'd forgiv hur for Raleigh's deth. Yeh, I know who wuz to blame. Yu do to. I had to laff loud at her foonrul. All you dumies stood aroun feelin sorry. I din't. I wood have told you, but yu think yur to gud to anser my calls. Raleigh wuz th only reezin I had to live an that womin tuk him. It made me mad to see that womin's famly ther lookin all tear eyed. They din't care what I lost. Raleigh won't be lone now. Im goin with him. Suzie King.

"Good gravy, Brown! Look at this."

"What? What did she say?"

"Read it for yourself. I cain't bear to look at it. I should have returned her calls."

The chief read quickly, looked at Art and asked, "Oh heck! Art, what are we going to do?"

"Nothin' at all, Brown. That's what I did when I read Leonnie's letter you handed me when we thought she took her her own life. She confessed everything and I lost the letter before I could get it burned. It couldn't help anybody out and I for one wasn't goin' to help the state prove cases against my friends. I believed, and they thought, she killed herself and that was that. Case closed."

This development was just one more reason why Art should give in and tell somebody about the letter, but he listened as Brown, realizing an awful truth, asked:

"Ain't you gonna face up to where you are and what's gonna happen in the next day or two?"

"Well, let me put it this way, Brown. I did what had to be done with the least possible harm to the majority way I see it.

"Yes, and I've heard you say that more than once lately. I just didn't connect it."

"Ain't that what politicians say when they vote the way they do? I made a choice and I have to live with it, Chief. Look after your own hide. Okay? Goodbye."

Brown left, shaking his head and not looking back. What good would it do? So many dead—unsolved murders hanging over a town steeped in vigilantism. Maybe next year would be better, or maybe he would step down.

Art's tacos were getting cold and he hated cold tacos. He poured on hot sauce, turned on the microwave and waited, but not for long. Sleep overtook hunger.

Chapter 22

Angel Visit

Body trembling from the cold of the room, Sheriff Art Simonds sat on the side of a hard bed kicking himself mentally for the mess he had made of his duty as a responsible peace officer. He draped a jacket around his shoulders, reached for a borrowed cell phone, hesitated, and then dialed a familiar number.

Naoma Lawrence answered on the first ring. Could she have been waiting for him to call? He hoped so. There was something he needed to say to her, hoping for the understanding that hadn't been in her eyes the last time he saw her.

"Hey," he said. "Art Simonds here."

"Hey," she answered. "Where are you?" She knew.

Ignoring her question as to his whereabouts, he asked, "Would you be willin' to listen to me talk about a nightmare I had last night?" Before she could answer, he said, "Also, I have somethin' to tell you since we've become good friends and before this relationship goes any further. Of course I wouldn't have nightmares if I didn't love tacos so much." Other nightmares could remain secret for the rest of his life.

"Well, lay the nightmare on me first," she said, her soft voice belying the lack of enthusiasm he noted the last time they talked. He relaxed. Her voice had a way of lulling him into warm comfort. The sound of it drew him back to the last time he sat with her in her church. He remembered the warmness of her body next to his. What was wrong with him? They were in church, for gosh sakes. He didn't like the churning in his belly as she turned and smiled at him that morning. He didn't like remembering it now. Could he be falling in love this late in life – one of those December romances he once heard it called. What in the cotton-pickin'-cornbread heck was he thinking? Dang! He had quickly looked away, thinking how he felt when he first met Nora, his late wife.

As soon as a large lady with a soulful, haunting voice quit singing, Art excused himself and left. He felt Mona's confusion as he marched out the double doors in the rear of the church. A man's not supposed to feel such stuff in a church. Enough of this remembering. He couldn't remember what the preacher said. His feelings for the woman beside him detracted from any message the Reverend was giving to the crowd.

* * *

Art inhaled, dragged his mind back to the phone call of today and began telling Naoma everything on his mind, beginning with "Are you sure it's okay to tell a private nightmare on the phone to a woman who don't know me very well?"

"Yes, Art, I think we know each other well enough for you to tell me a nightmare as long as it's clean," she said in that soft voice. He felt a thrill from long ago days. But last night, he ordered tacos again. Dang!

"Well, I woke up this mornin' scared out of my wits! When I dropped off last night, there was nothin' on my mind but rest. I was so tired I was gone as soon as my head hit the pillow."

"Go ahead, Sheriff," she teased.

"In this dream," he said, "I was standin' someplace like on a cloud and there were angels present, with folded wings, all except one. He was bowin' down with his wings folded across his chest, head down in front of a man, or somethin' so bright I couldn't look at it."

"And how could you tell if it was a man, Art?" Sometimes he allowed his prejudice to show.

"He would've had short hair. The angel had short hair," Art replied, stiffness in his voice. "It's obvious angels wouldn't have long hair or ponytails or earrings or such, Naomie. Don't you know that? They wouldn't be where I think I was in that dream if they did. Now, don't interrupt again until I get to the good part." He glanced at a distorted image in the mirror showing his own thinning head of hair. What was left had whitened. The black, unruly mane he had sported when courting Nora would be nice. He sighed.

"Okay, Art, I won't say another word," she promised, laughing, thinking of Art's prejudice. He drew up courage, knuckles white from gripping the telephone, settled his insides and told her how the angels motioned for him to step forward where they were looking at a big book.

"One of them angels looked inside and said, 'Sorry Sir, your name is not here.' "

"What do you mean? I asked. What is that book?"

" 'This is a record of your life, Arthur Simonds, and you have been found wanting.' "

"Look, I answered the figure, lookin' around at all the other angels. I don't even know where I am and I sure don't know who y'all are. I wanted to run, Mona, but one of them took me by the arm and none too gentle. Then his face turned dark. He said, 'You must hear this. Listen to what God has to say to you.' "

"Not wanting whacked up the side of the head with one of them big wings, I shut up and listened. I have to admit I was scared and shakin' in my boots. A booming voice of thunder—it sounded like the big horn I heard blown in your church, Naomie—deafened my ears and I fully expected lightening to come any minute. The voice said 'You have allowed your emotions to guide you in right and wrong. What do you think should be done to someone who does not follow the law, Arthur Simonds? Now return to your present situation where you may remedy your sins by confessing them.' "

"Naomie, I fell down on my knees, right there in the dream! When I looked up, the blinding white figure was gone. The large angel pulled me up from behind and led me to a hole in the cloud where I was dumped head first. I woke up screaming!"

"Art!" Naoma brought him back to the present. "What do you think the dream was about?"

"Oh, dang, Naomie, I don't know. I only know I shake every time I think of it."

"Well, let's lay that aside for now," she soothed him, "and you tell me the other thing on your mind. Okay?"

"Yes. But you have no idea of the dreams I have sometimes and this is not the time to go into them. You're not gonna believe what I'm doin' right at this time. Here I sit writin' a letter to the President of the United States, Naomie. Would you believe I'm prayin' for guidance in what to say?"

She mumbled something that sounded like "That would be a first. Are you hand-writing it?"

"No, I ain't doin' it by hand, if that's what you mean. I'm not a good writer. I'm usin' a laptop the system allowed me to have brought in–hunt and peck style. Me, once a good and honest sheriff of DeWitt County here in south Texas, thinkin' the President wants to hear from me. I'm not sure how to feel, Naomie, nor what to write. I'm just disgusted with how long it took Congress to pass a law puttin' the kibosh on sex offenders movin' freely over the nation, and then the president to accept and sign the order. He did it one night, July 26th, 2006, on national television, which won't help this county one hair right now. You know what I mean?"

Art waited for Naoma to ask him just what the Sam Hill he was talking about. Silence. He said, to cover the silence, "I'm workin' up the courage to tell our President just how everything happened to me, and what this soft-on-crime attitude where sex offenders are concerned did to the best little town in Texas—what it did to my career and life."

"Art, I thought you had a great career goin' what with you bein' appointed sheriff again," Naoma said, and fell silent again. What could one say to a man about the position Art found himself in today, short of putting in another year as sheriff.

Just hearing her voice warmed Art up inside and prepared him for what was to come. He was glad he called.

"Just listen, Naomie, then decide what kind of a a career I have goin' nowadays," he pleaded. He shook slightly as he gathered the strength to read what he had written so far.

"Dang it, Mr. President," he read, "I want to say you're too late to change the history in DeWitt County and the City of Cuero signing that Walsh bill thing in 2006, but if you're keepin' up on Texas legislative matters, the House just signed onto a bill which would require the death penalty for repeat offenders. How do you like them apples?"

Naoma interrupted: "I'm not so sure that Dang it, Mr. President is any way to begin a letter, Art. Couldn't you just say Dear Sir?"

Ignoring her question, Art continued: "Your big show in

front of the camera in July of 2006 was too late to save me and a lot of good folks who got caught up in a terrible situation. As President, you made this play on TV, signing' the Adam Welsh Child Protection and Safety Act."

"As soon as I saw you makin' that move," Art continued, "I hated how it wasn't done years ago. Now take an example from your own state: put it before the Congress and get this thing nationalized, not just Texas and a few other states. I'm gonna be behind this Texas bill one hundred per cent and I hope you are too. In fact, I just might pray for the bill to be passed by the Senate when it comes up—if the senate president or whoever is in charge of introducin' bills lets it go before our General Assembly. It disgusted me to think of the Walsh Act as years late, a law short, and too little to have helped prevent the most horrendous murder case to ever cross our paths."

"Mr. President, it was far too late to save the victims and their kin from this new-fangled phrase the news media throws around: *collateral damage.* It's blowin' around the nation like tumble weeds in a Texas wind. I'm wonderin' if I should even bother tellin' you how we faced this crisis and if it was solved. I don't know."

Art quit reading when Naoma tried to interrupt again, and said, "Dang, Naomie, just listen to the story I'm tryin' to tell, will you?"

"Okay, Art, I'm listenin' to every word," she said, "just don't cuss." He was in no position to treat anyone with disrespect, but then she wasn't sitting where he was sitting, sorting out his predicament. "Are you going to send one to the Governor of our state, supporting the House-passed bill?"

He waited. Maybe this was another mistake. He was too harsh with her. Here he sat, trying to justify a lot of things that happened to his town and to tell Naoma everything, hoping it wouldn't bear to much on her mind and deter her marrying him next Spring when the wild flowers were blooming along the highways in DeWitt County—"The Wild Flower Capital of Texas"—that is if he was available, if she was willing, he would marry.

Art didn't need or want another interruption, but his chief

deputy walked in without sending word ahead, and Art said "Naomie, hold on." He thought to punish the deputy for pushing in—interrupting the phone conversation— by making him listen to what he was saying to Naoma on the borrowed cell phone. He cupped a hand over the mouthpiece so she wouldn't hear.

"Walt, sit down," Naoma heard Art say. "I want to run something by you at the same time I'm tellin' Naomie what happened here a couple of years ago. I'm plannin' on doin' this if I can get my thoughts straight. Think maybe you can take time to listen?"

"Sure, Sheriff," he agreed and grinned as he sat down where Art jerked away a borrowed laptop from the only chair in the room. Walt wouldn't be ungracious and say no, Art. If he hadn't moved it, Walt could've busted the laptop.

"Did y'all catch George on TV that night when he made a production out of signing a new bill designed to protect kids and women?" Art asked, raising eyebrows at Walt at the same time.

Using his inside voice Art had trained his loud deputy to do, Walt whispered, "Yeah, I watched it for awhile, but I had better things to do."

Naoma said, no, she hadn't wanted to watch Bush say anything, and asked, "You got somebody there with you?"

Art didn't answer her question. Instead he said,"Well at least read about the Texas House signing the bill callin' for the death penalty, y'all." He couldn't hear what Naoma said, but Walt was nodding in agreement, so Art continued to read the letter to the President. He intended to copy it for the Texas Governor, not word for word, but how it applied to Texans.

"Well, if I understand it right, Mr. President, this new law is designed to prevent a pedofile from movin' state to state, molestin' and murderin' our kids without anybody knowin' he or she is around. Texas already has a law on the books coverin' out of state sex offenders as far as registration when they move into our territory, but this law, if it truly has teeth in it, maybe could've influenced the outcome of what happened to us.

"This big act, Mr. President, to allow the death penalty for murder of a child under the age of sixteen might deter a first-timer, but I keep askin' myself, would it penetrate the sick minds of repeaters."

"If your assistants are on the ball, they already know about the Texas House voting on the bill to render death to repeaters. I'm for that one hundred per cent and if you'll give us an audience, I'll tell the entire story just how it all happened here."

"Also Mr. President, maybe you heard about Lubbock, Texas where they have a good restriction which could be incorporated into all cities with enough man power. They check out each and every potential property buyer's background for sex offender status before and after the purchases. We can only follow that lead here in DeWitt County and Cuero. I believe the known 600,000 sex offenders living in the United States might have to rethink their way of life. You know for sure that many children are unprotected where relatives and neighbors are concerned. That's a parental duty."

No sound from Naoma's end. She was appreciating how long it must have taken Art to pound out the letter so far using the hunt and peck system. She, herself, was a fast typist, having just retired from a career as a secretary.

"Y'all got an opinion on that?" brought her and Walt back to the matter.

Walt just sat there because he had to, not answering, but Art could tell he wasn't much interested. Walt was interested in arresting perverts and "convincing" them to confess. Too bad. Art had to bounce this off somebody and Walt was new enough to not know what to do with the story Art wanted to tell the two listeners. Besides, the deputy already knew something terrible took place here in 2004, so it wouldn't surprise him, maybe, and he wouldn't dare criticize the sheriff to his face.

"Maybe the powers that be," Art said aloud, "hope the new law will put the fear of God into these perverts, Naomie, maybe prevent them from killin' their victims. I don't know. If they get scared about leavin' witnesses, and they know it's likely they'll get caught, well, we'll see. We had no kids murdered during this particular time I'm tellin' you about, but we once had too many child molesters in our county. Y'all know what happened to them. Are both of you still interested?"

"Yes, Art, I'm listening' to every word." Naoma said and he

heard the sigh in her voice. "You didn't put that in the letter yet, I hope. It could get mixed up."

"No," he reassured her, "I'm puttin' this out in the open so as to straighten my thoughts before it's down in the computer or anything. I've heard that once somethin's on the hard drive of these things, it's never lost. The question now is," Art said and Naoma heard a smacking sound on the other end, "what law can prevent innocent victims and their kin from being swept up in the fall-out of sex crimes invadin' a town and changin' people from sane to crazy—changing law abiding citizens to vigilantes? I'll answer that for y'all. One like the Texas House just passed, that's what! We'll just have to pray the Texas Senate sees to the same action—maybe stop vigilantes from takin' the law into their own hands."

"Danged if I know what to say, Art," Walt whispered. He had jerked awake when Art slapped the chair the disinterested deputy was sitting in. "I'm a little lost on where you're goin' with all this. We have no vigilantes I know of."

"Art, do you believe in vigilantes for protectin' our children?" asked Naoma. "As you may know by now, I didn't have the privilege of bearin' children. I just have to help others."

Sheriff Simonds didn't really want input, just listeners. He stared hard at Walt, then dismissed him with a wave of his hand to go on about his duties. Walt jumped up.

The new deputy had been passed down to Art when he was named temporary sheriff until the next election. Walt hated how things turned out for his boss. Art had to take over when Bridges left suddenly. It was too long for the murders to remain a mystery and now Art was back in it–stepping back in from the retirement he had so long sought and bragged about. Gossip was Art had said he hated to take over but the old sheriff sure didn't act the part. It was rumored he was hiding something that caused the Rangers to be called in by Justice of the Peace Sorensen. Walt sighed as he left.

It was Art's turn to sigh. He would just keep thinking on these important letters, but meantime Naoma was listening and she was the only one he cared about deep down inside.

"I'm fully aware the President has daughters, Naomie," he

said to break the silence. Was she still there? She was.

"They're in the news enough. Me, I never had the pleasure, but if I had, I would've wanted this protection for 'em. Even sons have to be protected from a Pred-o-file."

Naoma waited, wondering where this conversation was going and wondering where he picked up the new word he used for pedofile, but said nothing. She lifted a hair brush with her free arm and began wiping back strands of brown hair falling into her eyes. No need to just sit there. This could take a while.

"Three years ago, Naomie," Art rushed on, "I didn't have a religious bone in my body, but I could've used God in workin' out the details of our infamous serial killings—I'm sure you remember the fallout—that plagued our town for over a year. Here I sit, Sheriff of DeWitt County again, out of retirement to take over the reins of a mess my chief deputy-turned-sheriff helped to create. It was me who pushed the county to elect Tom Bridges after I trained him for years. Never had a thought he would become fame-hungry and leave the office."

He stopped, waiting for her to comment on Bridges. She didn't. "I repeat, this story might have had a different ending if the law was tougher years ago and sex offenders were given the death penalty or incarcerated forever."

Naoma was waiting. Was he for sure fame-hunger drove Bridges to take a lesser position in another county? Did Art have anything to do with Bridges leaving? Would she ever know?

Art could hear the sound of gentle breathing and liked what it did to his heart, but he paused, wrestling with his conscience. Vivid memories of the past years shut down his thinking. She waited he hoped, until he was ready. His hand ached from holding the phone, and if he hadn't been on the phone, his trembling fingers wouldn't stay on the keyboard as the past swirled in to take over. Art reached out, put the presidential letter on save and reflected back to 2004.

"Naomie, maybe we'll talk later. Okay?"

Curiosity full blown, she agreed, after soliciting a promise that he would finish the story. She heard the phone click and hung up. Was she foolish to fall in love with an old fool like Art? He was at least fifty-seven, ten years her senior, maybe even sixty or sixty-one. Oh well. When he sat down beside her in church, her mid-life bones came to life. She gasped when the feelings came over her, coursing through her body. It had been so long since she felt anything for a man. What would happen if he ever dared to put his arms around her? That was outside church of course, and so far he hadn't. Once she casually asked why? He said:

"I didn't want to offend you."

Such chivalry in this day. Why? She was just as lonely as he appeared to be, but he was in trouble right now and his position of sheriff on the line. Better wait and see, but he had such a soft Texas drawl on the phone.

* * *

Once again Art woke up feeling more like a fool than a sheriff. Dang Taco. Putting aside a crazy dream he had, Art needed someone on which to vent his frustrations. He sat on the edge of the hard bed asking himself who he could call: who would listen and not condemn? It dawned on him that Leona Broughton's preacher, Rev. Lester, out at the church on the northern edge of town seemed friendly. The preacher always had a warm hand shake and a big smile when Art came in to sit by Naoma.

After all, preachers ain't supposed to betray a confidence, are they? And it was a strange church anyway. They would understand, wouldn't they? The preacher had been married more than once, and at least one of the deacons had been married more than once. They would understand, wouldn't they, that people could sin and be forgiven?

Art called from the borrowed cell phone and Rev. Lester said, "Sure, Sheriff, I'll be there."

Art relaxed, picked at the taco dinner Walt brought and let his eyes close in a quick nap until the preacher arrived. Was he sleeping too much?

Chapter 23

Confession

Jack Lester put in an appearance in thirty minutes, smiling and ignoring Art's surroundings. It wasn't his business why the sheriff was here.

Art was pleased to see the church man. They shook hands and Art felt comfortable in that he was about to open himself up for truth.

Now he could think back without interruption to gather thoughts on how to get his story straight enough that Naoma wouldn't hate him, or fear him when it was done.

With mixed feelings, Art leaned back against the wall, winched from the cold of it, loosened up and began his story for Rev. Lester, beginning with the incident in the sheriff''s office across from the courthouse one fateful day in 2004 when Leona Broughton busted into his office.

Rev. Lester sat through Art's story without blinking, although he hung his head from time to time. Maybe he couldn't look at Art's guilt. He didn't interrupt, not even once. His thoughts were not ones he could share. Guilt or innocence was up to the Lord, not Lester. He always tried to keep his judgements to himself and let God handle the sins of man.

Art ended the one-sided conversation with:

"Not that it's right, but nobody grieved over any of the perpetrators, especially me. Heck, I'm sixty now, Reverend, sheriff of the county again, and the sex offenders are staying away from a murderous town like ours. Don't that count for something? I'm still lonely, but that could end. There's the little brunette, Naoma, at your church who lets me sit by her if you noticed, Reverend, and who I'm planning on marrying if she'll have me. Y'all's music and dancin' ain't so much a bother now. And that strange-lookin' animal horn the young man blows—fair busts my ears—raises goose bumps on my body each time. It's somethin', ain't it? Actually I'm enjoying myself in the atmosphere of people who look for good in others. This God business is all right for my later years."

"Sheriff," Rev. Lester said, rising and reaching out to shake Art's hand, "you have to live with what happened and it's not up to me to judge. Vengeance is mine, saith the Lord. I'll leave it up to you to tell whoever needs to know outside the realm of Christianity and my office in the church."

Before he could slip away, Art exacted a promise:

"You won't spread this around, will you Reverend? This was just for gettin' my thoughts together for a couple of letters I'm writin'. Okay?" Art peered at a balding young man with his totally shaved head—was he trying to regrow hair—and hoped.

Jack Lester agreed, suffocating with the knowledge filling his head. Too bad he was sworn to confidentiality. He had only been Pastor of the church Leona and Naoma attended for the last two years, but had served as assistant before that. He had known the sheriff all of his life. Art was basically a good man, not much on going to church, but wasn't that between him and God? He would not betray any confidence, but would pray that Simonds would see the light and take his punishment like a man. That would go over well with the townspeople.

After all, the entire congregation was sinners saved by grace and not by confessing wrongs to the powers who held the county and state. God forgives, but not most people was Lester's experience. He was still young, not yet fifty himself, and he had a teenager. The knowledge was no prevention when it came to Art asking:

"How can I make this right with God, preacher? I don't want to die like Leona Broughton if she's going to hell. I don't want to burn in that eternal fire you talked about at your church. What can I do?"

"Sheriff, for one thing, Leona made peace with God. I was the only one she witnessed to. She told me everything about the killings. She got down on her knees and asked God to forgive her. If you know anything about the Bible, you know God is faithful and just to forgive us our sins if we ask. Do you understand you have to want to repent, ask Jesus into your heart and go on from here?"

"Hey, my mother made me do all that when I was a teenager. Do I have to do it all over again? They even dunked me under and almost drowned me in a pond."

"Sheriff, do you want God's forgiveness or not? He doesn't play games. Have you heard the story or read in a Bible how Jesus forgave the thief on the cross? Yes? Well, the same thing applies to you. Bow your head, repent and repeat after me: God I ask for forgiveness for all my sins in the name of Jesus."

"You got it, preacher. I said it silently and that's as good as it's gonna get."

"Art, only God knows if you're tellin' the truth. I forgive you for the critique of our church services. I'm not your judge. I trust you've made yourself right with God. I'll leave you with that."

"Before you go, one last question: If I accept this stuff you're talking about, does it mean I have to pray for sex offenders or try my best to keep rid of them here in DeWitt?"

"That's something you have to discover for yourself, Sheriff. See you around."

Dismissing the preacher from his mind, Art deferred to Rev. Lester's admonition to tell whoever needed to know, promised to do his best, squeezed the preacher's hand and Jack Lester walked through the door not looking back.

Simonds opened the Bible lying beside him and read aloud aloud from a page in the back part of the Bible Lester had marked called the New Testament. Art wondered briefly why he didn't remember any of this from his childhood. He read from the book section named Romans 10: 9-11.

"That if thou shalt confess with thy mouth the Lord Jesus, and shalt believe in thine heart that God hath raised him from the dead, thou shalt be saved. For with thine heart man believeth unto righteousness; and with the mouth confession is made unto salvation. For the scripture saith, Whosoever believeth on him shall not be ashamed."

"Who you talkin' to, Sheriff? You gettin' spiritual on us?"

"Nobody! Mind your own business, deputy."

There had been no expression on the reverend's face. Would he warn Naoma? Art didn't dare ask and really didn't want to know. He had no idea about preachers. If they were like the rest of the citizens—talkative—heck, they might even be gossips for all Art knew of them, but he felt relieved to think he would be "saved" like his Ma always wanted.

The sheriff had plenty of time on his hands to think about all that transpired the last two years. Too bad about the new Child Protection Safety Act, Art wanted to tell the President. It might not be too late to scare somebody from molesting children and maybe there wouldn't be so many perps killing their helpless victims. At least, if they let them live there was hope, and the predators would only serve time for molesting instead of going on death row.

Maybe there wouldn't be so much collateral damage to the Leonas out there, to Judge Black and good men like Bridges, Roscoe Wilson and his family, all the senior citizens who knew another way of life years ago. Nobody said much to Leona's two daughters and their families at the funeral. Didn't anybody understand anything?

Art called for Walt, his deputy now in charge, and asked him to listen to a solution he conjured up about what to do about sex offenders. He kept to himself what the preacher had admonished him to do to seek absolution for sins.

"Okay, Art. I've got more time than you. Talk to me."

"The President needs to look into the idea of a separate colony for them, give them lifetime sentences," Art planned. They could open up Alcatraz again. That wouldn't take as much of the taxpayers money, especially if they made those monsters do all the renovation. I would back the idea to the hilt and maybe with everybody working on a solution, they could stop so much collateral damage and fall out from sex offenses in the United States."

"Yeah, go on," Walt urged out of politeness.

"Trouble is, Walt, sex offenders have become such a blight on our town, and swelled our land with such filth until they're a dime a dozen. How could we get Congress to finance such a project? From what I read, some of the congressmen were not innocent when it came to committing lewd acts. Our previous President wasn't. How many others, Walt?"Art asked.

"You got me there, Sheriff," Walt answered, not wanting to make a commitment.

"On top of that," Art reasoned, "there's all kinds of shows exposing sex offenders on TV and still the battle rages. Just yesterday they found two little boys—well, one was fifteen already—in a Missouri man's apartment after an eleven-year-old disappeared from right by the school bus. The man arrested was a known pedofile. Good gravy, Walt, it's 2007 already and nothin' happening."

He paused, but the deputy didn't take a cue.

"But one thing for sure, Walt, the sign that says 'Don't mess with Texas' is a clear warning that in the long run none of us will get away with anything in this state. A few years ago I would've said see you in Hell, but not anymore. God Bless this county! God bless this city and God bless this state! And God Bless the President."

Walt stared, backed out through the door and waved to the sheriff.

* * *

Art woke to wondering if all of the night before happened or was he just dreaming again? He sat up, finished a letter to George Bush and wrote one to Texas Governor Rick Perry not expecting to receive a reply from either one. Nobody but God cared about collateral damage in a small Texas county, Art thought, and he didn't really want to explain his own inaction in bringing all the killers to justice. Heck, if he was lucky, the President's term would be up before he knew about the letter and sent the FBI in to straighten up the county. No need for that, the Rangers would take care of Art and his town.

The Texas governor indirectly was responsible for sending in the Rangers. Art's heart had near burst with encouragement one day when he picked up the Victoria Advocate and read:

"Texas House approves death penalty for repeat sex offenders." And, if Art read the March 6, 2007 Victoria Advocate correctly, Gov. Perry "deemed passage of a child sex offender bill a legislative emergency." It was named Jessica's Law" after a Florida girl, Jessica Lunsford, who was abducted and killed. Art read that "more than a dozen states have passed versions of Jessica's Law."

He had been elated to read the news: "The Texas version

would make the Lone Star State the sixth to allow some child sex offenders to be sentenced to death." Wow! He noted— as he had discussed with Chief Brown some time back concerning teenagers getting labeled— the paper clarified there could be an exception where a "high school romance such as a seventeen-year-old senior and a thirteen-year-old freshman engaging in consensual sex." Statutory laws could apply, "but not the new , harsher continual assault law." He read on that "the bill also removes the statute of limitations for many sex crimes against children, including indecency with a child and aggravated sexual assault."

The embattled sheriff believed these considerations merited his support, because the current limit on charges being brought was 10 years after the victim's eighteenth birthday, according to the news article. Maybe he was behind the times, but if he was, so was his county.

Art hoped the reporter got his facts straight on the news. There was little said about the senate's part in the passing, except that the bill had to get a final vote before going to the Senate, "which is considering a similar measure," the article explained. Dang!

* * *

Art made what Leona had always called an "executive decision," and that was to not tell this new woman Naoma a dang thing about his past until after they married. Just mulling the story over in his mind was enough for him to realize guilt and fear. She couldn't love a man full of past regrets—not that he had any— but he happened to be part of the collateral damage since he did nothing to punish the killers. He knew he failed his county, his state and his nation.

"Hey, Sheriff, you gonna stay up all night?" a voice yelled. "I heard you talkin' in your sleep a while back. Anything wrong?"

"No Deputy," he answered. "Will you take this disk and print out some letters for me? I'll sign 'em and maybe you can mail 'em off?"

"Sure, Art, that's the least I can do."

You have no idea, deputy, no idea.

"Thanks, Walt. You've been a good deputy. Have I told you about the nightmare I had last night? Okay, I thought I did, but it bears on my mind so, I cain't remember who all I told. You know someday you could be sheriff, so take my advice and be a good one: stick to the letter of the law or don't run for election. Okay?"

"Sure, Sheriff, sure." *Like you have old friend.*

"And be sure to return this laptop upstairs, the cell phone to Brown, and turn out the lights. And, by the way, before you lock the door, would it be too much to ask a favor?"

"Accordin' to what it is Art. This ain't no hotel."

"Would you be the one to walk with me over to court tomorrow? It'd be a blessin' if somebody I know does the honors. I thank you for bringin' in the preacher. He didn't say much, but it was a comfort for an old fool like me. It's not like I killed anybody or anything. I ain't no vigilante, Walt, I was just too worn out to deal with all the fall out in our county."

Art thought about where court was held now that the landmark courthouse was under full restoration activity. It would be beautiful when done, but for now all prisoners were being taken before a judge in the temporary quarters at the old Weber dealership.

"Sure, Art, we understand about the collateral damage you keep mentionin'. Too bad the Ranger they called to straighten out your office didn't. Maybe they'll go light on you seein' as how you're sorry. They ain't proved anything yet, have they? But Art the whole county may turn out to watch us tomorrow, huh? And you know the Ranger ain't gonna let me walk you. He gave instructions that he and he alone would come by for you—none of us allowed. Sorry."

Art didn't answer. Fact was he was not yet sorry, and he was not apprehensive about the repercussions of his actions. That was between him and God, he told himself. Besides, there was this plan hatched up by Texas Ranger Boyd Irwin. Maybe Trent would not be surprised how things would turn out, and how it was, guilty parties being Art's friends and all. The Ranger was just doing his duty when he took over the reins of the sheriff's office on a temporary basis.

Art felt no resentment, no guilt, and that concerned him, but he had made his peace with God.

Walt gently shut the cell door.

* * *

Naoma sat in church on a Wednesday night knowing where Art was writing his letters. She was sorry—no, compassionate—he had to end a fine career in this manner. Perhaps she had been hasty in allowing him to believe she cared for him the way he wanted. Once in a lifetime a woman falls deeply in love and hers had been with a man she never could understand. He was no good, chased women, loved dancing and drinking too much. Art had seemed to be a god-send for her lonely life, but for now he was to all intents and purposes unavailable.

"Hi," a voice caught her attention as she sat in the back row, drinking in what comfort she could find in a spiritual world. Naoma looked up and there was Jack Lester. He was the youngest preacher she had churched under, but she respected his knowledge and insight.

"Hi, yourself, Reverend. I was just lettin' God soak into my soul in an attempt to sort out my feeling for Art Simonds. How are you?"

"Naoma, I've been meaning to talk to you about the sheriff. Do you think you might be serious where he's concerned? I mean, were you thinking of maybe marrying him when he's available?"

"Truthfully, Rev. Lester, I have to answer yes, but I have doubts invading my mind on that subject. He's a nice-looking man, he's mannered, self-assured, but not very tuned into what we're about here. Have you discussed our beliefs with him? I know he called you to visit him in the jail. He seemed so depressed, yet determined to alert the President and Governor of his desire to alter the law as far as sex offenders are concerned."

"Naoma, I did talk with him. He gave his heart to the Lord, he said, not out loud, but he did assure me he did it inside. It's a start and I'm going to believe he was sincere. Believers don't blossom overnight, you know. How long before we convinced you that your place was here with us? If I remember correctly you were actually frightened the first time you attended a service. Right? Well that's how I interpreted the sheriff when he came here seeking answers to Leona Broughton's bitterness and her a church member. We discussed it briefly one time. I don't know if he found the answer he was looking for or not, but, well— "

"It's okay, preacher," she interrupted. "I understand. Think I'll go home now. I'm still thinking of how Leona and the King woman died. I pray I don't get that depressed in this life. I think I'll pray for Art too. It's just not true what the people are saying about him."

She rose, shook Lester's hand, smiled and walked proudly out the door.

* * *

Art was ready when the Ranger opened the cell door. He smiled as they made their way to a squad car.

Chapter 24

Ranger Action

Three men, one older and two young, caroused on Broughton land, drinking, laughing, just plain celebrating. The older one with his big black hat, tight-fitting jeans and plaid cowboy shirt had just tossed a beer can onto a pile when a voice yelled:

"Freeze!"

The snickering men stopped in their tracks.

One of the younger men, not more than twenty, appeared to make a move but was grabbed by the older man.

"Don't shoot!" the careful one yelled.

"On the ground! On the ground!"

Not intending to be shot, all three dropped, face down, hands behind their backs like they knew the drill.

Three Texas Rangers approached the unarmed men, held them down, twisted arms and snapped on cuffs. The was no display of karate chops, resistance by force, or kick-boxing such as seen on television. The action was just plain leg work, intense investigation and forensics. No heroics, no showmanship, no sneaking from behind buildings. Three lean fighting machines did their job like clockwork, like a rehearsal. The leader was tall, slim, jean and plaid shirt dressed while the other two wore white cowboy design shirts and sported shiny leather boots.

They looked the part, but Captain Clint Morgan had to move around town unrecognized until he had gathered information on the actual killers. He had compassion for Simonds and his friends, but not to the point of letting unsolved murders stay on the books. It would lead the state into a killing frenzy if over zealous citizens thought they could get away with ridding the area of sex offenders.

"You're under arrest," Morgan grunted as he jerked the oldest man to his feet. "You have the right to remain silent....." he paused when he remembered the 1976 Revised Miranda Art Simonds showed him one day when they were talking about the tragic death of Raleigh King and who was guilty of the crime. He wondered where the sheriff could have found such an out of the ordinary Miranda. He didn't finish reciting the Miranda rights to the older man before he was interrupted by one of the younger men.

"What for are we under arrest? We ain't done nothin' and you got no right," he said from a face in the dirt. He was ugly enough with his pock-marked face, scraggly hair and beady eyes that he should not bring attention to himself, Morgan thought.

He finished the Miranda on Jordache and heard his men doing the same to the others.

One of the sons, Jake was whining and the older man yelled "Shut up, fool!" Jordache cringed as he was pulled up and spun around to face Morgan.

"You three men are under arrest for the murder of seven men found at Leona Broughton's cabin out at Concrete," Morgan minced into the snarling face. "Your game is over, Rudolph Jordache. We know you started the seven killings with the Murdock boy and buried them all out here on Broughton land."

"You're crazy. That fool northern woman did the killin's. She was helped and covered up by the Sheriff. Everybody knows that."

"We don't," Morgan said, "and in case you don't know what being under arrest is, you will when the local authorities are through, so shut up."

Along with the others, Jordache was shoved toward unmarked vehicles driving up in the overgrown weeds of the property where the accused and his sons were found lolling around, drinking beer and laughing about some imaginary feat they had pulled off. Nobody was laughing now. The younger men, Jake and Roger, had to be folded into waiting sheriff department vehicles.

Chief Brown stepped out of the last one. Art had called him to be in on the arrest since they used the chief to further the farce of Art's guilt where negligence of duty was concerned. It wasn't easy for Sheriff Edmonds to let himself be charged with false negligence of duty charges as he and the Rangers planned.

They had fooled the chief and the county into thinking the Rangers were after the sheriff.

The Jordache boys couldn't believe their Paw would let this happen. He had assured them nobody would ever know. It was the perfect crime. Where was Grandpa George and Elsworth? Did the Rangers have them already or did they even suspect. Rudolph kept his mouth shut.

A disgusted Sheriff Simonds had stuffed Jordache inside a county vehicle, making sure Rudolph's head was out of the way before he slammed the door. He had rolled down the window part way to allow air to stir in the hot sun, not that Jordache deserved it.

"Hey! I thought you got yourself arrested for bein' part of the killin' Sheriff," he objected.

"Not hardly. It was a ruse, a game—just like the one you and your boys played— but you lost this game, Rudolph."

"Go to h..." didn't get all the way out of his mouth as Art punched his face with no witness. The thud of his fist against snarling flesh was more enjoyable than he anticipated.

"You thought the killin's would be blamed on Leona Broughton and her old friends at the center downtown ," Art growled, his insides screaming to club the insolent fool. "It was easy from there on in to rid the town of the rest of them sex offenders to make it look like vigilantes on the loose. Why didn't you just run your n out of town? Was it necessary to kill? Just because we knew each other all our lives don't make no difference. You left things at the cabin—things you didn't think forensics would find. Morgan here got your number, Rudolph, your DNA, strands of tape, rope, and other stuff including the knife used to cut bodies you hung in the trees. All from your garage."

"You're crazy," Jordache said. "How could he get my DNA? I would have known it. Why would I kill my own son?"

"Oh, you should remember being in the hospital last year or so; DNA still good on that visit. As to killin' your own son, we know about that—your first victim. He wasn't yours, he was your step-son and you wanted the stench of him and his sex offenses gone from your house. Your woman knew. She talked and talked. He was the most decomposed, being your first, but forensics did a thorough job."

"Paw?" Jake yelled from his position of being stuffed into a squad car.

"Shut up, I said. They ain't got nothin' on us. We'll be free by mornin' and out on bond." Morning would make everything all right to Jordache.

Simonds signaled his deputies to load up for the ride to the county jail. How ignorant for Jordache and his boys to be drinking so close to the crime scene. Didn't killers often return for the fun of it? Well, this drunken celebration proved their undoing.

As he drove, he reflected on his memory of Jordache, just one of "the good ole boys." He spoke over his shoulder:

"You ain't nothin' but a murderer—a cold-blooded killer, Rudolph. How could we all have been mistaken all these years? Did you kill your first wife? Rumor had it that she wasn't happy with you and the boys and wanted a divorce. She died by your hand, didn't she?"

"Go...."

Art slammed on the brakes, smashing Jordache's face into the wire screen divider of the squad causing the vehicle behind him to slide on the blacktop. Without looking back he asked:

"Want some more, moron? Jordache, if I had my way, you'd be drawn and quartered like they did two hundred years ago. You and your family turned this town upside down. If you had a religious bone in your body, or belief in the hereafter—well, you don't. Why say more? "

No answer from the back seat. Did he get knocked unconscious, Art asked himself, but looking to the rearview mirror, saw a devil in human form scowling at the back of his head. Art thought of another thing Jordache might be interested in hearing. Nah! That spawn of the devil wouldn't care what his three boys thought of a man who might've killed their mother. Still—

"Hey, killer. What would your sons say if I proved you killed their mother? Think they'd look to you for help? Hah! Think I'll slip a bit of information to them when we get back to

Cuero. Think about that, killer. If y'all had left well enough alone, Texas is fixin' to do somethin' about child molesters and y'all wouldn't have had to kill poor Murdock and all them others to cover up the killing of your step-son."

Another case for Sturm, Art thought. He'd be on tap again no doubt. Art was glad Trent wasn't the Texas district attorney on NBC the other night who fell for a trap set up for predators of teenage girls. Another sex perverted idiot bit the dust. Why did he have to be a Texas DA? They don't ever learn. It was like Art wanted to tell the nation through the President, he told himself for the umpteenth time, but for now if Texas took matters into hand, he would be pleased.

"Sheriff, watch your mouth!" Jordache yelled, returning Art's attention to his presence. "I'm reportin' you for police brutality."

"Brutality? I never laid a hand on you—you got no witness. My mouth might've abused you, but you cain't prove it unless you got a tape somewhere in your pants. Them tight jeans? You're too old and ugly to wear tight jeans. Somebody oughta pass a law against old men and fat women wearin' jeans."

"Speak for yourself, fatso."

Art slammed on the brakes again. Walt pulled alongside and yelled through the open window:

"One more time, Art! And I'm gonna smash into you. It ain't only prisoners, I hit my head twice. Now move on or surrender the lead."

"Who's boss here, Walt?"

"You, but not for long. I know about the county meeting. You're gonna be replaced and it might be me take over."

Art wished he would, take over the lead that is. He could drop back, stop and handle the back-seat perp. It was the fault of idiots like Jordache that Art and his beloved county was the talk of the nation. Life would never be the same around here. It was his fault the town had become a hotbed of accusations against him and Brown. Men like Jordache deserved to go to prison to rot, but wouldn't it be better justice if vigilantes got a hold on him? Nah! That was Art's old way.

Walt honked. Art gunned the engine, spun out in anger.

He was heavy-hearted, disappointed in all the so-called Good Ole Boys of Cuero for the first time in his life—including his best deputy ever, Tom Bridges. It occurred to the new man of God that he was not living like the Bible said. Hadn't he read it over and over sitting there in the cell waiting on the Rangers to relieve him of his "undercover' part in the investigation and arrest of the Jordache men?

Where did it say in there "Vengeance is mine, says the Lord, like the reverend tried to point out? Well, God, if you're watchin' what I'm doin' to this man, do you understand how good it feels to shake him up a little? Will you forgive me and give me another chance? On the other hand—

"Hey, Jordache. I have an idea. Why don't the government open up that big federal unused prison building, Alcatraz, dump all the perverts in, throw away the key? Huh? That's for first time offenders. The repeaters could be executed and the rest could kill each other. Either way, we would be rid of 'em and you wouldn't be here with me like this. But then mavericks like you wouldn't have any thing to hide behind and blame other people for your killer instincts."

Nothing. No sound from the rear. He's thinking, Art told himself. He looked to the rear seat again and radioed for a stop to the vehicles behind.

"Now what?" Walt asked himself out loud. "What's that bone head sheriff doing now? I'll be glad when we get to town and I can get out of this squad before Art wrecks me."

"Did you say somethin' to me?" asked his handcuffed passenger Jake.

"No, I ain't talkin' to no killer. Just wonderin' out loud why the sheriff stopped."

"He's got my Pa. What's he gonna do?"

"Nothin' meat head. I'll be back in a minute. Sit tight." Walt left the vehicle and walked up to Art's squad car. "What's goin' on, Art? Why you pullin' off the road again?"

"Walt, I think my passenger's dead or somethin'. He ain't said a word for a while. I tried to get him riled up about his first wife and his boys and he didn't respond. Take a look with me."

Walt opened the back door, took in the blank, cold stare on

Jordache's face, and accused:

"Oh heck, Art. You done killed him."

"I did nothin' of the kind. Just stopped a couple times when he smart-mouthed me."

"We better get him to the hospital. Put your siren on and let's go!"

Sirens blaring and lights flashing, Sheriff Simonds and his deputy in the second vehicle pulled into Cuero Community Hospital. Emergency personnel rushed out with tight looks on their faces. Thinking there was no emergency inside the hospital, they saw fit to desert it.

"Hey!" yelled Art. "I think I got a dead man back here. Get him inside and find a doctor. I don't want no dead man on my hands. I didn't do anything to him."

Chapter 25

The End

Standing in the weeds of the Broughton land, totally unaware of the trauma taking place at the highway entrance, Morgan had watched the sheriff and his deputies until they hit the main road, alleged killers in custody. He didn't want to know why the sheriff kept slamming on his brakes. He turned and shook hands with Sgt. John Boyd Irwin and Corporal Jeff Thompson.

"Good work, men. Let's trail back to our pick ups over at the Stagecoach Inn driveway. I know it's a walk and a half, but how else could we sneak up on our suspects? We didn't pick up too many burrs and fire ants, now did we? We can head out for Dallas as soon as we pick up George and Elsworth Jordache and turn them over to the locals. We'll operate out of Dallas, still available for the trials."

He turned and faced Boyd. "That was a good diversion, Irwin, plotting with Simonds on an arrest warrant and jailing him like he was guilty of something— well, he was guilty of caring about his friends—but not so much we can't cover it. At least he wasn't an assassin like these four Jordache men would have us believe. They did their part to stir up the town against Simonds and Brown. Maybe these arrests will squash some of the rumors floating around about them and bring resolution to months of distrust. Do you want to stay at your post in Victoria, or do you want to meet us in Dallas? We're bound to get points out of solving this case."

"Hey, if you don't mind, go on back. I'll stick around here a little longer. I know these people. Known them for some time now and they might need help. Chief Brown is short on men as it is. There's a precinct constable, but he's busy serving subpoenas or warrants most of the time."

"Okay. We're thinking about taking a side trip up to Lubbock for a look-see at how their plans for new restrictions are working out on future property buyers. Just for the heck of it," Morgan added to squelch the look on his Rangers' faces.

* * *

Art drove away from the hospital after depositing a dead man, leaving the screaming Jordache boys trapped in the other vehicles driven by his deputy and Chief Brown. The worn-down sheriff closed his ears to accusations he had "killed their Paw." Hospital personnel determined that Rudolph Jordache died of a heart attack, but it would be Kate Sorensen's decision to call in a medical examiner to clear Art.

Dang! One more reason to pack it in. Art recalled the past three years of his life, sighed, gripped the wheel, leaned forward and drove with a purpose. This was his last case. Never again. This time, he was actually retiring—well, being replaced was more like it. The county and town were on his back too much and the county board listened. He sighed again.

Should I dare ask Naoma to marry me? Will she understand how we played out this plan to catch the real killers and let my name be blackened by that stint in jail? Will she believe we wanted to clear Leona, Laura, and the men at the center from all the deaths they didn't do? She knows like I do that Raleigh's death was carried out by these friends of mine, but they'll be cleared of the wanton killings of the rest of the perverts. Appeared from all reports and new acts of law by the state, Texas might be taking care of its own while the rest of the nation stewed. Yeah?

Yeah, he would ask Naoma right now! He turned his vehicle toward Morgan Street. He was going to do it—ask her to marry him. A thought of how her voice sounded on the phone pounded in the decision. She would make a great wife, one of them soft easy-going Texas women. Asking her couldn't wait. It was now or never. He made himself and a coffee buddy a promise:

I ain't gonna eat another taco Leona, and to tell the truth, I'm glad we're rid of them Pred-o-files. I ain't got no stomach for jellybeans anymore though. I sprinkled them on your grave like you wanted—all black.

* * *

Naoma threw open the door when Art knocked, pulled him inside and melted against him for the first time. Surprised, he leaned over and drowned in her soft lips, but then pushed back.

"I don't know how to do this," he said.

"Do what?" she whispered.

"Ask you to marry me." He knelt on the floor in the old-fashioned way which dumbfounded the surprised woman. No man had ever kneeled before her. At a loss for words, she stood smiling as he grew anxious. "Well— "

She stood still. In shock? Her brown hair parted on the side in a way he had not seen it spurred him to pray for an answer. *God, help me out here.* He grew nervous. Come on, his heart urged.

She reached down and pulled him to his feet. He knew Art Simonds was in trouble. Everything he had told her, everything he had gone through, ruined his chances.

"Art, I hardly know you, but...."

"Yeah, I know. I had to try, dang it."

"Yes! Yes, yes, and yes."

Was that angels he heard singing *Hallelujah*?